Tut

MY EPIC BATTLE

TO SAVE THE WORLD

ALSO BY P. J. HOOVER

Solstice
Tut: The Story of My Immortal Life

Tut

MY EPIC BATTLE

TO SAVE THE WORLD

P. J. Hoover

A Tom Doherty Associates Book

New York

TUT: MY EPIC BATTLE TO SAVE THE WORLD

Copyright © 2017 by Patricia Jedrziewski Hoover

Illustrations by Erik McKenney

A Starscape Book
Published by Tom Doherty Associates
175 Fifth Avenue
New York, NY 10010

www.tor-forge.com

The Library of Congress Cataloging-in-Publication Data is available upon request.

ISBN 978-0-7653-9082-0 (hardcover)
ISBN 978-0-7653-9084-4 (e-book)

Our books may be purchased in bulk for promotional, educational, or business use. Please contact your local bookseller or the Macmillan Corporate and Premium Sales Department at 1-800-221-7945, extension 5442, or by e-mail at Macmillan SpecialMarkets@macmillan.com.

First Edition: February 2017

Printed in the United States of America

0 9 8 7 6 5 4 3 2 1

For Jessica, who is always there
and always understands.

CONTENTS

CONTENTS

Tut

MY EPIC BATTLE

TO SAVE THE WORLD

1

WHERE MY CAT CONSPIRES AGAINST ME

I could outrun anything. Messenger bikes. Angry hippopotamuses. Cheetahs. Okay, I'd never actually outrun a cheetah, but I was sure, given the chance, I could. I was the Great Pharaoh Tutankhamun, after all. King Tut. Plus I was immortal. Except in this weird nightmare I was having, whatever was chasing me was gaining on me, and I couldn't seem to pull on any of my immortal powers no matter how hard I tried. It wasn't going to end well.

Just before my imminent doom, I woke up covered in sweat to the sound of someone pounding on the door of my townhouse, and a renewed sense of dread filled me. Something besides the nightmare was right at the edge of my mind. I knew when I remembered it, I wasn't going to be happy.

I stumbled downstairs, right as the shabtis were letting in my best friend, Henry. His messy blond hair looked like he'd passed through a hurricane on the way here, and his mouth was filled with a huge bite of bagel and cream cheese. He finished chewing and then uttered the four dreaded words that restored my memory.

"Time for science camp."

Things that an immortal fourteen-year-old pharaoh living in Washington, D.C., might do over summer break? Stay out late. Try out every food truck on Pennsylvania Avenue. Swim in the Reflecting Pool. Science camp was not on the list.

"I'm not going to camp," I said, rubbing my eyes to clear my head from the nightmare. It had felt so real.

"But you promised." Henry took another bite of the bagel. Pure disbelief covered his face as he chewed. Not that I had any clue how he could be surprised. The last thing I intended to do over summer break was go learn about a bunch of science stuff I already knew. Why anyone would willingly spend two weeks of summer vacation in camp was beyond me.

"I never promised," I said, trying to remember my exact words.

"You did, back in January," Henry said. "You said that it was the least you could do after your crazy uncle tried to kill me."

Ugh. He was right. My uncle had tried and nearly succeeded. If the god Osiris hadn't intervened and transferred all the energy from my scarab heart into Henry to heal him, Henry would have died. But afterward, I'd been caught in a moment of weakness. I'd been feeling sentimental. After all, I'd been willing to give up my immortality to save Henry. It was without a doubt the most unselfish thing I'd ever done.

But now science camp wasn't sounding like such a fun bonding experience. Images of boring classrooms and songs about the periodic table filled my mind.

"Hmmm . . ." I said.

"You were sitting on the futon when you said it," Henry said, like that would help refresh my memory.

"I always sit on the futon." I plopped down on it for effect. It was the only real seat in my family room besides Gil's chair, which was faded and covered in patches and was so old it had probably been made during the time of the dinosaurs. Gil was my older brother—or at least he pretended to be. His chair had been empty for the last six months, ever since he went away. The leader of my shabtis, Colonel Cody, asked if we could rid the apartment of it on a daily basis.

"That's beside the point," Henry said, eyeing Gil's chair and then opting to sit on the faded green camel seat instead. I hadn't sat in Gil's chair either. I kept waiting for him to come back. And if Gil sauntered in the door and someone had their butt in his chair—or worse, if his chair wasn't here—he'd be out for revenge. I wanted Gil back, but I didn't want him to put shaving cream in my pillowcase once he got here.

Two of my shabtis, Lieutenants Virgil and Leon, ran over with a huge glass of orange juice and a plate of scones. Now this, to me, was the perfect way to start the morning. Science camp was not.

I should explain about the shabtis. They were these six-inch-tall hand-painted clay figures that had been placed in my tomb to wait on me in the afterlife—365 of them, to be exact. But unlike me, who'd never actually been placed in the tomb, they'd been stuck in there until 1922. Then when my tomb had been opened, they'd found me here in D.C. Ever since, they've been my eternal servants. I know it sounds kind of weird, like I have pint-size clay butlers waiting on me hand and foot, but they'd been bound to me from the moment they were created. The spells written on them made it that way. Also, it made them really happy.

Horus sat silently on the top of his cat scratching post, swatting his tail back and forth, watching scarab beetles scurry across the room. He'd softened a bit toward Henry in the last six months, but he still kept his distance. I think he never got over the fact that Henry had almost chopped his tail off with a sword.

"Then what is the point?" I said. I grabbed my spiral notebook from the coffee table in front of me and flipped through it. In the last six months, I'd listed out every place in D.C. that I'd searched for Gil and also all the places I still planned to go. I was getting way closer to the end of the list than I wanted to be.

Henry grabbed a scone from the plate and started picking little pieces off it. It looked like blueberry today. That or maybe rhubarb. Lieutenant Virgil made a different flavor every day. It was a new thing he'd been trying, part of his effort to serve food befitting a pharaoh while still staying up with the times. Scones were great and all, but I was hoping he'd go through a doughnut stage soon.

"The point is that you promised you'd go. I asked, and you said, 'Yes,' and if that's not a promise, then I'm not sure what is."

It wasn't exactly how I remembered the conversation.

"I said maybe."

"You said yes."

"Henry's right," Horus said, finally deciding to enter the conversation. "And if you two don't stop bickering about it, someone's going to get eviscerated."

Coming from Horus, that wasn't an idle threat. Horus was a god, and things like evisceration were nothing unusual with the gods. Also, seeing as how I'd known Horus forever, I figured Henry was the one in danger. Horus would never eviscerate me. I think.

"See? Even Horus agrees," Henry said, edging away.

"Horus just wants you to stop complaining. Right, Horus?"

Horus jumped down from the top of his scratching post and onto the coffee table in front of me.

Yes, Horus was a cat, in addition to being a god. A talking cat. It was a god thing. And when he wasn't a cat, he was a falcon. It was a little confusing, but those were the basics.

He narrowed his one good eye at me. The other had been scratched out in an epic family disagreement. Losing an eye might seem horrible, but Horus definitely came out ahead in that fight.

"What I want is for you to do something besides look for Gil," Horus said. "You haven't done anything else since school let out, Tutankhamun."

This is probably a good time to address that Tutankhamun thing. Yes, I was King Tut, Ruler of Upper and Lower Egypt. At least I was before my uncle, the worst relative anyone in the world could have, yanked me from the throne and tried to kill me.

Thankfully, the gods smiled on me and made me immortal. Pretty cool, right? Except they'd made Uncle Horemheb immortal, too, which wasn't quite so cool. It took a long time, over three thousand years, but I was happy to report that Uncle Horemheb was no longer a problem in my life. He'd been cast into the underworld. Devoured by the crocodile goddess, Ammut. She probably had indigestion.

Me? I was still immortal. I got to live forever. I could never die. What wasn't quite so lucky was that I was stuck at fourteen. I used to rule Egypt. Now I was never going to get out of middle school.

"That's because I intend to find Gil," I said, holding up my notebook and flipping open the pages. They were filled with everything I could remember about Gil.

Yes, that Gil, as in Gilgamesh, former Sumerian king, who also happened to be immortal. Or at least he used to be. But I'll get to that. The thing was that Gil and I had been living together, roaming the earth, for thousands of years. He'd been the older brother I'd never really had the chance to have. And then he'd just up and left, leaving me no clue about where he'd gone.

I'd been mad at first. Okay, furious. I deserved more than that. I at least deserved a goodbye. But then I started getting worried. Because—and here's where we get into the immortal thing—Gil used to be an immortal, just like me. But then that whole mess with my uncle happened, and Henry was dying. I wasn't going to let that happen. I had to do something. That's when, with Osiris's help, I transferred all my immortal energy to

Henry to heal him. My scarab heart drained, and it left me . . . mortal, just like everyone else in the world. And that was fine. I was prepared to grow old and die.

But I guess Gil wasn't quite so prepared for me to die, because without even asking, he'd shoved his scarab heart inside me, making me immortal once again, and dooming himself to mortality. And then he'd just taken off, without even saying goodbye. After three thousand years together, that was not cool at all. I was going to find him and . . . well, I wasn't sure what I'd do then. I'd figure that out when the time came.

Oh, and as to whether Henry was now immortal or not, since he got pumped full of all that scarab heart energy . . . that was still up for debate.

"You're obsessing about Gil," Horus said. "You need to do something else, because you're driving me crazy, and you're not making any progress."

"That's not true." I tried to find something in the notebook that would prove him wrong. It was filled with lots of stories of me and Gil facing perils of extreme danger during heroic adventures. Or at least that's how they sounded when I wrote them down. I'd been revisiting all those places, searching for him. But my list of places here in D.C. was almost done. I planned to continue my search overseas next, where ancient Babylon used to be. One of my shabtis, Captain Otto, was working on my passport.

"Then what have you found?" Horus asked, sitting on his haunches and flicking his tail back and forth. "Tell me one thing that's given you any clue as to where Gil is."

I stared at Horus. I tried not to blink. From the camel seat, Henry sat silent, picking at his scone. Even he knew that interrupting Horus wasn't a great idea. But my efforts at a staring contest against Horus were more futile than hunting Bigfoot.

I blinked and looked away. "Fine. You're right. I haven't found him yet. But you know, it would be nice if someone else helped me."

I said it way more sarcastically than I probably had to, but Horus was a god. It seemed like finding an eighteen-year-old formerly immortal ancient Sumerian king should be simple for him.

"I am helping," Horus said.

"How?"

"I have feelers out."

"What kind of feelers?"

"Just feelers," Horus said. "Now go to camp with Henry. You need a change of pace. And it's only for a couple weeks."

I turned to Henry. He grinned at me like he'd just beaten me in a game of Tetris. With both him and Horus after me, there was no getting out of it.

"Just today," I said. "I am not committing to the entire time."

"Perfect," Henry said, standing up. "We are going to learn so many cool things."

That, I highly doubted.

I glanced around the townhouse. There were no less than fifteen shabtis scurrying around, cleaning the place, but their leader was nowhere to be found.

"Where's Colonel Cody?" I asked a purple shabti named Lieutenant Roy. The shabtis came in all sorts of colors. It had something to do with their ranks and specialties.

Lieutenant Roy stood on the bookshelf directing the cleaning efforts. It's what he did best.

"I believe he had an errand to run, Great Master," the purple shabti said. He snapped his fingers and pointed to the shabtis scooping up the scarab beetle shells that decorated the wooden floor of my townhouse. Horus ate the insides, but refused to clean up after himself.

"What errand?" I asked.

Lieutenant Roy crossed his arms over his chest and bowed. "Great Master, he didn't tell me."

"When's he going to be back?"

"Great Master, he didn't tell me."

Colonel Cody had been running lots of errands lately. I'd tried to figure out what he was up to, but he'd managed to keep it from me so far.

"When he gets back, tell him not to leave again. I need to talk to him." I'd tasked Colonel Cody with helping me find Gil.

The shabtis and Gil kind of had a love-hate relationship. They thought Gil was a heathen since he didn't worship the Egyptian gods. Gil got annoyed when they wouldn't do simple things for him, like wash his dirty socks and underwear. But I think the real reason the shabtis didn't like him so much is because Gil didn't, in their opinion, show me, the former ruler of Egypt, the proper respect. Respect or not, I wanted Gil back, and the shabtis would help me.

"Very good, Great Master," Lieutenant Roy said.

I looked to Horus one last time. But he was staring out the window, lost in whatever kitty-god thoughts ran through his head. And then he jumped out the window onto the fire escape, with no explanation of where he was going. So I changed out of my pajamas, and Henry and I set off for science camp.

2

WHERE I GO TO SUMMER CAMP

Science camp was at the zoo. We walked to Woodley Park because it was way faster than taking the Metro. Henry, unlike me, had dressed for the occasion. He wore a bright blue T-shirt with $\boxed{O}\ \boxed{Mg}$ in yellow lettering. He caught me staring at it.

"Do you get it?" Henry said, pointing to the letters. "Oxygen. Magnesium. OMG."

Even though I didn't want to spend my day at science camp, that didn't mean I wasn't smart. I could recite the periodic table backward if required. Not that it had ever been required for anything in life. For that matter, neither had been reciting it forward. It was just one of those random skills I'd developed over the course of my immortal life. Scientists kept changing it, adding more elements. I hoped that one of these days they'd name one after me. Tutankhamunium. It had a great ring to it.

"I get it," I said.

"I could order you one," Henry said. "Two-day delivery. It would be here by Wednesday. We could wear them on the same day."

I liked Henry—he was my best friend—but I had no plans to be all twinsies with him.

"No, that's okay," I said. "Then it wouldn't be as special."

"I wouldn't mind," Henry said. "Maybe for your birthday."

"Maybe," I said. My birthday wasn't for another month. Camp would be way over. Not that I'd technically be older on my birthday, but it was still nice to celebrate. Every year Gil got me some stupid gag gift and we went out for pizza. I had no intention of letting that tradition die. I had to find him.

Henry then proceeded to start reciting random animal facts.

"Did you know that an octopus has three hearts?" Henry said.

Amid all the knowledge I'd gained in the last three thousand years, octopus anatomy was not part of it.

"Not eight?" I asked. I could see the logic in eight: the same number of hearts as tentacles.

"No, Tut, not eight."

"Sounds like somebody didn't think that all the way through," I said.

"Well, it does have nine brains, but only three hearts. There's one for each of the gills, and one for the body."

"Huh. Do all fish have three hearts?"

"Just all cephalopods," Henry said. "Do you know what a cephalopod is?"

"Yeah, I know," I said quickly, because one, I did know, and two, I didn't want Henry to tell me any more about them.

We were just outside the zoo now. A giant mural of a snake covered the wall. I'd never noticed it before, but it could have been new. Fancy murals were going up all over the district. Last I heard, there'd even been talk of painting one on the Air and Space Museum.

"Okay, did you know that snakes don't blink?" Henry said, pointing at the mural.

Snakes were a little more common that octopi. "Yeah, that I knew." I also knew that snakes smelled with their tongues.

"Don't you think that would be super-uncomfortable?" Henry said, blinking for effect. "I mean, let's say you get a piece of dust in your eye. How are you going to get it out if you can't blink? It's not like snakes have hands or arms. They can't just wipe it out."

"I never really gave it much thought," I said.

"You should study animals more," Henry said. "I've been researching them since school let out."

Henry had been researching way more than animals this past month. He challenged me daily with odd science facts and quizzed me on obscure vocabulary words like "phrontistery" and "podobromhydrosis."

"Okay, one more," Henry said. "Did you know there's this weird jellyfish that's basically immortal?"

I laughed. "Yeah, whatever."

"No, it's true, Tut," Henry said. "Its cells can revert back to their original form moments after being injured. And if we look at the principles in this immortality versus scarab hearts—"

I put up my hand to stop him. "Enough." Immortal jellyfish were nothing like scarab hearts. I was willing to bet that the jellyfish would die if someone accidentally put it in a blender, immortal or not.

Okay, that would probably be pretty uncomfortable for me, too. I had no intention of testing the theory.

"But what if it's true, Tut?" Henry said. "What if all your god stuff can be explained with science?"

This is what Henry's research came down to. He was convinced that all the crazy stuff he'd seen in the last year had a perfectly scientific explanation, even things like Horus talking. I hadn't shared this little tidbit with Horus yet. It would only make him grumpier when Henry was around.

"Where are we supposed to go, anyway?" I asked.

Henry pulled up some sort of camp brochure on his phone and zoomed in. At the top of the screen were the words SCIENCE MADE FUN—YOU'LL NEVER WANT TO LEAVE.

This was completely not true. I already wanted to leave, and it hadn't even started.

"It says here to meet at the elephants," Henry said. "We're supposed to look for a camp counselor with the red shirt that says, 'Science Rocks.'"

This was much easier than I would have thought. The camp counselor stood by the elephants, camera ready. The second we walked up and Henry asked about camp, she snapped a picture of each of us and printed out badges, laminating them on the spot with our names. TUT JONES was printed in block letters. But the picture of me was horrible. She'd totally caught me off guard. My hair in real life was dark brown and fell wavy to just below my ears, and my skin was sort of a dark tan color. But in the picture, my hair looked yellow and my skin looked green. I thought about asking her to retake it, but seeing as how I'd only be here one day, I guess it didn't matter.

"I'm Camp Counselor Crystal," she said, pointing to her name badge, which, unlike my photo, looked like one of those glamour shots. In the photo, her bright red hair was piled on top of her head, like it had been styled for a wedding. But here, in real life, she had a ball cap on, and her hair looked tangled and stringy. "Wear your badges at all times so we know you're part of the group." She eagle-eyed us until we clipped them on.

Maybe if I took it off later, I could sneak away.

Thanks to Henry's promptness, he and I were the first ones to get to camp, but other kids filed up as the minutes passed. There were at least five kids I recognized from school, including Joe Hurd and Brandon Knauss. I'd never pegged them as science nerds. Their parents must have signed them up. I was friendly enough with them at school, so they came over and stood by Henry and me.

"Science camp sucks," Joe said.

I completely agreed. I was going to have the shabtis put sour milk in Horus's bowl to get back at him for making me come.

"Give it a chance," Henry said. "It's going to be awesome."

"What would be awesome is being home playing video

games while my parents are at work," Joe said. "Do you have any idea what game just got released?"

If Gil were around, he'd have told me. Between the two of us, Gil was the one who was way more into video games. I played mostly so we could hang out together. The thought kind of depressed me. Why did Gil have to go away in the first place? Playing games hadn't been the same since.

Just then a girl I'd never seen before skipped up to join us. Her hair was blond and so super-curly that it bounced up and down with every step she took. It was like she had a cumulus cloud attached to her head.

"Am I late?" she asked, completely out of breath.

Henry took one look at her and grinned like a puppy dog letting its tongue hang out. And then I saw why. She had the exact same T-shirt on as Henry. It was like they'd texted each other ahead of time and planned it.

"I'm Henry Snider," he said, sticking his hand out like he was some grown-up or something.

The girl grabbed it and shook it so hard that I thought Henry's arm might fall off.

"Blair," she said. "Blair Drake. And, seriously, I can't believe today is finally here. I have been waiting for this camp, like, forever. Did you see the list of places we get to go?"

"It's not at the zoo every day?" Brandon said.

I was glad I wasn't the only clueless one around.

"Did you not check the camp website?" Henry said, as if Brandon's comment topped the stupid scale.

"There's a website?" Brandon said. "Joe, did you know there's a website?"

"For what?" Joe said.

Blair stared at them like they should actually live at the zoo.

"I'm Tut Jones," I said, pointing to my name badge.

"That's kind of a weird name," Blair said.

The name thing was nothing I hadn't heard about a gazillion times before. "Yeah, Jonas was my first choice, but my parents didn't listen. They didn't go for the whole Jonas Jones thing."

"You don't look like a Jonas," Blair said.

I guess that meant I looked like a Tut.

Now might be a good time to mention why I continued to use my real name. You might argue it would be easier to just pick a fake name and go with it. Like John. Or Mike. Or even Jonas. But I really liked my name. It defined me. And it was something I was not willing to give up. I'd lost so many other things in life: my family, the throne of Egypt. My name was staying forever. Anyway, plenty of people had weird names these days.

"My sister's name is Atlas," Brandon said, helping my case without even realizing it.

"Oh, yeah, and did you see that some Hollywood star named their kid Saber?" Joe said. "That's what I'm going to change my name to when I turn eighteen. Saber Hurd. Man, I love the sound of that."

He, unlike me, would turn eighteen someday. And he was right. Saber Hurd did sound pretty cool.

"Hey, what ever happened to that girlfriend of yours, Tut?"

Brandon asked. "Did she get in a fight and get kicked out of school again?"

"What girlfriend?" I asked, even though I knew exactly who he was talking about. Tia was this amazing, awesome girl I'd met at the beginning of the school year, back during the Uncle Horemheb fiasco. I hadn't seen her since before school let out. And I had no way to get in touch with her.

Joe looked at me like I was a few fries short of a Happy Meal, but I kept up the act because I didn't trust myself when talking about Tia. My heart was already thumping in my chest.

"You know," Joe said. "That girl who wore the combat boots and dyed her hair a different color every day? She dropped off the face of the earth."

I shrugged. "Oh, that girl. I have no clue. The last time I saw her was probably the last time you did, too. I totally forgot about her."

Complete lie. I thought about Tia all the time.

"My dad owns a carnival," Blair said, as if somehow that was the next obvious direction for the conversation. Or maybe she didn't like us talking about some girl she didn't know.

"I love carnivals," Henry said, moving right along in the conversation with her. He hadn't taken his eyes off her.

"What carnival?" I asked. I was happy not to be talking about Tia or the oddness of my name anymore. Normally I could pull together a combination of herbs and scents and say a small spell, and people around me would forget small things that didn't really make sense. Powers like that came from my scarab heart. From my patron deity, who happened to be Osiris, god of plants and bugs. Osiris was also why my skin did actually look green from time to time, like in the badge picture.

But ever since I gave Henry all the energy from my scarab heart, my immortal powers had been sporadic and weak. I couldn't even make grass grow anymore. I'd tried to recharge my heart—to fill it with immortal energy by channeling that energy through an obelisk—but it hadn't made me feel any different, which was weird. Recharging my scarab heart used to be one of the best feelings in the world.

Blair pulled a handful of brochures out of her pocket and handed us each one. "You know. That new one over across the river. It's a charity carnival. We're raising money to save endangered snake species around the world. Do you know people hunt snakes and kill them for horrible things like voodoo rituals and fake medicine? It has to be stopped. And my dad and I . . . we are totally doing our part."

"It sounds . . . um . . . interesting," Joe said. He glanced at the brochure like he wasn't sure if he could stick it in the nearest trash can or if that would be too rude.

"Do you have jugglers?" Brandon asked. I guess the charity aspect wasn't a big enough draw.

"Do we have jugglers?!" Blair said. "We have jugglers and a Ferris wheel and even a funhouse."

I was about to ask something else, but then she turned back to Henry, and their eyes locked. And I swear I could almost see little hearts floating in the air above their heads. Which was good news, now that I thought about it. I could ditch science camp after today and get back to looking for Gil. The problem was that if Gil wanted to be found, he would have left me clues. It was like he'd been erased from the same reality as me.

Still, I had no intention of giving up that easily. I could visit Auntie Isis. Maybe she knew where Gil went. Not that any part of me wanted to visit Horus's mom. The last time I'd seen her, she'd tried to mummify me. I didn't particularly want to give her the chance to finish the job. Maybe Horus could check with her. Even if she was the queen of the gods, she was still his mom. I'd ask him when I got home.

"You should totally come to our carnival," Blair said, licking her lips like she was checking if she had lip gloss on, which I don't think she did; her lips were really pale. "But if it's not your thing, my dad has a bunch of other businesses that all raise money for the same charity. Like a wax museum. And a restaurant. That really nice new place in Old Town. It's reservation-only. I'll bring you guys some information tomorrow. And next year, my dad is running for senator of Virginia. He's going to make a difference. If I were eighteen, I would totally vote for him."

"He's running for sena—" Henry started, but he got cut off by Camp Counselor Crystal.

Camp Counselor Crystal launched into a ten-minute-long speech about all the amazing places we were going to go for the next two weeks. Sure, they were all cool places, but my summer was not about going to camp. I needed to find Gil.

"Stop staring at her," I whispered to Henry while our group walked through the zoo. Henry hadn't taken his eyes off Blair, not even to listen to the science counselor lady.

"Huh?" I don't think Henry even blinked.

I smacked him on the arm. "Blair. You're completely staring at her."

He didn't reply.

"Henry," I said, a little louder, trying to get his attention.

Camp Counselor Crystal whipped around. "Quiet voices," she said, putting her finger to her lips. "We're getting ready to enter the reptile house. Reptiles do not like loud sounds. It makes them agitated. Very, very agitated."

The last thing we needed was some angry iguanas chasing after us, so I let it drop. I'd give Henry a hard time later. But the weird thing was that Blair was also sneaking looks at Henry. She was barely even glancing at me. It made no sense. People were always drawn to me. I was King Tut. I'd been the pharaoh of Egypt.

But as soon as we entered the reptile house, Blair looked away from Henry and started staring around at everything else. Her eyes got super-wide, and I'm pretty sure she stopped blinking. Slowly she edged her way to the back of the group. Henry looked at her, then at Camp Counselor Crystal. It was a huge dilemma for him, but nice timing for me. I could finally get his attention. I wasn't here to stare at lizards.

"You need to help me find Gil," I said. "I'm not having much luck on my own."

"Uh-huh," Henry said, still glancing back at Blair. She'd stopped at one of the displays—I think it was for a Gaboon viper—and she had her cheek pressed up against it, like she was trying to listen through the glass. Maybe it had something to do with her endangered-snake charity.

But before I could comment on this, images of a snake began

to flash through my mind. A giant snake, devouring something, like the stories I'd heard growing up. Snakes were revered back in ancient Egypt, but they were also feared. One bite from the wrong kind of snake—which in my opinion was any kind of snake—could be deadly, at least for a mortal. I didn't have anything to worry about. Except then the images became way more real. I was sitting in the dark, and things slithered around me, making hissing noises like snakes. And in the vision I wasn't me. I was Gil.

I tried to jump up, to get away from the slithering, but I couldn't move. Everything was really foggy, and my head felt so heavy I was having problems holding it up. My eyes were closed and I fought to open them, using every bit of strength inside me.

I called on my scarab heart powers. They didn't work.

My eyes finally snapped open. I was still here, at the zoo. What I'd just seen had been a vision. Some kind of daydream. Everything was exactly as it had been. I stood by Henry, and Blair was still by the snake display with her face pressed against the glass. But the weird thing was that the snake inside was nose to nose with her. And all the other snakes, in the other display cases . . . they were hissing and looking right at her. It was like my vision had done something to the snakes.

I tore my eyes away from Blair, but the reptile house was hot and muggy and freaky and what I really needed to do was get out of here and get on with finding Gil. That's what this daydream was trying to tell me.

"Dude, what's up with that girl?" Brandon said. "She's a little freaky."

Henry whipped around to face him. "You're freaky." And he looked angrier than I'd ever seen him look. But it wasn't just Henry's anger that took me by surprise. It was the confidence that poured off him. Immortal confidence. It had to be coming from the scarab heart energy inside him.

Brandon backed away. He looked like he might pee his pants. This was a bad situation getting worse.

I rested my hand on Henry's arm, trying to calm him. The last thing we needed was Henry picking a fight. Whether he was immortal or not, he still had immortal energy pumping through him. Someone could get hurt. And he'd get kicked out of science camp for sure.

Wait, maybe that wasn't such a bad idea.

No. It wasn't a good plan. Henry would never get over it.

"Henry, come on. You're missing what Camp Counselor Crystal is saying." I didn't care about missing her speech, but Henry would. Or at least he should. But he didn't move. So I dragged him away from Brandon and out of the reptile house. Maybe the heat was just getting to him, too.

But even as we left the reptile house, images from the vision returned to me. I felt like Gil was in trouble, and I was the only one who could help him. I had to find him.

3

WHERE I PLAY WITH FIRE

Great Master, we have a problem."

I nearly tripped over the army of small clay men in front of me as I walked into my townhouse. It was the shabti leader who spoke, Colonel Cody, finally back from whatever errand he'd been running. He stood there wringing his hands frantically. His golden face looked ashen. Or maybe that was my imagination. His face never really changed color, seeing as how it was painted on. Behind him stood twenty shabtis, also gold, but with green clothing. My special fighting unit. This couldn't be good.

"What kind of problem do we have?" I asked, trying to keep my voice steady. I didn't want to upset the little shabti. Since he'd returned from the underworld, he'd been trying extra hard to please me. I'd almost lost him during the whole Uncle Horemheb debacle. But thanks to Horus, I'd gotten him back. Sure, Horus had to travel to the underworld to retrieve Colonel Cody, but since Horus was a god, it wasn't as epic as it seemed.

He steadied his hands in front of himself, like he was trying to stay calm. "There seems to be an issue in the basement. We believe your assistance might be required, Great Pharaoh."

Oh, the shabtis. How I loved them. After nearly a hundred years together, I always knew when they were holding out on me. They never flat-out lied, but they did have an amazing ability to dance around the truth.

"The basement?" I almost never went down to the basement of my townhouse. If there was ever a problem with the plumbing or electrical work, the shabtis took care of it. They were way better at that kind of stuff than me, which made me sure this wasn't some sort of loose wiring or something like that.

"The basement," Colonel Cody said, nodding. Since he was the leader of my shabtis, he took charge of pretty much anything that went wrong.

"And you're sure you need my help?" I asked. I needed to find Gil. I'd already mapped out the places I was going to search for the rest of the day.

"Absolutely certain," Colonel Cody said. His eyes were wide and unblinking.

Whatever was going on in the basement, I wasn't getting out of it. So I followed the army of shabtis down two flights of stairs.

Colonel Cody held a tiny torch that looked like it had been

constructed from a Q-tip and a Band-Aid. It wasn't doing much to light up the place, so I let a small amount of light escape from my scarab heart. Gil's scarab heart. I was still trying to get used to it, and it didn't feel right to call it my own.

"Open the door, Great Master," Colonel Cody said. But right as he spoke, something slammed into the wooden door from the other side.

My gut reaction was to step back, but then my brain took over. I was not stepping back from whatever was behind this door. I was the Great Pharaoh Tutankhamun. I'd hunted jackals and ridden on the backs of rhinoceroses. I was more than capable of facing whatever dust bunnies the shabtis might have uncovered. I opened the door.

The light from my scarab heart bounced off the thing in front of me, and instantly I regretted it. It was about the size of a polar bear. I knew this because I'd just seen one at the zoo. Except unlike a cute little polar bear face, the thing in front of me had the head of a lion with bright white fangs popping out on either side of its ginormous mouth. Drool spilled from its black lips and dripped onto the concrete floor of the basement. Its tail stood straight up behind it. Actually, it wasn't really a tail. It was a snake, which hissed as soon as it saw me.

The thing lifted its upper lip into a snarl, exposing two rows of terrifying teeth that could rip my arm off in one solid bite. Armless was not how I intended to spend the rest of my immortal life.

"What. Is. It?" I asked Colonel Cody, keeping my voice low so I wouldn't upset the monster. But it didn't work because that's when the ears on the thing perked up; they were at least a foot tall. With those ears, it could probably hear a grain of sand fall in the Potomac River from ten miles away.

"It appears to be a monster," Colonel Cody said. He stood bravely at my feet, and with a small wave of his arm, the twenty battle shabtis moved forward, forming four rows of five. And though my shabtis were fierce when it came to protecting me, I was pretty sure this thing could step on them with its huge lion paws and crush them.

"What kind of mon—" I started, but I didn't have time to finish, because the thing let out a huge roar that made my bones vibrate. Globby drool spewed from its mouth and drenched me. And then it pounced.

It jumped twenty feet from a sitting position and flew through the air. Luckily I still had scarab heart reflexes, so I leapt out of the way, vaulting through the air and landing on the opposite side of the basement.

I rooted around behind me, trying to find something I could use as a weapon. I didn't dare take my eyes off the monster. My hand latched on to something, and I yanked hard, pulling it free. I held it out in front of me menacingly.

Colonel Cody said, "I'm not sure the toilet drainpipe is the best idea, Great Master."

Smelly sewer water gushed around my feet. But the shabtis could fix the pipes later. I swung the pipe hard, right at the monster's lion head. I swear it blinked out of existence, or else it was just really fast. In a split second it was ten feet to the right of where it had been and coming at me from the side.

"How is it so fast?" I said, and swung again. I hadn't actually hit the monster, but the pipe did seem to keep it back.

"It appears to have special skills," Colonel Cody said, stating the obvious.

"Skills! What is this monster?" With the way the thing kept flitting around, I had to keep changing directions.

"I'm certain that I don't—" Colonel Cody said.

"Don't say you don't know," I said. "Tell me. What am I fighting?" If I didn't know what it was, I'd have no clue how to defeat it. As it was, I wasn't sure that would help anyway. I let a bit more light escape from my heart, casting it on the monster. Maybe enough light would make it blind.

The light hit the monster, and instantly it stopped moving and closed its eyes. And then it sniffed the air, deep and steady, sucking in for a good thirty seconds. I know I could have swung the pipe at it in that moment, but something held me back.

"Colonel Cody," I said, prompting the shabti.

"We can't be completely certain," Colonel Cody said.

"If you had to make an educated guess?"

Colonel Cody looked to the monster, still with its eyes closed, and then back at me. "Humbaba," he said.

"Humbaba?" It sounded really familiar.

Colonel Cody nodded. "Humbaba. Guardian of the Cedar Forest. Destroyer of millions. Devourer of the living and the dead. Completely indestructible, at least according to our best translations of the Epic of—"

"The Epic of Gilgamesh!" I said. "Why is there a monster from the Epic of Gilgamesh in my basement?" Roaches. Spiders. Maybe even the occasional mushroom. These are things I would expect to find in my basement. Not mythological monsters intent on killing me.

It was about this time that Humbaba stopped sniffing at the air. His eyes flew open and fixed on me. He took a step forward. I gripped the pipe. I was in serious trouble here.

"Indestructible?" I asked Colonel Cody.

"Only so far," Colonel Cody said. "But we believe in you, Great Master. We know you will find a way to vanquish the monster."

At least one of us had confidence.

I wracked my brain, poring through everything Gil had ever told me about his history. He'd told me stories about his adventures before he met me. He'd battled gods and monsters alike. Gil was the most epic immortal the world had ever known. I vaguely remembered him mentioning this Humbaba monster, about trapping it, but I had no clue how to get rid of it.

I swung the pipe again, but this time, instead of moving around, Humbaba only stepped backward, out of the reach of the pipe. So I swung again. He jumped straight up in the air, and when he landed, his snake tail started wagging back and forth, like some kind of puppy dog's. He let out another roar, but it sounded like an invitation instead of a threat. And then he grabbed hold of the pipe with his fangs and pulled at it, as if it were some kind of oversized puppy toy.

Power started building up in my fingertips. But what was I going to do? Grow some plants on him? That's all my immortal skills had ever been good for before. Growing plants and summoning bugs. Plus my powers were flaky at best these days.

A couple dozen cockroaches wouldn't do much to vanquish this monster.

As the power in my fingertips grew, Humbaba's eyes widened, and his tail started wagging faster. He let the pipe go. I was sure it was all some trick and that he was going to pounce on me and rip my head off at any second. I raised the pipe to swing again, but . . .

. . . I couldn't do it. Humbaba looked too happy. So I threw the pipe backward over my head and I let the power flow.

Flames sprung from my fingertips and grew into a great ball of fire. I stared at it, not believing what I was seeing. I didn't have power over fire. That was all Gil. He got it from his patron god, Nergal. Except Gil didn't have that power anymore. I had his heart, and maybe, unless I was hallucinating, I had his powers, too.

I let the fireball grow until it was the size of a basketball, and then I pulled my right hand back and threw the fireball as hard as I could, directly through the open door.

Humbaba took off, chasing after the fireball, moving so fast I lost sight of him in under a second.

"Good boy," I said, and then I turned my sights to Colonel Cody.

He shrank under my gaze.

"Do you want to tell me what happened?" I asked, and then I shook my head. "Never mind. I'm going to shower first." I was covered head to toe in toilet water and monster drool.

"A very, very wise plan," Colonel Cody said, nodding agreeably. But he looked everywhere except right at me, like he didn't want to make eye contact, and I knew he was hiding something.

4

WHERE THE SHABTIS TRY
TO BURN ME ALIVE

Colonel Cody summoned Lieutenant Roy to the basement
to lead the cleanup effort and to fix the pipe. I stumbled
back up the stairs in my townhouse. I knew there was a
reason I never went into the basement.

"Great Master, we have a wonderful idea," Colonel Cody
said no sooner than we had walked into the family room.

"Does it involve my shower?" I asked, after tearing off my
clothes and tossing them in a pile.

Faster than you can say "stinky monster drool clothes," Colonel Cody snapped his little fingers, and four shabtis ran over to
the pile of laundry. I made a beeline for my bathroom.

"Well, sort of," Colonel Cody said.

I raised an eyebrow and looked down at him. "The only thing I'm doing right now is taking a shower."

Colonel Cody nodded, and I couldn't help but notice at least half the shabtis had covered their noses. I guess even six-inch-tall clay men aren't immune to the smell of sewer water mixed with monster drool.

"If my master would honor us with one minute, I would be happy to explain," Colonel Cody said.

I shook my head. "I'll be out in a few minutes."

A few minutes turned into half an hour. Halfway in, I'd wished I'd brought a scrub brush in with me. No matter how hard I washed, I felt like I was still coated in sewage and drool. It was only the water finally turning cold that drove me out.

The shabtis stood waiting, but I ignored them. Colonel Cody opened his mouth at least ten times to try to talk, but I put up my hand. The only thing I wanted to do right now was fall asleep.

I woke up the next morning on the futon to the smell of thick incense. And then I felt my scarab heart burning.

"What in the name of Amun Ra is going on?" I jumped up off the futon and brushed the burning incense from my bare chest. I looked around, sure hippie assassins were lurking nearby. No one was around except the shabtis.

I narrowed my eyes at Colonel Cody, who looked the other way and started whistling.

"What's going on?" I said.

He cocked his head at me. "Great Pharaoh was sleeping."

I took a step closer, but almost tripped on twenty shabtis running by with some old towels. I stepped over them.

"And I woke up because . . . ?" I said. Great Osiris, the shabtis avoided the truth like a plague of locusts. They always did exactly what I told them—except when they could sidestep around it.

The little shabti shrugged. "Great Tutankhamun was no longer tired?"

I reached down and picked him up, holding him near my face. "Did you light incense on me, Colonel Cody?"

He broke down. "Oh, Great Master, please order me to end my own existence if you must, but we were only trying to help you."

"Help me? By burning me alive?" I set him back down on the coffee table.

"Not burn you alive," Colonel Cody said. "We were cleansing you."

"Cleansing me?" I said. Hadn't the half-hour shower been enough?

"To cleanse the heart of the heathen within your chest," Colonel Cody said, jumping off the table and back onto the floor.

If he hadn't looked so earnest, I might not have answered. But I could tell that he believed every word he said.

"Gil's not a heathen and my scarab heart is fine," I said.

"As you say, Great Pharaoh."

But I knew no amount of talking would convince the shabtis. Once they got an idea in their heads, there was no stopping it.

"No more burning incense on my chest," I said.

Colonel Cody nodded. "Yes, Great Master."

I knew how the shabtis operated. "No more doing anything to me while I'm asleep without my direct spoken approval," I said. "Swear it on the tomb of Great Osiris himself."

I didn't pull out the threat of Great Osiris very often. But my townhouse was my refuge. I might not have been pharaoh of anything in the world anymore, but I still had my townhouse.

All the shabtis bowed their heads. "On the tomb of Great Osiris himself, we swear it," they said in unison.

"And what are you doing, anyway?" I turned to the window. A stack of towels flew out from the fire escape where I knew they'd land in the Dumpster below.

"Spring cleaning," Colonel Cody said. He snapped his fingers, and a set of black sheets went out the window next.

"It's summer," I said. Then it registered. "Hey, those are Gil's sheets."

Colonel Cody bowed. "We were taking it upon ourselves to rid the townhouse of the heathen lord's belongings."

"You're throwing out Gil's bedsheets?"

"They were very threadbare," Colonel Cody said. "I would take my own life before I would allow you to sleep on sheets of such inferior quality. Many of his possessions we've started moving to the basement."

"The basement," I said, and it clicked into place. "You let out Humbaba!"

"A most unfortunate accident," Colonel Cody said, pressing

a hand to his forehead. "He was stored in a clay tablet. I believe the heathen trapped him there. But"—he let out a small laugh—"you know how things are. Tablets are old. And, well, one small bump and . . ."

"Why are you moving Gil's stuff to the basement?" I asked. "He could come back any day."

"Gil's not coming back," Horus said, dodging towels as he walked in from the fire escape. "You know that."

I tried not to take the bait, but Horus and Gil . . . well, there was always this strain between the two of them. They argued about the best ways to protect me, when I didn't need their protection at all. But my fourteen-year-old mind took over and I couldn't help myself. "He is coming back," I said. "I know he is."

"If Gil wanted to be found, then he'd have been found by now." Horus flicked his paw dismissively in my direction.

I closed my eyes and counted to ten. Horus's lack of concern was infuriating. But he hadn't had the vision that I had. He didn't understand that Gil could be in trouble.

"Where did you go yesterday?" I asked. Maybe he did have feelers out and was secretly searching for Gil. I really hoped so, because I was running out of options fast.

Horus normally at least gave me an idea of where he was going to be. Sometimes he went to visit his girlfriend, a cat goddess named Bast. She was shiny and gold, and she and Horus had been on-again-off-again for centuries. Also, I was used to him disappearing around the new moon. He went crazy and blind when there was no light in the sky, and it was just safest when he went away. Otherwise there was the unpopular risk that he'd try to kill me. But the moon right now was a waxing crescent. He had a good three weeks until he was supposed to go away again.

"Ah, you missed me," Horus said. "I knew you cared." But then he walked to his milk bowl and frowned. It was empty. "Tut?" He narrowed his good eye at me.

"What?" I said, pretending I didn't know what he was talking about. I was still mad about him making me go to camp.

"I'm kind of thirsty." Horus licked his lips. His tail flicked back and forth patiently, as if he were willing to play this game as long as I was.

"Whatever," I finally said, and I looked to Colonel Cody, who summoned two shabtis to fill up the milk bowl.

"So really, where'd you go?" I asked. I wouldn't dare say anything, but Horus's normally shiny spotted Egyptian Mau fur looked dull and clumpy, almost like he'd been rolling in dirt. It was very unregal.

"I was watching the tides," Horus said.

"And?"

"And what?"

"Did you see anything interesting?" I asked. "No, never mind. Just play your games. Don't mind me."

"I won't," Horus said. He finished drinking his milk and jumped on top of his scratching post. It, like lots of the things around my townhouse, was covered in Egyptian hieroglyphs. We'd had it forever, also like a lot of the things around my townhouse.

Just then the doorbell rang.

"Expecting someone, Tut?" Horus asked.

Options of who would come by my townhouse were pretty limited. Nobody really knew who I was or where I lived. I mean, sure, I went to school, and kids in my grade knew me. But nobody knew I was the actual King Tut from ancient history. Nobody except two people.

Tia, the girl Joe and Brandon had been asking about yesterday, of course was one. And seeing as how it had been months since I'd heard from her, the odds were against her being at the door, no matter how much I might have wanted her to stop by and see me. Henry was the other. I was betting on him.

I opened the door.

"Am I late?" Henry asked.

I hated when I was right.

"For what?" I asked.

"Science camp," Henry said. "Day two."

"I'm not going today," I said, crossing my arms. "There was this Sumerian monster, and then the shabtis tried to burn me alive."

Henry's mouth formed a small O as I talked, but he had to realize by now that normal things didn't happen around me. I was about to tell him how I'd vanquished the monster in a heroic moment of glory, when I saw what was going on in the kitchen.

At the top of the basement staircase were twenty shabtis hauling some kind of large wooden chest on their heads.

"Stop!" I said, barely in time. Two more seconds and the chest would have gone flying down the steps. "Bring that to me now."

"But, my lord," Colonel Cody said, "as we were discussing earlier, it is best to rid ourselves of the heathen lord's possessions."

"We're not getting rid of Gil's stuff," I said. "And he's not a heathen."

"As you say, Great Master," Colonel Cody said. "But as we were agreeing upon, it would be prudent to place unneeded belongings into storage."

I imagined it would be eternal storage if the shabtis had their way.

"Bring it to me."

Panic grew on the shabtis' faces. They looked to Colonel Cody, then to me, then back at Colonel Cody. He sighed and nodded his head. So they trotted over with the chest on their heads.

Henry and I sat down on the futon, and I shoved the coffee table aside. The shabtis dropped the chest in front of me and backed away. The thing looked older than Gil's chair, and that was really saying something. I didn't see any kind of lock or key or even hinges, for that matter. I reached down to pull off the dirty wooden lid. Except it didn't come off. It didn't even budge. I bent down to look closer, but I couldn't see any opening at all. Maybe it wasn't a lid. The whole thing could have been a decorative cube, like an end table.

"How do I open it?" I asked Colonel Cody.

Henry started prodding at it. Clumps of dirt fell to the floor.

"My lord, I don't know," Colonel Cody said.

I rolled my eyes. "You don't know how to open it, or you don't know if you want to tell me?"

"That is an interesting question," Colonel Cody said.

"And the interesting answer is . . . ?"

"The answer to what?" Colonel Cody said.

I blew out my breath and put my hands back on the chest. Henry hadn't made any more progress than I had. "Let's take this one step at a time. Do you know how to open the chest?"

Colonel Cody crossed his hands over his chest. "No, Great Master."

"Okay," I said. "Do you know how to find out how to open it?"

He shook his head. Behind him, more shabtis scuttled to the basement steps with other things I didn't recognize.

"Nothing else goes to the basement," I said. "Didn't you guys learn anything from the monster? And bring anything that was Gil's to me right now." I fixed my eyes on Colonel Cody. "Even stuff already in the basement."

He snapped his fingers, and the little clay men began to obey.

"Did you ever see Gil open the chest?" I said.

Colonel Cody's face fell. "One time, Great Pharaoh, but I swear I don't know how he did it."

I smiled. Finally I was getting somewhere. "Do you think there was a key?"

Colonel Cody frowned. "No, there was no key. But . . ." He scratched his head. "I do remember something. He spoke some word and the next thing I knew, the lid popped off."

"It just popped off," I repeated.

Colonel Cody nodded and smiled like he'd solved world hunger.

"What word did he say?"

Colonel Cody sighed. "I don't remember. But the cat was here. Perhaps he would remember."

Horus opened his eye from the top of his scratching post.

"He's a god," I whispered to Colonel Cody, hoping Horus wouldn't hear.

"Yes, the cat god. He should know," Colonel Cody said. It was the best I was going to get out of him.

By now a pile had started growing in front of me. Sure, there were things like Gil's toothbrush and his dingy old Washington Bullets sweatshirt that he refused to get rid of, but there were also lots of other things I'd never seen before in my life. Like a bunch of clay tablets and a rusty old crown.

"Horus, do you know the word to open this chest?"

Horus put on his best bothered look. "What do I look like? A wordsmith?"

"No, you look like a cat," I said. "But that only cloaks your secret identity. You could be a wordsmith, too, for all I know."

I'd been around Horus forever, but he still remained a mystery. He wasn't just any god. He was a super-important god, the son of Osiris and Isis, who were kind of the king and queen gods. And he hung around with me for some strange reason. Not that I was complaining. I liked Horus—most of the time.

"Gil never opened that thing around me," Horus said. "Maybe it was for decoration."

Given the fact that it was secretly locked, I highly doubted that.

"Can you try to remember?" I asked Colonel Cody.

He nodded happily. "It would be my greatest pleasure."

But if he was going to remember, it wasn't happening right away.

"What about science camp?" Henry said.

I stood up and brushed the dirt and dust that had come from the chest off my jeans. Or maybe it was still some of the incense powder.

Henry stood up next to me. A shabti ran by with a paint-brush. It must have had something to do with repairs in the basement. On the scratching post, Horus again closed his eye.

"What about it?" I said.

Henry didn't say anything. He only stared me down. And as he stared, I remembered the weird vision I'd had about Gil from the day before. Maybe the shake-up in my normal routine had triggered it. As much as I hated to admit it, Horus could be right. Maybe I did need a change of pace. That could be the best way to find Gil.

"I have other things to do," I said, in one last-ditch effort to not go to camp.

"Great," Henry said. "We'll do them together after camp."

And so day two of science camp loomed before me.

5

WHERE THE GODS
VANDALIZED D.C.

Science camp day two was at the Tidal Basin. Across the water sat the Jefferson Memorial, glistening in the sun. Bright and shiny and polished. That's what Egypt used to look like, back when the buildings were new. Most people thought of them as always being a bunch of crumbling ruins, but that's completely not how it was. Egypt had been a shining star. It made me kind of sad when I thought about how it would never be restored to its full glory ever again, just like I'd never again be the king of Egypt. But, hey, I got to relive middle school forever.

Yeah, you feel my pain.

"Best shirt ever, Henry," Blair said, running up to us the second we crossed the street and met up with our science camp group. Here at the Tidal Basin, tourism was definitely picking up. There were already at least fifteen paddleboats out on the water, but none of them was moving very fast.

I glanced over at Henry's bright yellow T-shirt. It read, N Er Dy.

Nitrogen. Erbium. Dysprosium. I couldn't have hand-picked a better shirt for him.

"Thanks," Henry said, turning thirty different shades of red. "Do you know what happens when you mix two atoms of nitrogen with three atoms of dysprosium?"

"Please don't tell me," I said.

Blair looked at me, and it was like she really saw me for the first time. Like yesterday I'd been more of an accessory to Henry, but today I'd magically turned into a real person.

"You smell funny," Blair said. She leaned close and sniffed me.

I took a step back, bumping into Joe. The weird vibes were kind of rolling off Blair. Or maybe it was just the pungent odor coming from the Tidal Basin.

"It's the water," I said. I didn't smell the least bit funny. Colonel Cody never let me leave the apartment without deodorant.

Blair glanced over my shoulder at the mucky water and wrinkled her nose. "Yeah, maybe." But she sniffed me again. And then she sniffed Henry. And then she moved on to Joe and Brandon. She tried to act casual, like she wasn't doing it, but there was no missing it.

Behind me, Joe whispered, "Cray-Cray," and Brandon laughed.

I cringed, hoping Henry hadn't heard. We didn't need him threatening to pick another fight.

Henry started muttering words under his breath, things

that sounded like they'd come right out of the *Book of the Dead*. Around us, the air started to churn. It was like he was chanting some spell and actually making it work. Like maybe powers were finally coming out of him as a result of all the immortal energy I'd pumped into him. I had to do something.

I grabbed Henry's arm and started dragging him. "Come on, Henry. Let's get up front so we can hear better."

I couldn't believe the words had actually come out of my mouth. The things I would do for friendship amazed me. But it worked. Henry stopped whispering the spell and the air settled down.

"That was weird," he said. He seemed as surprised as I was.

"Yeah," I said. "We can talk about it later."

Henry let me lead him up to where Camp Counselor Crystal was already deep in lecture mode. She droned on and on about the waters in the Tidal Basin, talking about the directions they flowed, where they came from, how its whole purpose was to safely release water captured during the high tide. She was trying to make it sound fun, like all the different currents were racing at the Indy 500, but she kept glancing back at the water and frowning. I didn't give it much thought until I actually looked at the water myself.

Here's the thing. I'd been living in D.C. for over two hundred years, ever since it was built. I knew the place pretty well. The Tidal Basin had only been around for about a hundred of those years. But in those hundred years, I'd never seen the water acting this way. The tides around here were always predictable. Always the same. Except for today. Because today the water was almost not moving. There were some places where it was so still, I could see the ground through the water. I glanced toward the inlet bridge that let in the water, but the water looked completely still. And then my vision sort of clouded over, where I couldn't see anything at all. But I could hear all sorts of things. There was a bunch of pounding, almost like construction noise. And two people talking, arguing.

"It's your turn to watch him," one of the voices said. It was super-high and thin, to the point where it almost squeaked. I still couldn't see anything.

"I watched him already," the other voice said. Unlike the first voice, it was deep and gruff. "I'm sick of watching him. It's boring watching him. He's not doing anything."

In the vision, I felt really groggy, almost like I'd been drugged. My head was heavy, and all I wanted to do was lay my head down and sleep. But I also knew I had to listen. I tried to summon fire to the tips of my fingers, but it didn't work.

"What do you want him to do?" the first voice said. "Better for him to sit here doing nothing than to try to escape. I hear these immortals are ninja masters."

Escape? What was that about?

"He can't escape," the second voice said. "We got him secured pretty good."

The words faded and the darkness disappeared. The real world returned around me. I was still at science camp. Still watching the water. It had just been some kind of daydream. Another vision like I'd had at the zoo.

I was sure the vision was about Gil again, but what was it

trying to tell me? Gil wasn't immortal anymore. And I couldn't imagine where he'd need to escape from. Maybe I was just going crazy and it was all a bunch of weird stuff my mind was making up.

If anyone noticed me slip out of reality, they didn't let on. Henry was caught trying to split his attention between the lecture and Blair. The words he'd been muttering flitted around in my mind. If he did have powers, I'd have to work with him on getting them under control. I'd also have to get my own under control.

I still couldn't get over the fireball thing with Humbaba. Gil would be completely impressed. When I found him, it would be the first thing I told him. Speaking of which, I wondered where Humbaba had gone off to. I hoped he wasn't wreaking havoc on some small country.

I edged away from our camp group, wandering over to the inlet bridge so I could get a better look at the water. I sat down in the dirt, watching the lack of waves. Something was definitely up. The tides should not be acting this way. What was it Horus had said this morning, when I'd asked him where he'd been? Watching the tides. So he'd noticed it, too.

My phone buzzed, stirring me from my thoughts. It was probably Henry, telling me to get back to the group. I almost didn't look at it. But when I finally did, my heart started pounding like a herd of gazelles running across the plains. The message was from Tia.

did you miss me?—tia, she texted.

Finally, after six months of not seeing her, she decided to

get in touch. How was it that she had my cell phone number? I didn't have hers.

A million possible responses ran through my mind. Things like "hardly" to declaring my undying love for her. I opted against that since I could almost see her roll her eyes.

tia who? I finally texted.

ha, ha, she responded.

where've you been? I typed.

busy looking for something, she texted.

what?

Her reply came quick. it's secret. Sry tut. gtg.

Perfect. Just when Tia finally gets in touch with me, she ditches me once again. My fingers hovered over the keyboard. I typed out will you call me? but I deleted it before sending. I didn't want to seem pathetic, even if I was. Then I typed out call me but I deleted that, too. I settled on simplicity.

bye, I typed, and I hit *send*. Then I added her number to my contacts and pocketed the phone before I typed anything else and ruined my cool image.

Henry was just walking over. Blair was nowhere to be seen.

"You're missing everything, Tut," Henry said.

I'd had another vision about Gil, and Tia had texted me. I was definitely not missing anything. But I let Henry drag me back to the group.

Camp felt like an eternity. I tried to focus on what Camp Counselor Crystal was saying for the next couple hours. I really did. But my mind kept jumping back to the tides and then Gil and then Tia. It was only made tolerable by Joe and Brandon's unending string of sarcastic comments. They were actually pretty hilarious. Even Henry laughed a couple times. Finally it ended.

"Hey, you guys want to grab a burger or something?" Joe said.

Even though my stomach grumbled at the thought of a juicy hamburger, I had to search the rest of the places on my list for Gil. My scarab heart thumped in reply. Also, I wanted to ask Horus about the tides.

"Not today," I said, even though Henry looked like he was about to say yes. He'd been eating everything in sight these days. "Henry and I have something to do."

"Next time for sure," Joe said. "We should hang out more often."

It was weird. In the past, I'd always gotten along with everyone. But I'd also remained pretty unnoticed, thanks to my spells. But Gil's heart was different. It made me feel more visible. More the center of attention. I wondered if it was how Gil had felt all the time.

"Next time," I said, though I couldn't imagine having burgers with the guys at school. A year from now, when I wasn't looking any older, they might not want to be my friend so much.

"I keep having these weird visions about Gil," I said as Henry and I started back toward my townhouse. I half expected him to laugh as I told him about them, but he nodded and hung on my every word.

"You think he's in trouble?" Henry asked.

"I don't know," I said. "I don't want to think that, but it's like my mind is trying so hard to figure out where he went. But you know how Gil was. He kept his private life so . . ."

"Private?" Henry suggested.

"Yeah. Which I know sounds obvious, but with Gil it was almost like he was hiding things."

"So you think he's hiding now?" Henry said.

I'd thought this out, plenty of times. Sure, there was a part of me that thought Gil was hiding just around the corner, still watching out for me. But Gil was mortal now. He could die. And he would die if he didn't watch out. This latest vision had mentioned escaping. That wasn't good. Gil could be in serious trouble.

"Gil would have found some way to get in touch by now. Something to let me know he was okay."

I was about to go into some lengthy story about all the great times Gil and I'd had together, but a Japanese family stopped us to ask for directions—in Japanese. No problem. I'd lived in Japan for years. I could totally tell them where the Smithsonian was. Before I had a chance, Henry answered instead . . . in Japanese. Perfectly fluent conversational Japanese.

The family beamed at Henry and must've bowed twenty times in thanks. Henry bowed in return, and the family set off toward the museums.

"You know Japanese," I said, stating the obvious.

"Yeah, weird," Henry said. "I had no idea I knew Japanese." He acted like it was no big deal.

"And . . . ?" I said.

"And what?"

"How do you know Japanese all of a sudden?"

Henry shrugged. "Maybe my mom's been playing those 'Learn Any Language' audiobooks for me while I've been sleeping. You know scientific data suggests that people can even learn to do things like play the guitar while asleep."

"You didn't learn Japanese while you were sleeping," I said.

"Google Translate?" Henry said, but even he didn't seem convinced.

I was about to point out the impossibilities of it being Google Translate, but I never got the chance because we turned the corner and came to a stop along with at least fifty other people.

We'd stopped under a bridge in Georgetown. It was right near where this super-cool music club used to be called the Bayou. They'd closed the club years ago. Gil would sneak me in to listen to music since the entry age was eighteen. It was one more annoying reminder of what a pain it was to be stuck at fourteen.

"I've never seen graffiti like that," Henry said, pointing. It's what everyone was looking at.

If there was one thing D.C. had plenty of, it was graffiti artists. But the guy in front of us had turned it into a contact sport. He jumped up high on the wall, grabbed hold of the rafters from the bridge above, and hung by one arm as he sprayed more paint. Next he flipped over in the air and landed on the ground, then proceeded to spray the entire base of the wall from left to right while sliding across the pavement on a skateboard. When he finished with one paint can, he snapped it into a belt he wore slung low around his waist, like some sort of Batman utility belt, but with paint instead of grappling bat-hooks, and grabbed another.

His white tank top was covered with paint of every color, as were his faded jeans, which hung as low on his waist as his belt.

The crowd started clapping. The guy bowed and waved in reply. A few people even handed him money. It had to be a way more fun way to make cash than bagging groceries.

People took pictures, and the guy posed. The graffiti was amazing. The only problem was, it wasn't just random graffiti. Not that anyone in the crowd would recognize it. What was written was a bunch of lines and symbols and didn't look like any language that had been used in the last three thousand years.

It took forever, but finally everyone wandered off except Henry and me.

"Give me a word," the guy said, snapping the red paint can into place in his belt and turning to us. He was Asian and lean and muscular and only looked a couple years older than me or Henry, about sixteen. His eyes landed on me and narrowed, as if he was searching deep inside my soul.

And even though I had no intention of doing it, a single word popped out of my mouth.

"Obelisk," I said, without even thinking. But I guess the whole thing with recharging my heart at an obelisk not making me feel any different was weighing on me more than I knew. I had no idea if Gil's heart would recharge the same as mine. Or if it even needed recharging now that it had been transferred to me. My level of immortal energy was stable, even after fighting Humbaba. And Henry . . . he didn't even have a scarab heart to recharge. I'd given him all the energy from mine, but that was it. I had no idea if or when it would run out.

The guy shrugged. "Makes sense. Just don't worry about it. Things will work themselves out."

He couldn't be talking about anything to do with my thoughts. Could he?

His eyes moved to Henry next, and they narrowed even more. "Give me a word."

Henry didn't hesitate. "Immortal."

The graffiti artist cocked his head. "And are you?"

"I don't know," Henry said.

I elbowed him. We had no clue who this guy was or why he'd be asking us for words.

He jumped forward and got right in Henry's face. "I don't know either. I mean, you seem like you might be, from the energy coming off you, but then again, you seem like you aren't. Do you want to find out?"

Henry took a step back and crossed his arms over his chest. "No. Not particularly." For Henry to find out if he was immortal, he'd essentially have to die. Or at least almost die. His not dying is what would prove his immortality. But that would kind of suck if he were only mortal. I'd gotten really used to having Henry around.

"What do you think, Tut?" the graffiti artist said, looking down at his paint-covered hands.

"How in the realm of Anubis do you know my name?" I asked, before I could think about what I was saying.

The guy smiled. "Interesting choice of words."

"Um, what?" I said, trying to play stupid.

"The realm of Anubis," he said.

"Yeah, way to be discreet, Tut," Henry said.

Nice to know that he had my back.

"Oh, that," I said. "That's just my polite way of referring to the underworld."

"Anubis wouldn't think it was very polite," the guy said. "But you'd know that if you'd ever been to visit. Not that I'm suggesting you go visit. Anubis has been a little cranky these days. He claims someone escaped from the underworld, but it's probably just an eternal shortage of chew toys, if you ask me."

Even though Anubis was a jackal, which was sort of related to a dog, I didn't imagine an Egyptian god ran around playing with chew toys all day. Then again, Horus sure liked catnip a lot.

Whatever the case, this was not just some normal D.C. graffiti artist.

"And you are . . . ?" I asked.

But Henry raised his hand and waved it around, like he was in the middle of class or something. I'd seen him do it enough times this past year in school. "Oh, I know!"

How Henry had any clue about this guy's identity was beyond me.

The artist smiled at Henry. "Of course you do," he said, like that made perfectly logical sense.

I turned to Henry. "How do you know who he is?"

Henry smacked me on the arm. "Don't you get it? The words. The . . ." His voice trailed off.

"What about the words?" I said.

"I don't know. Just the words. That's enough."

"See? Henry's smart," the graffiti guy, who I pretty much decided had to be a god but I wasn't sure which one, said.

"Smart" was one word to describe Henry. And I will say that Henry loved research. I'd never spent so much time in the library before I'd met him.

Henry beamed under the praise.

"So who is he?" I asked.

Henry reached forward and grabbed one of the spray cans from the guy's belt. He squatted down. And, like he'd been drawing them forever, he painted three Egyptian hieroglyphs on the ground.

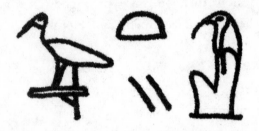

"Thoth," I said.

The guy looked like some grungy teenager, nobody I would bow to. Not that I bowed to the gods. They had so many issues and problems, it's not like they were role models.

"Nice, Boy King," Thoth said. "Way to figure it out once your friend spelled it out for you."

Yeah, that was pretty embarrassing. I still wasn't sure how Henry had figured it out before me. Or how Henry had pulled hieroglyphs out of nowhere. Unless he'd learned those in his sleep, too.

"Aren't you supposed to have the head of an ibis?" I said.

The ibis was this sacred bird with a long pointy beak from back in Egypt. Thoth, at least according to everything I'd ever heard, was the ibis-headed god.

Thoth ran a hand across his short dark hair. It was way shorter than mine or Henry's. But unlike Henry or me, Thoth had the start of a mustache over his top lip.

"I'm a god," Thoth said. "I can look like whatever I want. I can do whatever I want."

"So you vandalize D.C. for fun?" I said.

Thoth cracked his paint-covered knuckles, then took his paint can back from Henry and clipped it into his belt.

"It's art," Thoth said.

"It's illegal," I said.

"I've seen your art before," Henry said. "Didn't you have something last week over near the convention center?"

Thoth smiled. "As a matter of fact, I did. Do you remember what it said?"

Henry made a move to push his glasses up on his nose, but then he stopped when he remembered he didn't wear glasses anymore. The energy from my scarab heart had not only saved his life, it had improved some of his deficiencies also. His eyesight was now perfect.

"Sure," Henry said. "It said 'darkness.'"

"Right," Thoth said. "How about over near Ford's Theatre? Did you see that one?"

"What are you doing here?" I asked, interrupting. From the way things were going, it seemed like Henry and Thoth could have carried on this conversation all day.

"I have a message for you," Thoth said, and he started patting the pockets on his baggy jeans. If he really did have a message for me, it was probably covered in paint by now.

The first thing that sprang to my mind was Tia. Maybe after our wonderful text conversation, she'd decided to send a message via carrier-god.

"It's not from your girlfriend," Thoth said, like he could read my mind.

"She's not my girlfriend." My face got super-hot, and I knew that even with my tan complexion, it was probably bright red. I figured dropping the subject of Tia was my best tactic. "So who's it from?"

Great Osiris, please don't let it be a message from Set or anything like that. I'd had enough of the god Set and his crazy cult to last me the rest of eternity. Deadly snakes. Near-mummification. The last thing I wanted was anything to do with Set.

"Not Set either," Thoth said.

"Thank Amun," I said. "Then who's it from?" But the second I said it, I knew, deep in my scarab heart.

Thoth's eyes softened. "Right. It's from Gil." And then he pulled a piece of crumpled brown paper that looked like it had been torn from an old lunch bag from his pocket and handed it to me.

6

WHERE GIL SENDS A MESSAGE

looked down at the paper for one second. I swear it wasn't any more time than that. And when I looked up, Thoth was gone, along with his skateboard and all the paint cans.

"Where did he go?" Henry said.

I scanned the area, but aside from the graffiti-sprayed wall and the hieroglyphs on the ground, there was no sign of Thoth. I thought my immortal powers made me pretty quick, but they were nothing compared to Thoth's.

"Welcome to dealing with the gods," I said. "They never explain themselves to anyone. And what was up with all that attention he was giving you?" I'd have sworn that Thoth was way over-interested in Henry, and I had no clue why.

"I dunno," Henry said, but the way he said it, it seemed like he knew more than he was letting on.

I didn't push it. I had bigger concerns than the gods being nosy. For the first time in six months, I had a real sign that Gil was alive. That Gil was okay.

I unfolded the wrinkled brown paper and pressed the creases out between my fingers. And sure enough, there was Gil's handwriting: perfect script that was intentionally made to look sloppy. No matter how hard Gil tried to shake his royal background, he never could.

"What's it say?" Henry asked.

I had to squint because even in the bright sunlight, the letters were pretty faint, and where the folds had been, they were hard to read. It was almost like he'd written the note and then balled it up, like a piece of trash.

Tut—
I feel you looking for me. I know you're trying to find me. Seriously, just stop. Okay, I know you're going to ignore what I just said, so I'll say it again. Don't come find me. I don't need to be found. Really. Just go on with your life. Forget about me. And because I know what you're thinking, listen to me this one more time. Don't come find me. I mean it. You'll be fine.

−Gil

"He can't be serious," I said, once Henry had read the note also.

"Pretty sure he is," Henry said. "He said it, like, four times."

"But still, he can't possibly think I'm not going to look for him. And what about this part? 'I feel you looking for me'?"

"Yeah, that is a little weird," Henry said.

"Not too weird, though," I said. "What if the visions are real? What if he's feeling them, too?"

"You're just worried about him," Henry said. "Your mind is messing with you."

"Well, yeah, sure. I am worried. But this note? It's a complete cry for help. Like Gil is saying not to come find him, but what he's really saying, if you read between the lines, is to find him."

"I don't think so," Henry said. "He says it right here: 'Don't come find me.'"

Henry didn't get it. He hadn't had the vision of Gil in trouble.

I crumpled the paper into a ball. "And what? You think I should just listen to him? Be fine with that?"

I was all set to continue on my tirade when Henry stopped me.

"I never said that," Henry said. "In fact, I think you'd be a complete idiot if you didn't keep looking for Gil."

"You do?"

"Sure," Henry said. "It's what we're supposed to do."

What *we* were supposed to do. I liked that. It had been so long since I'd had a real friend, I'd forgotten how great it could really be. I wasn't in this alone.

When we opened the door back at my townhouse, I nearly tripped over a pile of junk in front of me. The whole place was jam-packed with so much stuff, my eyes could hardly focus. There were Sumerian tablets and leather-bound books and mugs and cups of every size. Gil had given me the hardest time about keeping so much stuff in the townhouse, things I didn't want to get rid of for sentimental reasons, and he was a way worse pack rat than I was. No way had all this been in his bedroom. This much stuff would've filled five bedrooms. It must've been down in the basement. And yet looking at it now, knowing it was his—well, it made me miss him that much more. I couldn't believe he'd just taken off like that. Without even saying goodbye. I should sell everything here in a dollar garage sale, just to get back at him.

I felt a tug on my jeans.

"What's up?" I asked Colonel Cody.

"Would Great Master and his friend care for anything to drink?" Colonel Cody said. Next to the shabti leader stood Lieutenants Leon and Virgil, balancing a tray on their heads. On it were two sodas.

"Sure," I said, reaching down.

But the shabtis shifted the tray around before I could grab the soda. "Not that one," Colonel Cody said. "That is Master Henry's drink." He pointed at the other glass on the tray. "And this is the Great Pharaoh's."

"Master Henry," Henry said. "I like the sound of that."

"Don't get used to it." I narrowed my eyes, picked up the soda, and smelled it. "What did you put in here?"

"Herbal supplements," Colonel Cody said, but I could hear it in his voice. He was definitely hiding something.

"What kind of herbal supplements?" I asked.

The lieutenants bowed and backed away with the tray.

"Those guaranteed to exorcise heathen spirits from any unfortunate situation," Colonel Cody said.

"I don't have heathen spirits," I said, even though I knew he'd never believe me. "And this is not an exorcism."

Henry licked his lips. "Does this mean I can't have my soda?"

"Go ahead. The shabtis aren't worried about cleansing *you*." I set my soda down. Colonel Cody frowned, but I didn't want any part of this cleansing.

Where the coffee table normally was, the chest still sat, unopened in front of the futon. Henry slurped his entire soda through the straw, eyeing the chest the entire time. And when he finished, he skipped around all the stuff scattered about my townhouse, knocking a bunch of stuff from the piles, and walked over to it.

"I know the word," he said. And he uttered something in ancient Sumerian that he couldn't possibly have learned in a book since he got the pronunciation perfect and everything.

No sooner was the word out of his mouth than the lid of the trunk popped open.

7

WHERE WE HACK INTO GOOGLE MAPS

How'd you do that?" I asked Henry. It's not like my scarab heart energy gave him some sort of magical power over words. Or at least it shouldn't have. But Henry now not only spoke Japanese, he also spoke ancient Sumerian. For all I knew Mandarin Chinese would be next.

Henry stared at the now-open trunk, like he'd just performed some hocus-pocus magic trick. "I just knew it."

"It was a heathen word," Colonel Cody said, and he started waving his hands in front of him as if he were warding off any evil that might have been released.

"Gil's not a heathen," I said, but Colonel Cody was right in that it was a Sumerian word. Osiris knows I'd heard Gil utter enough ancient words under his breath in the last thousand years, including some I definitely shouldn't repeat. "Do you know what it means?" I asked Henry.

Henry ran a hand through his messy blond hair and narrowed his eyes to slits, like he was thinking super-hard. "Away with thee?" he said, as if he wasn't really sure.

I nodded. "Or in twenty-first-century English it means 'Keep out.' It must've been Gil's password. But that doesn't explain how you knew what it was."

Henry ran his hands over the top of the lid. "It was the word Thoth painted on the side of the wall."

Henry was right. It's exactly what Thoth had graffitied near the Bayou club.

"Last time I checked, you didn't know ancient Sumerian," I said.

"Perhaps your friend is infected with the same heathen virus that you are, Great Master," Colonel Cody said.

"I'm not infected with a heathen virus," I said. "I have Gil's heart. That's all. It's not a virus."

"Of course, Great Master," Colonel Cody said, but he edged my untouched soda closer to me.

"And the Japanese thing, too," I said. "And that spell you started muttering at camp. Something weird is going on with you, Henry."

Henry tried to recover from the weirdness. "I'm sure there's a perfectly scientific explanation for it all."

I was sure he was wrong.

"What is all this junk, anyway?" Henry asked, leaning over to peer into the trunk.

The chest was packed full of trinkets and bobbles and papers. It even looked like there were some granola bars tucked around the edges.

"Gil was a worse hoarder than you," Henry said, bumping his hand against a bunch of golden charms that were sitting on the top. They spilled from the trunk and onto the floor. A shabti dove for one before it ended up under the futon.

I rolled my eyes. "I am not a hoarder just because I collect a few things here and there." I reached in and pulled out a big bundle and untied the string holding it together. "It looks like a bunch of letters."

Okay, part of me felt a little intrusive—like I was violating a secret slice of Gil's life. But that didn't keep me from reading at least a couple of the letters. My face grew hot as I read.

"They're from Gil's girlfriend," Henry said, reaching for the third letter. "Did you even know Gil had a girlfriend?"

I pulled it out of his reach and put it back with the others. "Are you kidding? Gil's had, like, a million girlfriends."

But none that I knew he wrote love letters to. A weird wave of . . . jealousy . . . ran through me. The fact that Gil had a complete life that had nothing to do with me. Maybe he was off living that life and was happy to be rid of me. Maybe I should just let him be. My visions could be a bunch of nonsense. Except they didn't feel like nonsense. They felt real. Gil was in some sort of trouble. He needed my help.

"Who?" Henry said.

I tucked the letters away, out of reach. "I don't know. He never introduced me to any of them." Introducing your girlfriends to your kind-of younger brother must not've been on the top of his priority list.

"What's this?" Henry said, picking up a pointy bronze object with two intersecting angles. He pulled at it, and it snapped in half. I cringed. If Gil had seen that, he would have wanted to pull Henry's hair out.

"Let's just put that down," I said, taking the broken pieces and setting them on the coffee table. The shabtis could fix anything, even ancient Sumerian artifacts. Whatever it was didn't give me any hint as to where Gil might be. I reached into the trunk and grabbed a round piece of paper that looked like a miniature vinyl record. At the top of the record, printed in silver foil, were the words THE BABYLON CLUB, along with some kind of weird picture of eight eyeballs centered around the middle like spokes of a wheel.

"What's The Babylon Club?" Henry asked.

"No clue," I said. I looked around the apartment until I found Captains Otis and Otto. They were master hackers. They always solved any computer issues I had. "Hey, bit heads, I got a problem for you."

They scrambled to unplug a bunch of cords and then hurried over, carting a laptop on their heads.

"What site do you need us to hack into, Great Pharaoh?" Captain Otto said.

Captain Otis set the laptop on top of the coffee table and unlocked it by typing in twenty characters that made up the password.

"Yes, perhaps the FBI? The CIA?" Captain Otis said. "Or is it the middle school again to make a grade adjustment?"

"You have them change your grades?" Henry said.

"Only once," I said. "But it was an honest error. I was just fixing it."

"I don't know, Tut," Henry said. "You should talk to the teacher next time."

Of all the things I may be, a cheater was not one of them. But I didn't want to take the time to defend myself right now.

"No hacking required today," I said to the shabtis. "Can you tell me where The Babylon Club is?"

"Directions," Captain Otis said, shaking his head. "Such a menial task."

Menial, maybe, but the last time I'd tried to use Google Maps on my own, the shabtis had started changing the computer password daily.

"It shall be done exactly as you ask, Great Pharaoh," Captain Otto said, and he and Captain Otis landed on the laptop and started typing and clicking the trackpad buttons so fast, I couldn't hope to keep up.

They started mumbling a couple minutes into the search, and when they hadn't sent the directions directly to my phone within five minutes, I got worried.

"Did you find it?" I asked.

"One moment," Captain Otis said, holding up a tiny pointer finger.

Another moment went by. Then another. After a solid five minutes, the two shabti hackers turned around and lowered their heads.

"It seems we have failed you, Great Pharaoh," Captain Otto said.

"You couldn't find it?" They'd found everything I'd ever asked, even the official middle of nowhere, which happened to be somewhere in Idaho, according to Google.

"It's not that we didn't find it," Captain Otis said. "It's that there is no such place as The Babylon Club."

I held up the paper record. "But I have proof that it exists right here."

"Great Master, perhaps you would care to refine your search terms," Captain Otto said.

I shook my head. "No, that's okay." All this meant was that whoever was in charge of The Babylon Club kept it off the grid, the same way Captains Otis and Otto kept me off the grid.

"Tut, look. There's a date." Henry flipped the paper around in my fingers. "From last fall."

He was right. It was written in silver Sharpie on the back.

"That's almost exactly when Gil went away. And maybe . . ."

Henry's eyes widened. My immortal energy had given him a sense of adventure. "Maybe if we go to this place, someone there might know where Gil is."

"But Great Master, as we were just saying, there is no such destination as The Babylon Club," Captain Otto said.

I folded the miniature vinyl-record paper and shoved it into my pocket. "No, it just means we need to use some new tactics to figure out where it is."

8

WHERE HENRY LOSES AT SCRABBLE

As much as I tried—and trust me, I tried—I couldn't talk Henry out of skipping science camp. Today it was at the Air and Space Museum. We were supposed to meet in the main planetarium, but the planetarium was closed, so we met under the *Spirit of St. Louis* instead. Of course, Blair was already there, along with the rest of the group. She waved frantically as we walked in, blond hair bouncing up and down, and before I could stop him, Henry hurried over to join her.

"Why's the planetarium closed?" Brandon asked.

"It's probably broken," Joe said. "Right, Tut?"

"Sure," I said, not sure why he was asking me. "That stinks." I'd been there lots of times before, so I wasn't sad to miss it. But it seemed like the right response.

"Hey, what are you guys doing this weekend?" Brandon asked me and Henry. "My parents said I could have people over."

Us? Like he was suggesting he'd have Henry and me over . . . for a playdate?

"Um . . . I think we have plans." It was so spur of the moment, I had no idea how to respond. I wasn't used to this kind of attention. What I was used was being invisible. But Gil's scarab heart had changed that. And I wasn't sure how I felt about it.

"You don't have plans the whole weekend," Brandon said. "It's Saturday night. You and Henry should both come."

"What about me?" Blair said. "Can I come? I mean, I have to be at my dad's carnival during the day for some super-important charity fundraising stuff, but we could all go to the carnival. It would be amazing and awesome and fun, and totally for a great cause. And then we could head to your house after."

Brandon looked to Joe, who looked to me like he thought I was going to save him. I pressed my lips together.

"No girls," Joe said. "Duh."

"Are you kidding me?" Blair said. "That is so twentieth century."

Twentieth century or not, there was no way Blair would magically become one of the guys. But she still looked like she was going to stomp her foot in protest.

"I'll let you know," I said to Brandon. "I'll text you."

Camp finally started. I thought about Gil's note while Camp Counselor Crystal rambled on about lunar eclipses and solar eclipses and binary star systems and stuff like that. When she started in on planets, she and Henry got into a heated debate about whether Pluto should be a planet or not. Henry started ticking off debate points on his fingers, and I knew they'd be at it for a while.

"I have to go text someone," I whispered to Brandon while Camp Counselor Crystal listed off the differences between planets and dwarf planets. "I'll be over there." I pointed to the closed door of the planetarium. Blair watched me as I walked away, not blinking, even as I overheard her saying to Joe, "No way does IHOP have better funnel cakes. The funnel cakes at my dad's carnival are the best ever."

Funnel cakes were pretty tasty, but they weren't what was on my mind. Neither was Pluto. I needed to figure out where this Babylon Club place was. And maybe . . .

I sat on the ground outside the closed-off planetarium and pulled up Tia's number. My scarab heart clenched up, like I was nervous. But that was ridiculous. I wasn't nervous to text Tia. I was King Tut. Ruler of Upper and Lower Egypt. Lord of the Two Lands. Reformer of Egypt.

Okay, fine, I was a little nervous. My heart skipped a few more times in my chest and then finally settled down.

have you ever heard of a place called the babylon club? I texted.

If she knew, this might be enough to get her attention. If she didn't know, maybe it would pique her interest.

I waited, watching Henry and his continued debate on Pluto and its hopeful replanetification—his word, not mine. Blair had finally stopped pestering Joe and Brandon about the carnival and now alternated between staring at me and Henry. Behind the closed door of the planetarium came loud banging, like they were dismantling the entire thing. It had been built eons ago, so an upgrade might be in order. A sign out front read, Renovation in Progress. Building a Brighter Future.

Tia never responded to my text, and Henry finally finished debating and noticed where I was. He waved me over, so I gave up on Tia and headed back to join the group.

You like Blair," I said to Henry after we left the museum.

"No," Henry said. "I mean, yes. I mean, she's really nice, I guess."

"You do like her," I said.

"Ugh. I don't know," Henry said. "Do you think I do?"

"Of course. It's really obvious." It didn't take Hathor, the Egyptian goddess of love, to know that Henry thought Blair was cool.

"Well, don't tell her," Henry said.

I was pretty sure Blair already knew . . . unless she was as clueless as Henry.

"I got an idea," I said, as we started back in the direction of my townhouse. Huge flocks of all kinds of birds swarmed overhead, like they wanted to roost somewhere but weren't quite sure where to go.

"I got an idea, too," Henry said.

"What?"

"We should go to Blair's dad's carnival," Henry said.

Seriously? He was thinking about cotton candy? We needed to find Gil.

"We have to go to The Babylon Club. Remember?"

"After the carnival?" Henry said.

"We're not going to a carnival right now," I said. "What we're going to do is have Thoth deliver a message for us to this club, the same way he brought that message from Gil to me. Then, we can follow him and see where he goes. If he delivers messages to people, he should know where everyone and everything is, right?"

Henry seemed to consider this. "Right, I guess. But couldn't we just ask him?"

That was a possibility. It's just that nothing in my life seemed to work that easily.

"We could try," I said, as we walked up the steps to my townhouse.

No sooner were Henry and I inside than Horus launched himself at the door, slamming it behind us.

"You shouldn't be out there," Horus hissed at us. His good eye was wide and filled with an almost feral look. I'd seen this look before, when the new moon approached. It was when Horus went blind. And when he went blind, he went crazy. His fur, which was dirty and dull before, was matted like he'd been drenched in Sumerian monster snot.

"We're fine," I said, moving in front of Henry. If Horus was having some sort of freak-out, I didn't want Henry to get caught in the middle. I still didn't know if Henry was immortal, and having Horus try to disembowel him wasn't how I wanted to find out.

"It's not safe out there," Horus said, waving his paws in front of the door. The protective wards on the townhouse snapped into place. "There are demons out there. Monsters. They're coming for us. Coming for you, Tut."

I had to be careful here. Horus was not himself and I didn't want him to go crazy and start clawing my face off. My eyes flickered to Colonel Cody, but he and the shabtis held back. This was super-crazy talk. I guessed that the shabtis were beside themselves with worry, trying to decide if they should attack Horus.

"It's perfectly safe," I said, stepping to the side. I needed to get on the other side of Horus, because there had to be something in the family room that could help. I looked around at the piles of Gil's stuff, but nothing seemed the least bit useful. Maybe a spell from the *Book of the Dead*? Or a catnip toy?

"Haven't you seen the sun?" Horus hissed. He stood arched on the tips of all four of his paws with his tail straight up in the air.

"The sun is setting," I said. "It's getting dark."

"Exactly!" Horus said. "And have you seen the birds? The grackles and pigeons and geese. They don't know what to do."

So there *had* been something off with the birds.

"Maybe they're migrating," I said. "Birds do that, you know."

"Not in the summer, Tut," Henry said.

I could have kicked Henry, drawing attention to himself like that. Horus whipped around to face Henry. I was sure Horus was going to rake him with his claws.

"How dare you—" Horus started, but that's when the door flew open.

"Is there some kind of problem here?" Thoth said, standing in the doorway. He raised a spray paint can in either hand, like he was prepared to strike, graffiti-style.

Horus spun and leapt in Thoth's direction. But he stopped short of attacking Thoth. Thoth stared Horus down. Silent words seemed to pass between the two of them. As the seconds ticked by, Horus's tail lowered, and he sat down and started licking his hind leg. Finally he pounced on a nearby scarab beetle and sucked its guts out.

"Well, that was weird," Henry said under his breath.

It summarized the encounter perfectly.

"What are you doing here?" I asked Thoth. "How'd you get in?"

Five shabtis ran over and slammed the door. Seeing as how there were now two Egyptian gods in my townhouse, it was a good idea.

"Just thought I'd visit," Thoth said.

"But the wards..." I said, waving my hand at the door. Whatever Horus had done to protect my townhouse had not kept Thoth out.

"Wards," Thoth said, as if the mere thought of them was laughable. "How would I ever get my job done if every single little ward I came across blocked my way?"

He had a good point.

"You guys don't need to bow," I said to the shabtis, who lay prostrate in rows on the floor in front of Thoth.

Colonel Cody raised his little head just enough to peek at me. "But, Great Master..."

"Really," I said. The gods were cocky enough for five immortal lifetimes.

"You got shabtis," Thoth said. "Do they know any words?"

This immediately got Colonel Cody to his feet. "Great God of Knowledge, we have all sorts of words. I, personally, have taken it upon myself to memorize—"

Thoth put up a hand. "Sure, you know words, but do you always know the right word?"

Colonel Cody froze. "I'm sure should the situation arise where—"

"Wonderful. It's always nice to see shabtis with words." He turned to Henry. "How about a game of Scrabble?"

Henry looked super-happy, like Thoth had just asked him to recite the first hundred digits of pi. I guess having a god ask you to play a board game might be considered something special.

"I'm extremely good at Scrabble," Henry said. I loved how his confidence in matters of the brain took over, even in the face of an Egyptian god.

Thoth smiled. "I'm better than you."

"Yeah, not to brag, but I don't think so," Henry said.

I figured I'd let them duke it out, so I dug my Scrabble board out of the closet. It was buried under a stack of scrolls and some dirty boxers. Weird. Normally the shabtis were all over doing my laundry.

"Any reason you're keeping my dirty clothes around?" I asked Lieutenant Roy.

He fell to the floor. "Our Great Pharaoh deserves better than this. All your clothes should be burned. You should buy new ones." He pulled out a stick of incense and a match. I managed to grab both before he set my underwear on fire.

"Do not burn my clothes," I said. Okay, that probably wasn't good enough. "Do not burn anything of mine." There. They'd have a hard time getting around that. I grabbed the Scrabble board and brought it over to the coffee table.

"Funny enough, I wanted to ask you a question," I said to Thoth.

"Once the game is over," Thoth said, grabbing the board.

"What do you mean, once the game is over?"

He pulled a bunch of letters from the Scrabble bag and handed it to Henry. "Once the game is over, you can ask me a question."

"You have to finish playing just for me to ask?" I said.

"Those are the rules," Thoth said. Then he lowered his voice and leaned toward me. "And I don't think your cat is feeling so good."

Yeah, that was the truth. There was definitely something wrong with Horus, but I didn't know what.

I picked through the piles of Gil's stuff for a while, wishing he were back. But no amount of wishing was going to make him magically appear. I ate a scone because I thought it might help me feel better. I even flipped through the scrolls of the *Book of the Dead*, pretending I had power over the spells in the book but knowing I didn't. The only way I got power from the scrolls was when one of the gods gave it to me. Earlier in the year, Horus had given me power for three spells, but the way Horus was acting now, I didn't think he'd be giving me much of anything except a headache. Finally, when I couldn't stand it any longer, I wandered back to the game board.

"Who's winning? Are you guys almost done?" I asked.

The scarab beetles and Thoth's presence seemed to have brought Horus back to normal. He sat on his scratching post so he could look directly down on the game.

Henry frowned. "Thoth. I swear he's cheating."

Thoth laughed and cracked his knuckles. "You seriously think I need to cheat? I played Scrabble for three days straight one time. And I won." He looked up at me. "Could you have the shabtis get me something to eat? I'm starving here."

"Hey," Horus called out. "The Lord of Divine Words here wants something to eat."

Colonel Cody looked at me, and I thought he might implode. The shabtis couldn't stand taking orders from anyone but me. Not even Horus.

"Yeah, get him something to eat," I said, and the shabtis ran off, returning with my plate of scones. I only managed to get one more before Thoth and Henry devoured the rest.

"I used to be really good at this game," Henry said when it was finally over. Crumbs covered the game board, sprinkled between the letters.

"Well, he is the god of words," I said. "You should cut yourself a little slack."

"How was the word I gave you the other day?" Thoth said. He started putting the letters back in the bag, like they were going to play again, but I grabbed it from him. No way was I letting that happen.

"How'd you know what word we needed?" I said, handing the Scrabble board to Lieutenant Roy. He ran off to de-crumb it and put it back in the closet.

"Yeah, that was weird," Henry said. "You painted a word, and then we needed that word, like, five minutes later."

"You just said it yourself, Tut. I'm the god of words," Thoth said. "It's what I do. Words are my thing. So what's your question, Boy King?"

I shuddered but said nothing about the "Boy King" comment. This was a god I was talking to, after all. An important god. And possibly a god who could help us. Henry, on the other hand, snorted while trying to hold in his laugh.

"Your message was from Gil," I said.

"Is that your question?" Thoth asked.

I shook my head. "I'm trying to find him. Do you know where he is?"

"Maybe," Thoth said, super-slowly.

"Where?" I asked.

"Yeah, see, that's where the problem comes in," Thoth said. "I know where everyone is, at any time. I can't see them, but I know. It's just what I do. It comes with the job. Someone needs a message delivered, and I deliver it to them."

"So what's the problem, then?" I asked. It seemed simple enough to me. He could tell us exactly where Gil was. No more searching required.

"I don't tell," Thoth said.

"What do you mean, you don't tell? That's ridiculous."

"No, it's not so ridiculous," Thoth said. He pulled a can of paint from his belt and uncapped it. Before I could stop him, he started spraying something on the center of my coffee table.

"Great Master, he's a god. What should we do?" Colonel Cody said. From the side of the table, he clasped and unclasped his hands furiously, like he could hardly hold himself still.

I put up a hand. "It's okay." The coffee table could always be replaced. "Is there a reason why you're vandalizing my town-house?"

"No reason," Thoth said, but he continued to paint.

"So why, then, can't you tell me where Gil is?" It was a simple, straightforward question.

Thoth didn't even look at me as he answered. He changed out one can for the next, and continued on with whatever he was painting.

"See, here's the thing, Boy King. Let's say this past year when the Cult of Set was after you—you remember how fun that was, running from them?"

"Of course I remember," I said. "What does that have to do with anything?"

"Well, let's say that your crazy uncle had asked me where you were so he could pinpoint your location and kill you."

"Yeah," I said, and even as the word came out, I saw where Thoth was going with this whole thing.

"If I'd just told him, would that have made you happy?"

"It's not the same thing," I said. "Gil needs help. He could be in danger. You have to tell me where he is."

Thoth clipped the paint can back onto his belt, and then

took his finger and smeared a line through some of the wet paint in a few curls.

"It's exactly the same thing," Thoth said. "I can't choose sides. I deliver messages, I give words, but I don't give away secrets. If I did, nobody would ever trust me again."

I clenched my hands because there had to be some way to get past Thoth's logic. But as much as I tried, I couldn't think of anything.

Once Thoth finished smearing the line through the paint, he stood up.

"Okay, fine," I said. "I get that you can't tell me where Gil is, even though I think it's stupid. But can you at least tell me where a certain place is?"

"Sure," Thoth said. Then without another word, he walked to the front door of my townhouse and left. I ran after him, but he was already gone.

"Ugh," I said. I slammed the door after him, making a bunch of stuff on my walls shake. I hadn't even had a chance to ask him to deliver a message for me.

"Great Master, we formally request permission to repaint your coffee table," Colonel Cody said.

I waved my hands. "Whatever." Why did the gods have to be so infuriating? They were all the same. Full of tricks and games and caught up in making both mortal and immortal lives miserable.

"Very good," Colonel Cody said.

"Wait, Tut."

I looked back into the family room. Henry stood over the coffee table, staring down at Thoth's painting.

"What?"

"I've seen this before."

I joined him and studied the painting, too. There on the coffee table was a smeared letter *B*, done up in all sorts of cool colors. It looked really familiar.

"You remember from yesterday, right?" Henry said. "When we first met Thoth."

I thought back. We'd been near Georgetown, under the bridge. Near the old Bayou club. Painted on the door of the closed-down club had been this same letter *B*. To the right of the image was a small group of eight eyeballs. The same eyeball symbol from the paper vinyl record I'd found in Gil's trunk.

"Great Amun, the gods are annoying," I said.

Horus hissed from the top of the futon.

"I mean, not you, Horus," I said. I'd nearly forgotten what had happened when we'd walked into the townhouse to begin with. "You aren't annoying at all."

This was a lie. Horus was as annoying as every other god I'd met. He knew this. I knew this. But he only glared at me with his good eye.

"It's The Babylon Club," I said, pulling the piece of paper from my pocket and holding it up.

"Thoth told us where it is," Henry said.

And we hadn't even asked. It would be so great to actually get a straight answer out of a god, but given that that was never going to happen, I'd have to be happy with the clue that Thoth left us here.

9

WHERE WE MEET THE WORST BOUNCERS IN THE UNIVERSE

We waited until it got dark, which weirdly was way earlier than it should have been. It was summer and the sun should have been setting close to eight-thirty, but it was only seven o'clock when the sun dipped below the horizon. I wanted to ask Horus about it, but he sat out on the fire escape, watching the sky, watching the birds, hissing low under his breath. In the last few days he hadn't even mentioned Bast, his cat god girlfriend. Something was definitely wrong.

One of the shabtis cleared his throat, so I looked down. There stood Colonel Cody, next to my gym shoe.

"Respectfully, I must disagree with this plan," Colonel Cody said. "Your possibly immortal friend and you should not seek out the heathen."

Henry quirked up his face, I guess trying to decide if this was an insult or not.

"Of course we should look for Gil," Henry said. "We can't just sit here doing nothing."

"Yes, I see the argument," Colonel Cody said. "But it's bad enough that great Tutankhamun has the heathen's heart."

"What do you mean, bad enough?" I asked. "Is this about the incense again?"

Colonel Cody shook his head frantically. "Of course not." But I knew it was. I was going to have to find a way to keep the shabtis from trying to cleanse me anymore. Earlier today the shabtis had begged me to let them do some sort of oatmeal scrub cleansing thing. I'd said no, but to tell you the truth, I was tempted to say yes. It sounded like the perfect way for a pharaoh to be pampered.

"We're looking for Gil," I said. Henry, I knew, was with me. We'd been through enough together already. And the shabtis . . . they'd do what I asked, even if it didn't make them happy.

Henry and I headed out of the townhouse, three shabtis in tow. There was no way Colonel Cody was going to let me go to a heathen nightclub without him. Even though I knew exactly where we were going, Colonel Cody took charge of the whole operation, searching the streets before he would let us follow. Gil didn't have anyone to watch out for him like the shabtis watched out for me. And with each day that went by—each hour—I was more certain he was in trouble. Serious trouble. I had to make sure he was okay.

After a couple covert detours suggested by Colonel Cody,

we finally came to the place under the bridge in Georgetown where the Bayou club used to be. The whole area was pitch black and boarded up. If the painted *B* hadn't still been visible above the door, I would have sworn we were in the wrong place. But this was where Thoth had told us to come.

Colonel Cody bowed low. "It would be my greatest desire to scout out the club for you ahead of time. Defeat possible foes."

My heart hummed with the anticipation of what was ahead. I had enough energy to fight a herd of angry elephants with my bare hands. Gil could be here, in this club.

"It's fine," I said to the shabti. "In fact, it's best for you guys to wait out here."

His face remained deadpan. "Certainly you jest, Great Pharaoh."

I glanced around to see if anyone had heard the "Great Pharaoh" thing, but there was no one nearby except Henry. The people who'd been here watching Thoth paint yesterday were long gone. Actually, Thoth's Sumerian graffiti was gone, too. City officials must be cracking down.

"Not kidding," I said. "We aren't sure what we'll find inside."

"Precisely why we should accompany you," Colonel Cody said. He snapped his fingers and Majors Rex and Mack stepped forward, arms crossed over their chests. They each wore a small sword and a bow and arrows slung across their backs.

"Not this time. Just wait out here." And then I stepped forward, around the shabtis.

Henry and I walked to the boarded-up door. There was no movement and not a single light that I could see.

"You think it's the right place?" Henry said.

There was no doubt that the symbol above the door matched the one Thoth had painted on my coffee table.

"It has to be." I reached up to yank the piece of wood off the door. But my hand passed right through it.

"It's an illusion," Henry said. He shoved his hand in and out, testing it.

I didn't have time for games. This was the way in. I took a deep breath and stepped through.

It was pitch black. Deathly quiet. All I could hear was something breathing, slow breaths, almost like a soft snore. My scarab heart sensors went into high gear, but I took another step forward because Henry followed me in. Whatever was ahead, I wasn't backing away. Gil had some kind of connection to this place, and I needed to find Gil before it was too late.

I raised my finger to my lips so Henry would know to be quiet, but right then my cell phone buzzed with an incoming text message. It was the worst possible timing in the world.

Something moved in the darkness.

"Watch out!" I said, but it was too late. Whatever was hiding in the dark landed on me, knocking me flat on my stomach and squashing me underneath it. My arms were pinched behind me. The thing had come out of nowhere.

Correction. Things. I discovered there was more than one when I let the light escape from my scarab heart. I turned my head to look over at Henry. He, too, was pinned to the ground, except he was face-up and could see his attacker—which made his situation all the worse.

A giant scorpion sat on top of Henry.

"What is this thing?" Henry called.

"Push it off!" I twisted my arms around over my head, breaking the grip of the scorpion. I rolled out from under it and got the great idea to make vines grow from the ceiling, but when I tried—when I summoned the immortal god-given energy that Osiris had granted me—nothing happened.

Curse the gods. Why wouldn't my powers return?

I went for plan B instead. I focused all my energy and concentrated. I'd managed to summon a fireball the other day. I held out my hands and waited for it to appear. Except it didn't. And my attempts only gave our attackers a chance to regroup. They came at us again.

"Can't you do anything?" I asked Henry. I hated that I felt so helpless. Gil giving me his scarab heart should have made me even fiercer than before, but I was nothing but a weakling. It stunk.

All the confidence I'd seen on Henry's face in the last couple days evaporated. "I don't know how."

The scorpions advanced on us, clacking their pincers together. They might not be able to kill me or Henry—if he turned out to be immortal—but they could pull us apart, limb by limb. That was no way to spend eternity.

"Who dares enter The Babylon Club with no invitation?" the scorpion on the left called out. Its voice screeched like nails on a chalkboard. Chills ran under my skin and my heart glowed even brighter.

The positive side of things was that they hadn't attacked us again. The negative side was that they looked like they were ready to at any given second. I crouched down, ready to jump out of the way.

"I do." I pulled out my bargaining chip. Not like I was ashamed to; it just always seemed like such bragging. "Did I mention I'm King Tut?" I called, knowing they'd be dropping to their feet and bowing pretty soon.

"King who?" the scorpion said.

"King Tut. Tutankhamun. You know, from Egypt."

The scorpions slowly shook their heads back and forth. "Never heard of him," the scorpion on the right said. If possible, his voice was even more screeching than the first.

"Seriously? You've never heard of me?" For three thousand years, people have known who I was. I was the king of legends. The famous boy king. I had to work hard to keep my identity a secret. And now, when I actually wanted someone to recognize my name, they didn't know who I was.

The scorpion on the right looked to the one on the left. He shook his head. Or her head. I wasn't sure how to tell which.

"Nope, never heard of you, Tutty-common," the scorpion said.

We had to get past the scorpions. I'd never hear the end of it from Colonel Cody if we didn't. It would be years and years of "I told you so" and they'd never let me so much as go to the bathroom alone again.

"Here, you can Google it," Henry said. He reached to pull

out his phone, but the scorpions must have thought he was going for a weapon because the one on the left was on him in two seconds flat, pinning him to the ground.

"What kind of weapon is this Google you speak of?" the scorpion hissed, spraying saliva all over Henry.

"It's not a weapon," Henry said. "It's a—"

"Silence!" the scorpion boomed. "We will have no part of this deception."

I'd given up on Henry doing anything to help, so I tried again to summon Gil's powers from inside my chest. Fire. Smoke. Heat. Nothing worked.

My phone buzzed again with another stupid text message. I was going to mummify whoever it was.

The scorpion still standing eyed my pocket warily, like he thought my cell phone was secretly a hand grenade. "Do you have an invitation?"

I mentally tried to silence the phone. It didn't work. "Do I need one?"

The scorpion above Henry whipped its tail around, and when I saw the spike on the end, I grimaced. It reminded me of the immortal-killing knife that both Uncle Horemheb and I had been after. He'd cut me with it during a fight and nearly killed me. Thankfully, the knife wasn't here. These scorpions were. They were right in front of me.

"Don't let them sting you," I said to Henry.

"You don't say." Henry eyed the spiky stinger that hovered in the air above him.

"Everyone who enters must have an invitation," the scorpion

in front of me said. "No invitation means death." And then it pounced, landing on my chest.

A claw grabbed both of my hands, and the giant spike tail whipped around and aimed directly over my head.

These were definitely the guys you wanted organizing your next party. They took the RSVP thing way seriously.

A drop of the poison from the spike tail dripped onto my forehead. I tilted my head back, hoping it wouldn't go into my eyes. This was not how I imagined the evening would go.

"Wait, Tut. I think I got this," Henry called. As he spoke, he started to glow. Sort of like how my scarab heart glows, except the light was coming from all over him.

"You think you got this?" I repeated. I had no clue what Henry thought he would do.

But Henry obviously had some kind of plan. The glowing coming off his body brightened, and he started muttering words just like he had the other day at camp. I recognized a bunch of the words. They sounded exactly like spells from the *Book of the Dead*, except I didn't remember the spell he was incanting. The light coming off him grew with each second that passed. As I watched, the scorpions started twitching and flailing around like badly programmed automatons.

The claws of the scorpion holding me loosened enough for me to slip my arms out of its grip and shove the thing off me. It tumbled sideways, fell over, twitched a few times, and then lay still.

"What did you do?" I asked, hopping to my feet and brushing off my clothes.

"I paralyzed them." Henry scratched his head. "At least that's what I think I did."

"Where'd you get the spell?" I asked. I didn't remember a "How to Paralyze Scorpions" spell from the *Book of the Dead*.

"I don't know," Henry said. "I just knew it."

"Well, it was really awesome," I said. "You did that." I pointed at the two scorpions who were stuck helpless on the ground. Their eyes still followed us.

"Yeah, I think you're right," Henry said, and he couldn't help the stupid grin that crept onto his face.

One of the scorpions screeched, "Release us now so we may finish you off."

If nothing else, these guys were persistent.

"Are you kidding?" I reached into my back pocket and pulled out the paper vinyl record. "We're here for a reason." I shoved it into their faces.

It hissed, but in a weird, not-so-scary way. "An invitation," it said. "Why didn't you say so?"

10

WHERE WE SPIN VINYL WITH A SUMERIAN GOD

After the paralyzing spell wore off, the scorpions started moving again, but they didn't try to kill us. Instead, they showed us the trapdoor to the club below. I felt the walls shake when the piece of floorboard lifted, and flashing lights filled the room. We were definitely in the right place.

We weren't five steps down the ladder when the scorpions slammed the trapdoor closed above our heads. I guess they had to go back to work—preparing to sting to death the next hapless victim who happened to stumble into The Babylon Club. But despite the scorpion bouncers, the place was packed with a dance floor and an entire balcony level filled with tables and people hanging over the railing, watching below.

"You think everyone here had an invitation?" Henry said.

I didn't see how it was possible. There hadn't been anyone else standing around outside. And I hadn't spotted any dead bodies in the scorpion den. The only person who looked like he might work here was some bald guy with sunglasses who stood next to the soda machine. It had one hundred different buttons, which he pushed in all sorts of crazy patterns. He handed out sodas with both hands. So I walked over to him and pulled out the record invitation.

"We have our invitation," I said, holding it out. I tried to put all my pharaoh confidence into my voice, but the scorpion thing had shaken me. They'd never heard of King Tut? I still couldn't believe it. Colonel Cody would have wanted to execute them on the spot for their blasphemy.

The soda guy took the invitation from me and shoved his black sunglasses onto the top of his bald head.

"Great," he said. He flipped it over and froze.

"What?" I said. Aside from the date, the vinyl record was blank on the back.

He looked up at me and Henry and narrowed his eyes. "Where'd you two get this?"

I shrugged, going for the truth. "In my townhouse." No need to mention whose trunk it had come out of. Gil wouldn't be happy we'd gone through his stuff.

"It's not yours," the soda guy said.

"How do you know?" Henry asked.

The soda guy pressed his thumb directly into the center of it. "It doesn't have your name on it."

I'd thought it was blank, but a bunch of Sumerian letters began to appear. The soda guy was right. They didn't spell my name or Henry's name. They spelled Gil's name.

I grabbed the record from him and shoved it back in my pocket. "Do you know where Gil is?"

He lowered his sunglasses and went back to pushing buttons on the soda machine. "You need to talk to Igigi."

"Who?" I said. There were probably four hundred people in The Babylon Club.

"Igigi," the soda guy said, pointing up at the balcony. "He's up there."

It turned out Igigi was the DJ. Everyone knew Igigi. And seeing as how Igigi had eight eyes—two on each side of his head—he'd probably spotted us an hour ago. It's not like Henry and I had been trying to keep a low profile.

"Is your name Igigi?" I asked. After the scorpion bouncers and the soda guy, I didn't want to take a chance offending him. He towered over me by a foot and looked like he could squash me with his fist.

"Nope." He looked down at Henry and me with the two eyes on the right side of his head. Even from the side, I could see his smile. He reached up to peel off his knit cap, exposing a head full of thick dark hair. His other hand kept spinning records—old-school vinyl records, just like the one on the invitation.

"But the guy at the soda machine said you were," Henry said, walking around behind him.

Igigi kept his eyes on me, but I was willing to bet the pair on the back of his head watched Henry.

Igigi flipped a button on the turntable and turned to me. "I know. It's easier that way."

"So who are you?" I said, trying to stand a little bit taller so I didn't have to crane my neck. Thankfully, Igigi sat down, so Henry and I joined him.

"I'm Igigi," he said.

"But you just said you weren't Igigi," I said.

"No," the guy said. "What I said was that my name wasn't Igigi. That doesn't mean I'm not Igigi."

"So you are Igigi, but your name's not Igigi?" I said.

"Right," Igigi said.

"Okay, I'm confused," Henry said. "What's your name if it's not Igigi?"

"Don't have one," Igigi said, like he'd heard the question a million times before. "But you can call me Igigi." He raised his giant arm, and a waitress ran over with a gallon-sized soda for him. She smiled at me and Henry, but didn't offer to get us anything.

"You have eight eyes," Henry said.

Igigi felt his head, like he wanted to make sure they were all still there. Once he was satisfied, he said, "So you noticed?"

I looked down at the pumping dance floor. The lights flashed blue and red, and a disco ball spun above. "Doesn't everyone?"

"What, notice? Sure," Igigi said. "But then again, they don't really, because, you know, they're only mortal, and the music kind of makes them forget."

I figured this implied that Igigi knew about the whole immortal thing.

"Do you know who I am?" I asked. My confidence was shaken. I still couldn't get over those scorpions.

"Sure," Igigi said. "You're King Tut! Everyone knows you."

Relief flowed through me. I had not lost my mojo. The universe was making itself right.

I pulled out the invitation and handed it over to Igigi. He flipped it over, and the smile fell from his face.

"What?" Henry said.

"Gil," Igigi said, shaking his head. "Man, I miss that guy."

That made two of us. I missed Gil way more than I wanted to admit.

"You know him?" I asked.

"Sure," Igigi said. "He used to come in here all the time. The girls loved dancing with Gil."

Gil was a girl magnet. When we'd gone places together, everyone gawked at him. But it wasn't just looks. Gil drew people toward him. He'd always been that way. Kind of like what was happening to me more and more, and I still didn't know if I liked it.

"You said he used to come in here?" Henry said.

Igigi handed the paper back to me. "Yep. I haven't seen him in months. But . . ." And then Igigi stopped talking, and I noticed his eyes swiveling around in all sorts of directions—down at the dance floor, back to the soda machine, across the balcony.

"But what?" I said.

Igigi leaned close and so did Henry and I. "But I hear everything that goes on at the club, and I did hear a rumor." He reached over and flipped another switch on the turntable. The techno song changed to disco and the lights flashed to green.

"What kind of rumor?" Henry asked.

"I'll tell you," Igigi said. His giant hands gripped the side of the table. "But it will cost you."

I was King Tut. I'd lived for three thousand years. I had more money than I knew what to do with. I could handle this. "Name your price."

Two of Igigi's eyes got super-wide. "How did you know?"

"Know what?" I said, worried that if they got any wider, they would fall out of his head. Of course then he'd be down to six eyes, which was still two hundred percent more than normal.

"About the name?" Igigi said.

"What about the name?" I said.

"That's what I want," Igigi said. "If you give me a name, I'll tell you what I heard."

That seemed like a simple enough request. "Okay, like Jim or Billy or something like that?"

"How about Henry?" Henry said. "That's a good name."

Igigi waved his hands to stop us. "No, you guys don't get it. You see, the Igigi—like me—we're the lesser gods of Mesopotamia. Well, lesser according to the creators. Personally, I think we're way more awesome than those loser gods who created us. But they made us, and then they thought we'd be too powerful with names, because, you know, we were so awesome. So they didn't give us names."

"And will a name give you more power?" Henry asked.

"Maybe," Igigi said. "But what's wrong with power? Even you have power. At least that's what the rumors say."

Wonderful. There were now rumors about Henry floating around amid the gods.

"Why don't you just name yourself?" Henry said.

"I tried," Igigi said. "But I can't. Only a god can name an Igigi."

"I'm not a god," I said, even though it felt like I was stating the obvious.

"Duh," Henry said.

"I have faith in you, King Tut," Igigi said. "You look like you're going to accomplish big things in your life. You'll find a name for me."

No pressure or anything, but I wasn't going to disagree with Igigi. I wanted whatever information he had about Gil.

He snapped his fingers. "Oh, but I should mention that if I do give you this information about Gil and you don't find my name . . ." His voice trailed off.

"Yeah?" I knew there was a catch.

"Never mind," he said. "I don't want to worry you."

It was too late for that.

"What'll happen?" I asked.

Igigi patted the air with his hands, like he was trying to minimize it. "Oh, it's just this small technicality about debts being paid. Something about getting sent to the underworld without your hands or eyes. It's really nothing to worry about."

That was easy for him to say.

"Fine," I said. "Just tell me what you know." I had no clue where I'd get a name for Igigi, but I'd figure something out. I always did.

"Right, so I heard this story about Gil," Igigi said. "It seems there was this knife."

Not the knife. My side hurt just thinking about it.

"The immortal-killing knife," I said.

Igigi nodded. "Right. The knife of the gods. Well, it turns out that some punk pharaoh-wannabe used it, which was a horrible idea."

Punk pharaoh-wannabe. Uncle Horemheb would have spit cockroaches if he'd heard something like that. Wait . . . unless Igigi was talking about me.

"Why's that?" Henry asked. I was surprised he'd spoken. Anything about the knife freaked him out now, seeing as how Horemheb had almost killed him with it.

"Because this knife," Igigi went on, "when it got used— well, it never should have been used—"

"But it was," I said, trying to get him to get on with the story.

"Right. It was. And it cut the fabric of the universe. The stuff that holds everything together. Keeps everything in place. It was just a little cut, but it was enough."

"Enough for what?" I asked. A chill ran through my body at Igigi's words. Whatever he was about to say was not going to be good.

"Enough to weaken the world and let a god who'd been imprisoned for thousands of years escape," Igigi said.

"A god escaped?" Henry said. "From where?"

I went over in my mind all the stories from mythology I could remember about gods getting imprisoned. Gods had fought all the time. Set and Horus were a perfect example. And they'd fought because Set had killed Osiris. Killing a god was a horrible, unheard-of thing, and it didn't happen very often.

For that matter, neither did imprisoning gods. Having all the gods around is kind of what kept the universe in balance. But there had been one time when things got so bad that all the gods banded together to defeat another god. I'd heard the stories since I was a baby. Even Set and Horus had fought on the same side for that battle. Yeah, it was that rare.

"Apep," I said. I hadn't spoken his name in decades. It made Horus itchy. Once a god was locked away, it was where he should stay.

Igigi nodded his giant head. "Apep. The Lord of Chaos. The creator of darkness."

"The Devourer of the Sun," I said.

"What do you mean, the Devourer of the Sun?" Henry said.

Even though Henry was smart, he didn't have the thousands of years of mythology under his belt like I did.

"I'll tell you what he means," someone said, walking up to our table.

It only took me a millisecond to recognize her voice. Tia plunked down in the chair opposite me and dropped her elbows on the table. Bracelets draped around her wrists and jingled with her every movement. A bright yellow streak ran through her cropped dark hair, perfectly matched to the tank top she wore.

Henry cast a quick look at me and raised his eyebrows.

I had no clue what she was doing here either.

"Nice way to return my texts, Boy King," she said.

Me return *her* texts? "What are you talking about? I texted you."

She looked at me like I'd lost my mind. "I texted you tonight. I told you to meet me here."

"You did not," I said, but even as the words left my mouth, I remembered my phone buzzing. It's what had woken up the scorpion bouncers. I pulled my phone from my pocket, and sure enough, there were three text messages from Tia.

meet me at the babylon club at 9, was the first text.

you may want to come around back. bouncers are kinda mean, was the next one. Too bad I hadn't seen it before we'd met up with the worst bouncers in history.

you should check your phone more often, was the third.

"Thanks for the warning," I said. "There's seriously a back entrance?"

"Duh," Tia said.

"Okay, does someone want to tell me about this Apep guy?" Henry asked. "Not that this isn't fun and all."

"Yeah, I'll tell you," Tia said. "Apep is this giant snake-god who devours the sun during solar eclipses. He's over three hundred feet long and blacker than the deepest caves in the world."

"No one devours the sun during solar eclipses," Henry said. "Solar eclipses happen during a new moon when the moon passes directly in front of the sun. It's called astronomy."

"Believe whatever makes you happy," Tia said. "But if you want to hear the bedtime stories about Apep, I'll tell you. Back before he was imprisoned, he used to devour the sun every single evening. It was why the sun set. But he made a bunch of gods mad and got imprisoned by Ra. Safely tucked away until that stupid knife got used. And now he's free. Lucky us. And here's the really bad part. He's super-mad about being imprisoned for so long. And he's vowed to the other gods that he's going to devour the sun and cast the world into eternal darkness."

Henry looked like his mind was about to explode. The melding between science and mythology was too much for him.

"That's not possible," Henry said. "Giant snakes don't eat the sun. That's not how things work."

But I knew it was how things worked, at the core of everything. If Tia and Igigi were right, Apep being at large could mean the end of life as we knew it.

"Also, I thought Set was the god of chaos," Henry said. "Not this Apep guy."

That *was* a bit confusing.

"Set is more the god of storms and violence and disorder," I said. "Sometimes people lump it together into chaos. But Apep . . . he's the Lord of Chaos. Like with a capital *C*."

"So he's worse than Set?" Henry said.

"Yeah, he's worse than Set," I said. Admitting that any god was worse than Set was hard for me, but I couldn't lie about Apep. That was the reason he'd been imprisoned.

"Great," Henry said. "That's just what I don't want to hear."

"What does Apep have to do with Gil?" I asked Igigi.

"I was just getting to that," Igigi said. "So Apep, he's now loose in the world. And here's where the rumors come in. Apep started hearing stories. Stories about Set. And stories about Osiris. And about immortals. Scarab hearts."

My scarab heart started pounding in my chest.

"And he decides that he wants one," Igigi said.

"What do you mean, he wants one? He wants someone with a scarab heart?" I said. Little flashes from my visions started coming back to me. "It's not like you can just go out and find an immortal on any street corner."

Igigi raised one of his eight eyebrows at me. "No? Tell that to Apep. He hears through the rumor mill that there's this guy Gil who's an immortal. And he decides that he's going to find Gil and make him start working for him. He thinks it will make him more powerful. Make him invincible."

"What?" I said. "You're kidding. Apep has Gil?" But as the words left my mouth, I knew it made sense. The snakes near Gil in my visions. The note from Gil for me not to look for him, like he was still trying to protect me, even when he was the one in trouble. Even the weird dream I'd had where I was running away from something and my immortal powers wouldn't work. These were all signs that everything Igigi was saying was true.

"Gil's not even immortal anymore," Henry said. "So what good will that do Apep?"

I didn't know what good it would do Apep, but I did know what bad it would do Gil. When Apep found out that Gil wasn't immortal anymore, he was going to be furious.

Igigi raised his arms. "That's all I know. Apep is loose and bent on destroying the world. And he's kidnapped Gil to help make himself more powerful."

It was worse than anything I could have imagined. Apep would kill Gil. And then he'd destroy the world. We not only had to find Gil, we had to stop the most evil god in existence.

11

WHERE HORUS TRIES TO KILL ME

I could walk you home," I said to Tia after we left The Babylon Club. Thankfully we'd taken the back door out and avoided the scorpion bouncers altogether.

Tia laughed like I'd made some kind of joke.

Not like I wanted to walk her back to the Cult of Set headquarters. She couldn't still be living there. Or be a part of it anymore, even though she was related to the people who ran it. It was such a group of wackos. Like, who in their right mind would worship Set? But I didn't want to ask where she lived because that would sound way too creepy.

"I'm fine, Boy King," Tia said. She gave me a cute little pat on the cheek. "Text me."

"Yeah, whatever," I said, trying to keep the puppy dog look

off my face. But this was Tia we were talking about. She was about as close to an Egyptian princess as I could imagine. And she smelled amazing, like fresh lotus blossoms blowing over the Nile River in the morning. I watched her walk away, until she turned the corner. Okay, I watched longer than that, but Henry finally elbowed me to get my attention.

"I need to go, Tut," he said.

I blinked a few times to reorient myself. Tia made my heart do all sorts of weird flipping things like it hadn't done in hundreds of years. Why did she have to be so mysterious, anyway?

Fine, maybe I liked the mystery, just a little.

"Need to go?" I said. "Did you not just have the same conversation I did?"

He glanced at his watch. It was giant and digital and had more buttons on it than the bridge of the starship *Enterprise*. "I told my parents I'd be home an hour ago."

"And . . ." I said. Here Gil had been captured, Apep was bent on taking over the world, and Henry had to get home so his mom could tuck him in?

"And they're going to start getting suspicious," Henry said. "I can't just stay out super-late every night. That's how it works when you have parents. You have to tell them where you are and stuff."

Silence filled the air between us. As if the fact that I no longer had parents wasn't bad enough, Henry had to rub it in my face?

Henry looked down at his gray Chucks. "Okay, that didn't come out quite like I meant it."

"It's not like it's my fault my parents got murdered," I said. "I didn't plan to grow up alone." And I hadn't been alone, not for a long time. Gil had been there. And then he'd just up and left, leaving me with no one except Horus.

"I know," Henry said. "I'm sorry. It's just that sometimes I see you running around, doing whatever you want, no one to report in to, and . . ."

"And what?" I said. That was my life. The life of an immortal.

He kicked at the dirt with the toe of his gray high-top. "And I get a little jealous, I guess."

I laughed out loud. "Seriously? You get jealous of me? You, who gets to go home to your parents each night. They make you dinner. They take you shopping."

I left the rest unsaid. I didn't trust myself. But I still remembered how my mom used to sing to me, to tell me stories, to wrap her arms around me and tell me that she loved me. I'd never been so happy in my entire life, and it wasn't just because my family was powerful. It was because I'd had my special people. People who cared about me. Sometimes it felt like I'd never be that happy again. Amun above, I had to find Gil. If something happened to him, I would never get over it. I knew it deep in my soul.

"I know," Henry said. "But you forget I'm a teenager. My mom is constantly asking me what we're doing, where we're going. And I hate to lie."

"You don't have to lie," I said. "Just leave out anything that seems to imply immortality. Or special powers. Or Egyptian gods. Or . . . yeah, I guess that's a lot."

"You're not kidding," Henry said. "So we're cool?"

"Yeah, we're cool," I said.

He punched me on the shoulder, just to make sure, and then we parted ways, me heading back to my empty townhouse and him back to the familiar presence of his mom and dad.

There were spells and wards all over the door to my townhouse when the shabtis and I got there. I felt chills run over my skin as I pushed past them. But I didn't have time to ask Horus about it, because he came out of nowhere, landing in front of my feet.

He hissed loudly. "Go away, Tut." His good eye roved the room, not focusing on me. Huge chunks of his fur were missing, contributing to his mangy look. I'd never seen Horus look so horrible, not even when he'd gone missing with amnesia for a couple decades.

Maybe it was the stupidest thing I've ever done, but I needed to start making forward progress. I squatted down to Horus's level and slammed my hands on the ground.

"No, Horus. I am not going to go away," I said, letting all the frustration running through me filter into my voice.

"I mean it, Tut," Horus said, but his voice wasn't as certain as before.

I took advantage of it and moved forward. Horus scooted back. So I took another step. He did, too. And we continued this until I got him into the family room. Behind me, the shabtis slammed the door closed. The chill in the air evaporated.

"Great Master," Colonel Cody said. "It seems the cat is not feeling well."

"He's a god. He's Horus," I said, still not taking my eyes off Horus.

"Yes, exactly what I was saying," Colonel Cody said. "It seems the cat god is a bit under the weather."

"Horus is fine." I pressed my hand forward, hoping to make peace, hoping Horus didn't take this moment to swipe at me. To tear one of my fingers off.

I held my breath and waited, counting the seconds. One. Two. I got to twelve when Horus finally backed off. He hissed one last time, then scurried across the room, grabbing a scarab beetle and biting it in half.

I sank onto the futon. Lieutenants Virgil and Leon ran up balancing a tall glass of ice and a soda on a tray. There were also two warm scones on a bright blue plate. Cranberry, maybe? They always knew exactly what I needed.

I nodded at them in thanks, and they ran back into the kitchen.

"What in the name of Amun Ra is going on with you, Horus?" I said.

Horus chewed the scarab beetle slowly, almost like he wasn't planning to eat it. But then he swallowed it.

Uh-oh. This was not a good idea. He jumped onto Gil's chair and started heaving. I knew what was coming. I tried to cover my ears and close my eyes, but the heaves got louder and louder. Finally Horus hacked up a giant scarab-beetle hairball all over Gil's chair. Then, to make matters worse, he started digging his claws into the chair. It was the only time I was glad Gil wasn't around. He would have skinned Horus.

"It's the sun and the moon," Horus said, rolling around in the hacked-up hairball.

"What about the sun and the moon?" I said, trying to ignore what he was doing. It was gross. Horus went crazy during the new moon, but we had almost two weeks until then.

"It's growing darker," Horus said. "Everything about the world is growing darker. And the tides. Have you seen the tides? They're way off. The sun and the moon aren't in the right places. It's messing everything up. It's not good, Tutankhamun. I'm telling you that it's not good."

Moon. Tides. The world growing darker. It all fit together with what I'd just heard. "This is about Apep, isn't it?" I said.

Horus didn't act surprised that I knew. He only flicked his tail in acknowledgment.

"How long have you known?" I asked. The bigger question was, why hadn't Horus told me?

Horus eyed another scarab beetle, but he didn't pounce. Instead he dug his claws deeper into Gil's chair, pulling out stuffing. I cringed but kept my mouth shut.

"Since I went to the underworld," Horus said. "Remember that little trip? Where I went to check up on Horemheb?"

"Oh, I remember, Great Master," Colonel Cody said. "It's when the cat god retrieved me from an eternal life without you."

This must've rekindled some fond feelings for Horus because the little shabti immediately ran off and ordered the filling of Horus's milk bowl.

"You learned about Apep escaping six months ago, and you didn't think to tell me?" I said.

"There was no reason to tell you, Tut," Horus said. "I'm a god. He's a god. It's a god issue. I'm going to take care of the problem."

"By doing what? Hacking up hairballs at anyone who comes near you? Attacking people? Don't you see how this is affecting you? You aren't yourself."

"I'm fine," Horus said.

"Fine? Then why the wards? Why have you tried to rip my eyes out not once but twice in the last week? Why do you look like a rabid alley cat who lost five fights in a row? Does that seem like you're fine?"

Horus scowled, but he didn't have much of an argument to make.

"Did you know that Apep kidnapped Gil?" I said. I still couldn't believe it. Gil was in serious trouble.

Horus stopped digging. Pieces of stuffing clung to his claws. "He what?"

"He kidnapped Gil. He's looking for an immortal, and he thought he got one."

"Oh, you have got to be kidding me," Horus said. "He can't still be stewing over that whole mess. When I find that snake, I am going to pull his tail through—"

I put up my hand. "Enough." I didn't need a visual of what Horus planned to do to Apep.

Horus and Gil may have had their differences. They argued all the time. But Horus's claws went up and he snarled. Gil, like me, was one of Horus's people, whether he wanted him to be or not. And as such, Horus was going to watch out for Gil.

"How do we stop him?" I asked.

"Stop Apep, the Lord of Chaos? The Devourer of the Sun?" Horus said. "We don't. I do. You stay here and stay safe."

"Great Osiris, no!" I said. "I am not sitting in this townhouse doing nothing. I'm going to look for Gil with you or without you."

And this was when things turned ugly. Horus launched at me from Gil's chair and landed on my head. His claws dug into me, even as I grabbed at him, trying to get him off me. I fell from the futon onto the floor, and using strength I didn't know I had, I clenched my fingers around him and pulled him from my head, throwing him across the room. And before he could get up and come back after me, fireballs ignited in my hands. I held them out, menacingly.

"Don't take another step," I said.

Horus hissed and stared at the flames, but he stayed back.

"This!" I said. "This is why you can't stop him. He's affecting you. The darkness is getting to you. You're going crazy. You have to stay here. Stay safe. And let me go out and stop him."

Bitter silence filled the townhouse, only disturbed by the crackling sound of the flames in my hands. I was not going to back down. I was going to find Gil. Stop Apep. Horus was not going to get in my way.

"Tell me what to do," I said when Horus didn't reply. "Tell me how to kill Apep."

Horus let out a garbled laugh under his breath. "That's what you don't get. There's no way to kill Apep. That's why he was imprisoned so long ago. Nobody could kill him."

"Fine, I don't kill him," I said. "How do I re-imprison him?"

Horus blew out his breath, then sauntered over to his milk bowl, as if he hadn't just tried to tear my head off. I let the flames subside and waited while he lapped up the milk—he drank for a solid minute—and then I waited until he wandered back over toward me. The shabtis were picking at my hair, inspecting it to see if Horus had done any damage. If they had their way, I'd have a bandage covering my entire head like a real mummy.

"Okay, Tut, here's my theory." Horus jumped onto the coffee table, looking toward the open window of the fire escape. "Back when Ra imprisoned Apep, do you know how he did it?"

I shrugged. "Sure. Ra stunned Apep with his awesomeness, and then grabbed him and dragged him off to the underworld." Ra's powers were the thing of legends. That was why he was the most important god ever. If a mortal even looked at Ra, it could cause irreparable hypnosis.

"It wasn't quite that easy," Horus said. "And I need you to listen to this part, because I'm not going to repeat myself."

What? Did he think I was going to start playing video games?

"Fine," I said. "What am I missing?"

"So Ra. You know that giant disk he has on his head? The sun disk?"

"Sure." I raised my hands over my head, mimicking the sun disk. It was sort of like Ra's signature item. His crown.

"Good," Horus said. "Well, it wasn't just some fancy decoration. It's what Ra used to capture Apep and seal him away."

"The sun disk?" I said. "Really?"

"Yeah, really," Horus said with a scowl. "You thought it was just a fashion accessory?"

"Of course not," I said, though that was exactly what I thought. "So we just get this sun—"

"Not so fast," Horus said. "Ra had to catch a reflection of the setting sun, the last light of the day, and cast it onto Apep. Not the noon sun. Not the rising sun. The setting sun. Did you get that part, Tut?"

"I'm not remedial," I said. "So where is this sun disk? Where do we get it? Wait, please don't tell me that Ra still has it?"

That would be a serious problem. No one had seen Ra in ages. Rumor among the gods was that he'd gone away, never to be seen again. That he'd given up on the world. If that was true, then I would definitely need a plan B.

Horus shook his head. "No, Ra doesn't have it anymore."

"How do you know?" I asked.

Horus put a paw to his forehead. "My mom told me."

"Auntie Isis?" I said. My stomach clenched at the thought of Horus's mom. I really, really didn't want to have to go visit her.

"What? You think I have another mom?" Horus said.

My hopes fell into the basement. "So she does have it?"

"No," Horus said. "I never said that. You were supposed to be listening, Tut."

"I am listening," I said. "You said that your mom told you that Ra doesn't have the sun disk anymore."

"Right," Horus said. "I never said that my mom has it herself."

Relief flooded me. Things were looking up. I wasn't going to have to visit Auntie Isis after all. "Great. So where is it? Do you know?"

"Of course I know," Horus said. "I'm a god. I know everything."

Now was not the time to disagree with Horus.

"Where?" I said.

Horus swatted a paw on the side of Gil's chair, as if he were cleaning scarab-beetle guts off it. "My mom says it's totally safe."

"Okay." I waited for more, motioning with my hands for Horus to continue.

"You know how she runs those funeral homes?" Horus said.

I could almost hear the jingle in my head. Dynasty Funeral Homes were the biggest name in town. Everyone wanted to be buried by them . . . except me.

"Of course I do," I said. Auntie Isis didn't just preserve the bodies. She mummified them. And she had one of Horus's sons, Hapi, her grandson, working for her. Hapi had a baboon head. Not the most flattering face in the world, but he never changed it.

"Well, my mom says that she had Hapi bury it with one of the bodies." He licked his paw, like this was the end of our conversation and it was time for him to groom himself.

"Which body?" I said. "Where?"

He raised a paw as if to reassure me. "Don't worry, Tut. I've already got it taken care of. I'm supposed to meet Hapi Saturday night at ten. But instead of me, you can go. I'll let him know. He'll take you to it. It'll be simple."

Great. I had a date to go grave-robbing with a baboon god. Nothing about that was going to be simple. But if it got me one step closer to finding Gil and imprisoning Apep, then that's exactly what I was going to do.

12

WHERE I TRAIN A MONSTER

Horus told me where and when to meet Hapi and then jumped out the fire escape window. I thought about having a few of the shabtis trail him, to make sure he was okay, but if Horus found out I'd done something like that, he'd be furious. An even angrier cat god than my already angry cat god was not what I wanted on my hands.

I tried to fall asleep, but this whole mess with Gil made it impossible. I finally got up in the middle of the night and went downstairs.

"Breakfast, Great Master?" Lieutenant Virgil asked, even though it was nowhere near breakfast time. He stood at attention, next to the toaster, as if he'd pop a waffle in if I so much as raised an eyebrow.

"Just some water would be great," I said.

He bowed deeply, like I'd justified his existence. "Water it is," he said, and the refrigerator door flew open. A shabti he had stationed inside passed out a water bottle. I'd tried in the past to keep them out of the refrigerator, but Lieutenant Virgil swore they never got cold and insisted this allowed them to perform their duties more efficiently.

I walked back into the family room, but instead of sitting on the futon, I sank into Gil's chair. I don't know why. Maybe I wanted to be closer to him. I fell back asleep. And then my dream started.

There were chairs everywhere. I moved from one to the next, feeling them because I couldn't see anything. I tried to pull on energy from my scarab heart, to light up the place, but it was like I had ghost powers. I couldn't feel anything in my chest at all. And my memories of the visions returned. I wasn't me in this dream. I was Gil.

"Pretty sure that's Orion," a voice said.

"Not Orion," another voice said. "Orion has the five little stars in a row. That's Scorpioid."

"You're an idiot," the first voice said. "Orion has four stars in a row."

From the sound of it, they were both idiots. But as long as they were bickering about constellations, they might not be paying attention to me.

"And that one up there," the first voice said. "That's called Geminus."

"Not Geminus, moron," the second voice said. "It's Geminoid."

I craned my neck around, trying to hear anything else I could. And I kept moving. There must be a door somewhere. Some way for me to escape. But I bumped into something and the guards stopped arguing. I almost felt them look my way as goose bumps popped up on my skin.

"What do you think he's doing?" the first one said.

"Don't look at him," the other said. "Don't you know these immortals have superpowers? He might have laser eyes or something."

"He's blindfolded," the first said. "And the boss isn't even sure he's immortal. He's planning to come by later and do some tests."

Tests were not going to end well. I might be immortal, but Gil wasn't. He'd fail any tests Apep gave him. And then he'd kill Gil.

My eyes flew open and panic filled me. Three shabtis stood on the arms of Gil's chair, fanning me with long ostrich feather fans. My scarab heart pounded.

"Great Master," Colonel Cody said. "Should we attempt to locate the cat god?"

I ran a hand through my hair and tried to clear my mind. Gil was in serious danger. Time was running out.

"No, it's fine." With the state Horus was in, and the effect Apep was having on him, Horus was not going to be able to help. That much was obvious. He couldn't even help himself. If I didn't stop Apep, I could lose Horus, too.

"It is the heathen heart," Colonel Cody said, and he jumped around to my side so I had to crane my neck to see him. "Perhaps if our Great Pharaoh would allow us to perform a ritual, the heathen spirits could be eradicated." He whipped a lighted match and a piece of incense from behind his back and held them over me.

"It's not heathen spirits. It's Gil's heart," I said, swatting away the match. It fell on the arm of Gil's chair and started smoking. One of the shabtis doing the fanning jumped on it and put it out, but not before it left a huge burn mark in the patched fabric. "What time is it anyway?"

"Five a.m., Great Master," Colonel Cody said. He glanced quickly behind me.

An odd smell hung in the air, but I couldn't quite place it. Maybe it was the residual incense.

"Some breakfast?" Lieutenant Virgil said. He, like Colonel Cody, was standing in a completely awkward place, making me have to turn my head to see him.

"What are you guys hiding?" I asked.

"I'm sure I don't know what you're talking about, Great Master," Colonel Cody said.

I'd known Colonel Cody a hundred years. He knew exactly what I was talking about. I spun around, even as the shabtis tried to distract me. And then I saw why.

Gil's door, previously black with a giant red *X*, had been re-painted, which explained the odd smell. Instead of being black, it was now bright blue with gold stripes running horizontally across it and a shiny gold star in the middle.

"What did you do?" I asked.

Captain Otto hopped onto the stair railing. "A brilliant

thing," he said. "We are building Great Pharaoh a media room. Only top-of-the-line audio and video equipment will be good enough for—"

"You're not turning Gil's room into a media room," I said.

"Perhaps an exercise room?" Colonel Cody said.

I shook my head. "No! Gil is coming back. We are going to find him, and if he gets here and his room is . . ." I waved my hand in the direction of the blue and gold door. "Just . . . no. Put it back how it was."

Captain Otto's face fell. "But think of the movies . . ."

"And popcorn!" Lieutenant Virgil added.

"No movies! When Gil gets back, he is going to need his room." I spun back around. "And, yes, I would love some breakfast."

The doorbell rang at eight a.m. sharp. The shabtis checked through the peephole to see who it was.

"Should we allow Great Master's questionably immortal friend to enter?" Major Rex said.

Ugh. Henry. Not today.

"I'm not going to science camp," I yelled through the closed door.

The knob turned, and Henry opened the door, peeking inside. "Not to worry. It's Thursday."

I wasn't sure what that had to do with anything, but I didn't ask.

Henry took my silence as an invitation and stepped inside. He was eating a powdered sugar doughnut and had sugar all over his chin and red shirt. Today's shirt read, Ba Co N. If I'd still been hungry, I'd have asked Lieutenant Leon to make me some.

"Camp is only Monday through Wednesday," Henry said. "Thursday and Friday we can do whatever we want."

What I wanted to do was find Gil and save the world.

"So you'll help me look for Gil?" I said. With me not meeting Hapi until Saturday, I still had two days to spend searching for Gil.

Henry took another bite of the doughnut. "Sure. You have any ideas?"

I flipped to a page in my notebook. "I have a whole list. Today I'm hoping to hit most of the places near Georgetown. Oh, and I need your help with something Saturday night."

"Saturday?" Henry said. "What time?"

Oy. After the thing about Henry's parents, this was going to be tricky. "Ten o'clock. Tell your parents you're sleeping over."

"I told them that three days ago," Henry said, brushing the powdered sugar from his shirt onto the floor. Lieutenant Roy and another shabti immediately ran over with a small broom and dustpan and started sweeping up the mess.

"So? Tell them again."

Henry pulled out his phone but stopped before typing anything. "Wait. Why? What do you need help with?"

After the whole thing with the giant scorpions trying to kill us, I couldn't blame him for asking. So I told him about my conversation with Horus. And I told him about the Sun Disk of Ra.

"I don't think Hapi likes me very much," Henry said.

"That's because you called him a monkey when you met him," I said.

"That was six months ago," Henry said. "I've been doing tons of research on simians, and now I can totally see that Hapi is a baboon. Baboons have a longer nose and their eyes are way closer together. You know that almost gives them binocular vision? Oh, and they're nocturnal. There are tons of differences. I don't know what I was thinking before."

I wasn't sure what Henry was thinking much of the time.

"So you'll help me?" I asked. After the spell and the way Henry had paralyzed the scorpions, I really wanted him as backup. Plus, I liked hanging out with Henry. With Gil gone, and Horus permanently grumpy, things had gotten pretty quiet around the townhouse.

"I'll help you," Henry said. "If . . ."

"If what? Isn't science camp enough?" This was the fate of the world we were talking about.

"If you go somewhere with me during the day on Saturday," Henry said.

It sounded easy and straightforward, but I could tell by the way Henry wouldn't look me directly in the eye that he had some ploy going on.

"Where?" I asked.

"I want to go to Blair's dad's carnival," Henry said, pulling the brochure she'd given us from his pocket.

"The carnival? You're kidding."

Henry shook his head. "Blair keeps asking us to go, and she's really cute, and I don't want her to think I don't care about her charity. It sounds like it's a really great cause. Do you have any idea how many endangered species of snakes there are?"

Great Osiris, help me. If I ever acted this way about a girl, I'd mummify myself.

"Please don't te—" I started.

"Hundreds," Henry said, cutting me off. "And if I don't even do something like go to the carnival to support her cause, she's going to think I'm a horrible person."

I knew that agreeing was the only way Henry would help me.

"Fine," I said. "I'll go with you to the carnival on Saturday. But until then, you have to help me look for Gil."

This must've been totally cool with Henry, because he beamed and did some little cross-your-heart thing I'd seen girls in our grade do when they made promises. And so our plans for the next few days were set.

Henry and I spent all day Thursday and Friday searching one place after another on my list, looking for Gil, but we came up completely empty. I tried not to let it get me down. But when I thought about how every single place I looked was a dead end, it made me feel like I had a giant pit in my stomach that was growing bigger with each failure. I had to find Gil.

I wanted to spend Saturday looking, too, but I had made a

promise. I remembered this time for sure. Plus, all Henry could talk about was the carnival. He showed up super-early on Saturday morning with a bag of doughnuts, ready to go.

I'd seen the carnival going up for the last month. It was across the Potomac, on the Virginia side of the water. The Ferris wheel was tall enough to see all the way from my townhouse. And I liked a good carnival as much as the next immortal.

"You want a doughnut?" Henry asked, holding the bag out to me.

Even though I loved doughnuts, Lieutenant Virgil's chocolate chip scones from earlier were still sitting in my stomach. "Maybe later."

"There's only one left," Henry said.

"Then it's yours." I didn't want to interfere with Henry's insatiable appetite.

We walked south, toward the National Mall. The Fourth of July was next week, so they were setting up tents and stages everywhere. Hundreds of porta-potties lined the sidewalks, ready for the huge crowds that were sure to come. We crossed over the Mall and had almost reached the Jefferson Memorial when something slammed into me, coming out of nowhere.

I landed flat on my back, and stars filled my vision. When the stars cleared, I barely had time to register the giant blob of drool falling toward my face.

I closed my eyes . . . too late. Humbaba, the Sumerian monster from my basement, towered over me. And then he lowered his head and licked me across my entire face, taking the drool and most likely a layer of my skin with it.

"What is that thing, Tut?" Henry said. He stood ten feet away and didn't look like he was moving in to help.

"Good Baba," I said, but I still couldn't move. I had no clue where he'd been for the last few days. Truthfully, I hadn't expected him to come back.

Humbaba jumped up and landed back on me, knocking the wind from my lungs. And then his giant snake tail started wagging. It was so long that it hit the ground on both sides of me, the snake head hissing with each impact.

"Good boy," I said. The gender part was a guess. I didn't want to inspect Humbaba that closely. "Time to let me up."

Humbaba didn't move.

"Seriously, Baba," I said. "Time to get off."

Humbaba only pounced on me again. This was not going well.

I dug through my mind, trying to remember anything I could about dog training, but Horus had never let us have a dog. He said they barked too much and peed all over the place, marking their territory. But from back in Egypt, when I did have dogs, there were a few basics that came to mind. I had to let Humbaba know who was boss. And I had to reward good behavior.

"Give me your doughnut," I said to Henry.

Henry held the powdered sugar doughnut back, out of reach. "It's the last one."

"Yeah, and I have a monster on top of me. He wants a treat. Give me the doughnut."

Henry glanced longingly at the doughnut one more time and then edged forward, placing it in my outstretched hand.

I looked Humbaba directly in the eyes. "Okay, here's the

deal, Baba. If you get off me and be a super-good boy, then you get this yummy, yummy treat."

Humbaba's ears perked up at this and his huge lion eyes swiveled to the doughnut in my hand. I tensed for a second. I did not want him to bite the doughnut and accidentally take my hand with him. Another huge drop of drool fell onto my face.

"Come on, Baba. You know you want to be a good boy."

He wagged his snake tail, and his black tongue lolled out. His eyes roved back and forth between me and the doughnut. And then he jumped off, lifting so high in the air, he would have registered on the radar for low-flying airplanes. I finally sucked in a breath.

Humbaba landed next to me, sat on his haunches, and started panting, eyes fixed on the doughnut. His tail wagged so fast I could hardly see it.

"Tut?" Henry said. He still hadn't moved.

"It's Humbaba," I said. "I don't think he'll hurt you."

"You don't think so?" Henry said. "That's no reassurance."

"Good boy, Baba," I said. "You want the treat now?"

His snake tail wagged even faster, and he let out a roar that shook the ground around us.

"Here you go!" I tossed the doughnut to him.

He caught it easily and inhaled it. And then he tilted his head at me, like he was asking for more.

"That was the last one." I reached forward and scratched Humbaba on the head between his giant ears. He let out a low roar, and his back right leg started twitching.

"Is it a dog?" Henry said. "Because if it is, it doesn't look like any dog I've ever seen before. And I've seen a lot of them, Tut."

"It's not a dog." I kept scratching Humbaba because he seemed happier than a puppy at the park. "It's a Sumerian monster. He's the guardian of the Cedar Forest."

"A monster? You're scratching a monster's head? What? Are you going to rub his tummy next?"

At this, Humbaba's ears perked up. He rolled over immediately onto his back and exposed his super-hairy stomach. And he did really remind me of a dog, so I figured there was nothing to lose. I started scratching his stomach.

Drool oozed out of the sides of Humbaba's mouth, and his eyes rolled back in his head. It was like he'd died and gone to monster paradise.

"Who's a good monster?" I said. "Who is? Baba is, that's who."

"Are you kidding me, Tut?" Henry said. He'd finally dared to inch closer. "That thing looks like he could swallow me whole."

"Then don't make him mad," I said.

"Can you just make him go away?" Henry said.

"Go away? He's so cute." It was hard to believe the terrifying monster from my basement was now enjoying a tummy rub.

"Seriously, Tut," Henry said. "He's like a pit bull on steroids."

From behind us a car drove by, blowing its horn like an idiot. Humbaba must've taken this as a challenge, because he got up and lowered himself onto his front paws. His tail stopped wagging. And the roar that had been simmering in his throat began to grow.

I figured this was a good time to stop playing. Henry was right. Humbaba was bigger than a smart car. If he landed in the middle of traffic, that would definitely make the evening news.

So, like I'd done it a million times before, I summoned a fireball in my right hand.

"Ready, Baba?" I said.

He snapped his head in my direction. Thankfully his snake tail started wagging again. He let out a roar that sounded a lot like a bark. And then another one.

I pulled my hand back and threw the fireball with all my immortal strength. It whipped through the air like a comet. Humbaba didn't hesitate. He was after it so fast, it was like he hadn't been standing there one second before.

I brushed off my jeans and T-shirt.

Henry just stared at me.

"What?" I said.

"No more monsters," he said. "And fireballs? Seriously? You didn't think to tell me about that?"

It hadn't come up. Also, I hadn't been sure. But now I was. I'd summoned the fireball with hardly thinking about it. My powers, or Gil's powers, were getting stronger.

"I'll tell you next time," I said.

"Let's hope there's not a next time," Henry said, and we crossed the bridge to Virginia.

13

WHERE THE FUNHOUSE
ISN'T SO FUN

No sooner had we walked through the giant wooden gates of the carnival than Blair ran up to us. Well, she ran up to Henry. Me, she just kind of sniffed the air and shrugged and looked away. But I was covered in monster drool, which isn't attractive no matter how many fireballs I'd summoned.

"You came to the carnival, Henry. I'm so glad." She clasped her hands in front of her with glee.

Henry turned a shade of red I didn't think was humanly possible. It looked exactly like the inside of a pomegranate, splotchy and everything.

"Well, yeah," he said. "The whole thing with the endangered species . . . I've been doing a ton of research on it, and I can't believe some of the things they hunt animals for."

The smile slipped from Blair's face, and tears filled her wide eyes. "It's horrible. And snakes are the worst. People don't care about them as much since they aren't all fluffy and fuzzy and don't like to cuddle."

I kept my mouth shut, but I fell into that category of people. The last animal I'd want to cuddle with was a snake.

"It's a really great cause," Henry said. "Your dad must be an amazing person."

"He's the best ever," Blair said.

I cleared my throat because I'd had about as much of this conversation as I could without risking losing my breakfast.

"So . . . uh . . . where's camp next week?" I said, looking for a common thread between us.

Blair whipped her head around so fast that it took her hair a couple seconds to catch up. "You don't know?"

I took a step back. "Um . . . no."

From how excited she was, I worried it was a snake farm or something.

"We're going to the Botanical Gardens. I can't wait!"

"Yeah, you should like that, Tut," Henry said. "With as much as you like plants."

He was right. I did like plants—a lot—seeing as how my patron deity was Osiris. Or at least it used to be Osiris. I guess, with the whole fireball thing, maybe it was Nergal now, Gil's patron deity. But the thought of that made me kind of . . . I don't know. Sad. Sure, I was happy to be alive. And fireballs were really cool. I'd always been envious of Gil's powers. And even though I used to laugh about how silly my own Osiris-given powers were, I missed them. The number of scarab beetles in my town-house was declining fast. Horus was not happy.

Blair grabbed Henry's hands. He froze, and the red on his face deepened. His eyes darted sideways to me, but I didn't say a word.

"Make sure you both visit the funhouse," Blair said. "It's the biggest funhouse in any carnival this side of the Atlantic."

I'd visited pretty much every carnival in the United States. I'd seen lots of funhouses. I was about to tell Blair this, but I stopped myself since she wasn't paying attention to me.

She started pulling on Henry's hands. "Henry, you should come meet my dad."

"Wwwwhat?" he said.

"My dad," Blair said. "I've told him all about you. He wants to meet you."

This was too much for Henry. He shook his hands loose and took a step back, toward me. "Um . . . Tut and I are just going to walk around for a little bit."

I didn't think this was the right answer. Blair stared at him with wide eyes that didn't blink, and then she licked her lips.

"Right," I said. "We're just going to walk around."

At this, her eyes snapped to me. She licked her lips again, not breaking eye contact. She was kind of pretty, I guess, but she did have some serious social issues. Finally she looked away.

"Okay, whatever," she said. "Don't forget to check out the funhouse."

Henry nodded but didn't speak. I think the whole meet-the-dad comment had him freaked out.

"Sure," I said.

"Great. Bye." Without another word, Blair whirled around and skipped away, blond curls bouncing as she went.

"Your girlfriend's creepy," I said to Henry, once I was sure she was out of earshot. Or at least I thought she was out of earshot. But the second the words were out of my mouth, she stopped skipping. She didn't turn back toward us, but my skin prickled. How could she possibly have heard me? She was fifty feet away. I didn't say another word, but Henry and I both waited. Finally she started skipping again and vanished from sight.

"She's not my girlfriend," Henry said. "And she's not creepy. She's super-interesting. And very smart. We have a lot in common."

"She doesn't blink," I said. "Haven't you noticed?"

"That's a medical condition," Henry said. "It just means she has a reduced amount of dopamine."

"So you have noticed," I said. "It's weird."

"You're just jealous that she's not paying attention to you," Henry said.

"Hardly." But even as I said it, I couldn't help but wonder. Was that it? Could I possibly be jealous?

I shook my head. No. That was silly. I was not jealous because Blair Drake liked Henry and not me.

Or was I?

My phone buzzed, which saved me from having to think about it anymore. It was a text from Brandon asking when Henry and I were going to be at his house. I couldn't really tell him about the grave-robbing thing, so I texted back and told him that we couldn't make it. That something had come up.

bummer, Brandon texted back.

I'm not sure what possessed me, but I typed, maybe another time, and hit *send* before I could stop myself.

Was I really making plans with other people? It was so un-Tut-like, and yet part of me deep inside loved the idea of hanging out with other kids. Having fun. Not worrying about things like saving the world.

Henry and I stopped to get a funnel cake, because, well, funnel cake. The line was huge; all sorts of people were at the carnival. Most of the picnic tables were taken by families with strollers and balloons with scary clowns on them. But at one of the tables there was a single person I recognized.

Well, he wasn't technically a person. He was a god.

Thoth stood next to a picnic table, skateboard propped up next to it. He had a spray paint can poised in his hand and he studied the top of the table. It was already covered with a bunch of bright colors. As Henry and I walked over, the colors separated out into a giant grid.

"Give me a word," Thoth said, not even looking up.

"Graveyard," I said without even thinking about it. With the night I had ahead of me, it was most on my mind.

"Monster," Henry said.

He must've still been thinking about Humbaba.

Thoth nodded and kept painting. "Those are good ones. I'll take them."

"Stop doing that," I said. This power Thoth had to draw words out of people . . . well, it just left me feeling like I'd given away a deep secret.

Thoth switched out the paint. "Stop doing it? No way, Boy King. It's how I get words. People give me words. I give them words in return. It keeps the universe in balance."

I highly doubted that the fate of the universe rested on Thoth giving and receiving words, but there was no reason to pick a fight with an Egyptian god if I didn't have to.

"So what word do you have for me?" I asked.

Thoth clipped the paint can back into his belt and then clasped me on my shoulders with his giant paint-covered hands. "I got the perfect word for you, Boy King."

Henry laughed.

"Also, can we please stop saying 'Boy King'?" I said.

Thoth seemed to consider this. "We as in . . . you and who? Henry? Sure. You guys don't have to say 'Boy King.'"

It's not what I meant at all, and Thoth knew it.

"So what's my word?" I asked again.

"Bob," Thoth said.

"Bob? What kind of word is that?"

He flicked his hands upward, and drops of paint flew off, splashing across my face. Paint. Monster drool. Colonel Cody was going to insist on lye soap to get me clean.

"It's a palindrome," Henry said. "You know the longest palindrome sentence?"

I knew he'd tell me if I didn't stop him. "But what's it supposed to mean?"

"It's your word," Thoth said. "First word I think of when I look at you. Just like you give me the first word that comes to your mind." He turned to Henry. "What about you? Do you want your word?"

Henry wiped his finger in the paint on the table, but it had already dried. "Is it also a palindrome?"

"Maybe," Thoth said. "I'll tell you after you play a game with me."

That's what he'd painted on the picnic table. It was a giant Senet board.

I was about to explain to Thoth that the last thing we had time to do was play a game of Senet, but Henry sat right down like it was game day at school. "I have no clue how to play," he said.

Thoth sat across from him. "Don't worry. I'm a great teacher."

I'd played plenty of Senet before, back in Egypt. It was kind of like chess but much simpler and with a lot more luck. Gil and I used to play at the townhouse, too, from time to time. I probably still had a Senet board somewhere around there. But I had no intention of watching Henry and Thoth play. The game could take hours. So after finishing my funnel cake, I left them to it and wandered off.

I'll say this: Blair was right. This was the best carnival I'd been to in years. There were jugglers around every corner and food trucks serving everything from deep-fried pickles on a stick to Frito pie. But all the grease from the funnel cake had made my stomach start to hurt, so I followed signs until I found the funhouse.

It must've just been closed, maybe for cleaning, because

when I walked up, they were pulling the gate open to let people back in. I paid my ten dollars—way expensive; I don't care how big of a funhouse it was—and was about to go inside, when someone walked up and said, "Are you going to pay for me, too?"

My insides went to mush. Tia stood there tapping her combat boot, hands on hips, waiting. And I realized that there was nothing I'd rather do than go in the funhouse with her, so I pulled ten more dollars from my pocket and gave it to the tall, skinny guy who was taking money.

"Thanks, Tut," Tia said. "Maybe you can buy me a funnel cake later."

I would totally suffer stomach distress and eat another funnel cake for the chance to hang out with her.

I thought everything was cool, I thought Tia maybe just wanted to hang out or something, but no sooner were we inside than she whipped around to face me. "What are you doing here wasting time? Aren't you supposed to be looking for something?"

The streak in her dark hair was blue, and she wore a blue tank top to match. It matched her eyes really nicely, too.

"Looking for what?" I said. She may have been part of the conversation at The Babylon Club about Gil, but she didn't know anything about the sun disk. At least not as far as I knew. Unless, like before, she knew way more than she was letting on.

"Something important," Tia said, widening her eyes, waiting for me to tell her.

"Nope," I said. I liked Tia. A lot. But I still didn't trust her completely. I had no plans to give away all my secrets to her. What if somehow she was working with Apep? She'd been part of the Cult of Set before. Their sister, even! As much as I wanted to trust her, I knew that I couldn't.

"Whatever, Tut," she said. "Keep your little secrets." And she flipped her dark hair around in a completely cute way that made my face feel really hot.

"So you like carnivals?" I asked. It was a horrible way to change the conversation. I think it also sounded really stupid. But I didn't want to talk about the sun disk with her because I didn't want to get tempted to tell her.

"Yeah. I like carnivals," she said. "Or maybe I hate carnivals and I'm just following you."

Of course I wanted to believe that, but Tia was way too cool to ever let on that she might kind of like me. But she had to kind of like me. Didn't she?

For as crowded as the carnival was, nobody else had come into the funhouse behind us. The ten-dollar price tag probably kept them out. It was just me and Tia. Alone. She took off ahead of me, walking along the slanting floor. I slipped ahead of her, balancing without needing to hold on once, because I was an immortal, and that's just the cool kind of thing immortals could do.

"You're showing off," Tia said when she caught up to me.

"I would never show off," I said, putting on my best shocked look.

"Are you kidding?" Tia said. "You've shown off every time I've ever talked to you."

"That's completely not true," I said.

"It's totally true."

"Tell me one time."

"Okay," Tia said. "How about that time you accidentally cut yourself and then healed it?"

"You dug your fingernails into me," I said. "And it's not showing off. I was healing myself. It's cheaper than a Band-Aid."

"It's showing off," Tia said. "And then when you took the scepter for me, you jumped, like, twenty feet into the air."

Back during the Uncle Horemheb mess, I'd helped Tia steal the Holy Scepter of Set. It had been grasped in the hand of a giant statue of Set.

"It was the fastest way," I said. "What was I supposed to do? Climb?"

"Most people would have," Tia said.

"Yeah, but I'm not most people," I said. "I'm an immortal. It's why you needed me to get the scepter for you." Only an immortal could steal the Scepter of Set.

"It was showing off."

There was no way I was going to win this argument with Tia. That much was clear. But as I prepared to defend myself again, something jumped out at us from behind a doorway.

It was a life-size animatronic clown.

Tia actually shrieked. It was so un-Tia-like. And then her face, which was normally so cool and composed, grimaced.

"Ugh! I hate clowns," she said, kicking it in the chest with her combat boot.

"You're scared of clowns?" I laughed. "I didn't think you were scared of anything."

She hit me on the shoulder. "I'm not scared of clowns. I just hate them. They freak me out."

"You are scared," I said.

She narrowed her eyes. "Mention it again, Great Pharaoh, and I will find a way to get my revenge."

I couldn't imagine what worse thing she could do to me. When the Cult of Set had been chasing me, she'd nearly turned me over to her crazy brothers to be sacrificed and mummified for the good of Set. Speaking of which . . .

"Where are you living now?" I asked as we crept around the clown. I had no plans to admit it, but clowns freaked me out, too, what with their fake red smiles and their oversize shoes and polka-dot bow ties. Ahead of us was a mirror maze, which no matter how confusing would be way better than clowns.

Tia, maybe not even realizing it, had grabbed my hand during the clown thing. I didn't pull away.

"At the funeral home," she said, like it was no big deal.

"You're living with Auntie Isis?" Holy Amun. If that was true, then there was a really good chance she could know about Ra's sun disk.

"Sort of," Tia said. "My brothers were out to get me, in case you didn't notice. And after that whole thing with the Scepter of Set, I couldn't really go back. They're still looking for whoever took it."

Of course, when I stole the scepter, Set got angrier than the Hulk. No god wanted his sacred objects stolen from him. But this had been exactly Tia's mission. She was out to steal sacred objects from all the gods. It was some crazy scheme she had planned to reunite the Egyptian gods. It was never going to work. The last thing the gods wanted was to be reunited.

"So they still don't know?" I asked, silently praying to Osiris that she wouldn't pull her hand away from mine. I tried to pretend I was leading her through the mirror maze, making sure she wouldn't get lost. It wasn't far from the truth since the mirrors were everywhere and it was probably the most confusing mirror maze I'd ever been in. We turned left and right, trying to find our way out.

"They think you took it," Tia said.

"What?"

"Don't worry," she said. "It's no big deal."

"Um . . ." The last thing I needed now was the Cult of Set managing to get their act back together and coming after me again.

"They know Horus is protecting you," Tia said. "You're fine."

With as strange as he'd been acting, Horus wasn't protecting his kitty litter these days. I doubted his protective spells around my townhouse, if they were still in place, would hold out much longer.

Tia pulled her hand away from mine and pressed it forward on one of the mirrors. "Auntie N says there's something funny about this carnival."

"Auntie who?" I asked.

"Auntie N," Tia said. "Nephthys. She's taking care of the funeral homes while Auntie Isis is away."

"Auntie Isis isn't there?" I asked. Did Horus know that? It seemed like something he would have mentioned . . . if he'd been himself. Nephthys was Auntie Isis's sister, Horus's aunt. I almost never saw her. But here Tia was talking about her like it was just another regular thing on another regular day. How far enmeshed was Tia in this whole Egyptian gods thing anyway?

"She had to go away for a little while," Tia said. "But Auntie N is taking care of everything."

Keeping the mummification business going strong, I was sure.

"What did she say about the carnival? Funny how?" As far as I could tell, it was a typical suburban junk-food and money-making way to keep kids busy for hours on end, all for the good of some charity, of course.

"Funny like . . ." Tia leaned forward and pressed her nose against the mirror. "Do you see something in here?"

I leaned forward, too, pressing my nose the same way she was. And instantly I knew I'd made a mistake. There was something in the mirror. Something that started coming at me the second it saw me. It was long like a snake but had the head of a bird with eyes like black diamonds. Hypnotic eyes that refused to let my eyes go. Waving around it were tentacles covered in suction cups that looked like they could suck the marrow from my bones.

"Back away!" I yelled, yanking Tia with me as I retreated from the mirror. Too late. The image of the thing reflected in every mirror around us. I slammed against one after another, hitting them with my fists, but I couldn't find the exit. There was no way out.

"Tut?" Tia said. She clenched my arms.

Images of Gil, captured and trapped, flickered through my mind. Snakes everywhere. Darkness. Gil hurt. In trouble.

"It's some sort of creature of Apep," I said. "We need to find a way out."

I slammed my elbows into the mirrors. I tried throwing fireballs. I closed my eyes, hoping that when the visual connection through the mirrors was broken, the snake-bird creature would vanish. Nothing worked.

What would Gil do in this situation? If he were here with me, we'd find a way out. We'd fight this minion of Apep together. But Gil wasn't here. I had to do this on my own.

"I have your friend, scarab heart," a voice hissed through the air. It was the voice of a snake, and it made my skin crawl. Like Apep himself was somehow speaking through this monster.

"Give me Gil," I said, with as much command as I could. I'd never seen this creature before. Never even heard of anything like it.

"Gilgamesh is nearly mine," the voice of Apep through the creature hissed. "He always has been. But now I am stronger. No one will ever be able to defeat me again. I am invincible."

Gil was not Apep's. That much I would make certain of. I would die trying. And I had no intention of dying. I had to find a way to free Gil and destroy Apep, in that order. And I had to start by finding a way out of this funhouse.

"Return Gil to me now," I said, using my pharaoh voice. Not that I thought I was going to convince Apep, Lord of Chaos, to just hand Gil over.

The bird-monster darted its head from side to side, looking everywhere at once. Its tentacles waved around, reaching for me and Tia, but we kept skipping out of the way. And then it flicked a tongue out like a snake, smelling the air around us.

"I smell what's inside you, immortal," the bird-monster hissed. "Come closer so I can see you. Then you will be mine."

This had to end. If Apep captured me, too, I'd never get the sun disk. I kicked at the mirror in front of me. I jumped to the ceiling, trying to break through. But the mirrors seemed to be closing in on us, inch by inch.

"I always get what I want," the creature said.

"Not today," Tia said. She reached into one of the pockets of her cargo pants and pulled out, of all things, the Holy Scepter of Set. She threw it as hard as she could. It spun through the air and slammed into one of the mirrors.

All the mirrors shattered, raining glass down everywhere. Tia and I covered our heads and waited for the glass to stop falling. When I finally dared to open my eyes, there was no sign of Apep. No reflections left. The mirrors had not only shattered, they had turned to dust.

"You're horrible to spend time with. You know that, right?" Tia said. She grabbed the scepter from the piles of dust and shoved it back into her pocket.

"You keep the scepter with you?"

Tia brushed the dust from her dark hair. She, like me, was covered in a fine layer of the powder. "Weapons of the gods are useful when you're fighting other gods."

"But what about Set? What if he finds you?" It was like Tia was trying to get into even more trouble than she already was.

She patted my cheek. "He thinks you have it. Remember?"

Great Amun, it was a mess of epic proportions. But I couldn't worry about it now. If Apep had come after me because I was immortal, he could come after Henry, too. I had to warn him.

Tia kicked at the dust of the mirrors. "Auntie N is going to be furious about this. I need to go."

"Wait!" I said.

She spun on me, fixing her eyes on mine. "What?"

"That's it? We fight a monster together, and you just up and run away?"

Not that I was sure what to expect. But still.

She shrugged. "Yeah. I guess that's it." Then she grinned at me and sauntered out of the funhouse.

I could have gone after her, but I had bigger concerns. If Apep was after me because I was immortal, then Henry was in danger, too. Worry filled me. I couldn't let Henry get hurt again. I ran back to the picnic table, my panic increasing with each step. But I had no clue why I'd ever been worried. Henry and Thoth were still deep in the game.

"We need to go, Henry," I said.

Thoth put up a giant painted finger. "Not in the middle of a game. Do you realize how rude that would be?"

"But it's dangerous here," I said, glancing back in the direction of the funhouse. And in as few words as I could, I told them what had happened.

"After the game," Thoth said.

"But Henry—"

"—is under my protection," Thoth said. At this a ripple

seemed to pulse through the air, passing over the three of us, almost like a spell from the *Book of the Dead*.

Henry's eyes got wide—he must've felt it, too—but a huge wave of relief flooded over me. If that was true, if Thoth had truly just vowed to protect Henry, the same way Horus protected me, then Henry would be safe, at least while Thoth was around.

"Fine," I said. "But after this game, Henry, meet me back at the townhouse. Please," I added, because Thoth was, after all, a god, and the more gods I had on my side, the better.

14

WHERE WE GO GRAVE-ROBBING
WITH A BABOON

It was nine-thirty at night when Henry finally showed up.

"What have you been doing for the last ten hours?" I said the second he walked through the door. The shabtis had been trying to burn me alive with incense all afternoon. It seemed like no matter what order I gave them, they kept finding a creative way around it in their ongoing effort to cleanse me of Gil's heathen cooties.

"I'll give you one word," Henry said, holding up a finger. "Losing. I hate Senet."

"Then don't play," I said.

Henry shook his head. "You try saying no to Thoth. That guy has some weird power. Have you noticed?"

"He's a god," I said.

"And what about that protection thing?" Henry said.

"It's a pretty big deal," I said. I'd been thinking about that, too. With Thoth protecting Henry, I wouldn't have to worry so much about him. But why was Thoth taking such an interest? "Having a god protect you is pretty unusual."

Henry brushed funnel cake powder off his shirt. "It makes me feel indebted to him."

"That's because you are," I said. "What word did he give you?"

Henry kind of cringed. "He said I shouldn't tell you."

"Shouldn't tell me? Why not?"

"He said I would know when the time was right," Henry said. "That I should tell you then."

The gods and their games.

"Well, that's great. Make sure you don't forget, you know, just in case it's important or anything," I said. "Anyway, we need to go."

I felt the tug on my pants. "Great Master," Colonel Cody began.

I didn't have time for the argument. "Fine. But just you and a couple other shabtis. Nothing is going to go wrong. I swear, if it does, I'm never leaving the townhouse again." I didn't understand why it was so hard for things to go as planned. I'd been all set to tell Horus about the funhouse and the mirrors and the reflection of the monster, but Horus was nowhere to be found. He was as bad as all the gods. That's why I needed Gil back.

Colonel Cody beamed and immediately snapped his fingers. Majors Rex and Mack lined up, arms crossed over their green chests.

"Do I at least have time to go to the bathroom?" Henry said. I gritted my teeth. "Please just hurry."

Horus had told me to meet Hapi across the bridge, near the airport. We hopped on the Metro since Henry kept complaining about how beat he was. He'd been sitting on his butt all day. I was the one who'd had a confrontation with the Lord of Chaos at the funhouse. If anyone should be tired, it was me. But my heart raced. Once I got the sun disk, I could use this immortal thing to my advantage and find a way to lure Apep to me. I'd make him tell me where Gil was. And then I'd save Gil, imprison Apep, and be done in time for dinner.

We got off at the airport Metro stop and walked over to the bike trail. Hapi was already waiting, arms crossed and feet planted like he planned to wait the entire evening if necessary. Yes, he had a baboon head, but everything else about Hapi was normal, at least for someone who works in a funeral home. He wore a black shirt and black pants with a huge key ring attached to one of the belt loops by a chain.

"Tut, what are you doing here?" he said, with about as much emotion as a wad of chewed-up gum.

Had Horus seriously not told Hapi that we were coming instead of him? I was going to declaw Horus.

"Your dad isn't feeling so great," I said. "He sent us instead."

"You're late," Hapi said. No emotion about Horus. No emotion about seeing us. I dreaded the moment when Hapi would bust at the seams from holding in every feeling that ever ran through that baboon brain of his.

"It's great to see you, too," I said, flashing him what I hoped was an endearing smile. Sure, Hapi and I got along. Of Horus's four sons, Hapi was the most trustworthy, the most responsible. If I had to pick one of them, he was definitely the one I'd want to go grave-robbing with.

"It's my fault," Henry said, extending his hand for Hapi to shake.

Hapi only looked at it and bared his teeth.

When you considered what Hapi did all day, mucking around with dead people's insides, Henry was better off not shaking his hand, anyway.

"Okay," Hapi said. And then he swung his leg over a bicycle. I hadn't noticed before, but there were two more bikes lying on the ground next to him. Two. And it's not like Horus would have ever been caught dead riding a bike. Hapi had been expecting us after all. What a liar.

"Did you bring me a helmet?" Henry said. "I seriously never ride without a helmet."

"You might be immortal," I said. "You probably don't need a helmet."

"Might? Probably? That's no reassurance," Henry said. "People die without helmets."

I'd never had to worry about helmets in my life, but I could see Henry's point. Getting hit on his bicycle was maybe not the best way to test for immortality.

"We'll stick to the path," Hapi said.

"Just don't fall, okay?" I picked up one of the bikes and swung my leg over. Henry ran his hands through his messy blond hair and did the same. The three shabtis ran up my legs and perched on my shoulders.

"Don't forget the shovels," Hapi said, pointing to a nearby tree. Two huge shovels leaned against the trunk.

"How are we supposed to ride our bikes with those?" Henry said.

"Just grab one, Henry," I whispered under my breath. "Make it work."

For as little emotion as Hapi normally showed, as a baboon, he was really quick to get angry. I didn't think he would hesitate to pull off Henry's eyebrows, given the least excuse.

Henry and I grabbed the shovels and laid them across the handlebars of the bikes. And then we proceeded to follow Hapi down the bike trail toward Old Town.

"So where are we going?" I called ahead.

"To a grave," Hapi said.

"Whose grave?"

"Oh, I bet it's George Washington's," Henry said from behind me. With the shovels, there was no way we could ride side by side.

"It's not George Washington," Hapi said. "He's not in his tomb at Mount Vernon, anyway."

"What?" Henry said. "Of course he's in his tomb. I've been there five times."

"And you've seen his body?" Hapi said.

"Well, no," Henry said.

"That's because he's not in there," Hapi said.

"You're kidding."

"Hapi doesn't make jokes," I said. I couldn't believe Henry hadn't figured that out by now. "If he says that George Washington isn't in his tomb, then George Washington isn't in his tomb."

This, I think, was why Hapi liked me. I got his awkwardness in social situations. I got the way he didn't know how to react. I understood when I'd ask him a question and he wouldn't answer for ten minutes.

"Okay, then it's that Female Stranger," Henry said. "No one knows who she was. That would be the perfect place for us to go."

I figured this game could go on forever. There were about a million graves within biking distance.

"It's not the Female Stranger," Hapi said.

Henry hesitated, then tried again. "Okay, then, it's the Tomb of the Unknown Soldier of the American Revolution. Isn't it? Almost no one knows about it."

"It's not the Tomb of the Unknown Soldier of the American Revolution," Hapi said.

He might not have been getting annoyed with Henry's guesses, but I didn't want to hear any more of them. What I wanted to do was get on with finding the sun disk.

"Please don't guess again, Henry," I said.

He snapped his fingers. "But I have it this time."

"Are you two hungry? We could stop for clam chowder," Hapi said.

"I'm starving," Henry said at the same time I said, "No."

Hapi smacked his lips together. "Maybe afterward."

He and Henry could go hang out together. I planned to get the sun disk securely back to my townhouse and then plot out exactly how I was going to get Gil back and save the world.

"I hear you have some changes back at the funeral home," I said, going for a subject change. "Nephthys is there. Auntie Isis is gone. And Tia is living with you guys?"

"Tia makes good cookies," Hapi said. "Buttercream pistachio. Chocolate drop. Mexican wedding cookies. And last week, we had this funeral service, and she made these peanut butter cookies that were better than ambrosia."

That was a pretty big compliment, coming from Hapi. I would have sworn a scrap of emotion slipped into his voice. A normal human would have been drooling.

"Tia makes cookies?" I said. Of all the things I could imagine Tia doing in her spare time, donning an apron and using a hand mixer did not top the list.

"She said she's going to make a German chocolate cake next week," Hapi said.

It made me want cake really bad.

"And everything is cool with her living there?" I said.

"Sure," Hapi said. "Except we all miss Granny. You remember how much Granny likes cookies."

I hadn't remembered this small detail, but I filed it away in case it might come in handy in the future. If I ever needed a favor from Auntie Isis again, I'd make sure to show up with a plate of macaroons as a peace offering.

"Wait. Auntie Isis isn't there?" Henry said, and he sounded

really worried. I couldn't imagine why Henry would care one way or the other.

"Nope." Hapi looked up at the sky while he biked, like he didn't even have to watch where he was going.

"Where did she go?" I asked.

"You'll have to ask Auntie N," Hapi said.

I had no plans to visit the funeral home, Tia or not, so I figured I'd just ask Horus.

"Who's Auntie N?" Henry said.

"Nephthys," I said. "She's a goddess just like Auntie Isis."

"She's nothing like Granny," Hapi said. A hint of agitation crept into his voice. I'd better be careful.

"Right. But they're sisters. And they both like mummification and dead people," I said, because that at least kind of justified my remark. Truth was, I hardly knew Nephthys. I had creatively found ways to avoid her over the years. Sure, she was Anubis's mom, and he wasn't all that bad, but she was also married to Set, of all people. And hanging out with the wife of Horus's sworn enemy was not how I chose to spend my immortality. It was one more very good reason not to go anywhere near the funeral home.

"Lots of people like mummification and dead people," Hapi said.

I didn't know what kind of people he hung out with, but I didn't say a word.

We got to Old Town, and Hapi slowed down. He wove his bike around people, but if anyone noticed his baboon head, they didn't say anything. Nobody even looked his way.

It was times like this that I was reminded just how powerful the gods were. For thousands of years, I'd lived my immortal life, pulling on my Osiris-given powers. I'd used the *Book of the Dead* a handful of times—not nearly enough. But the gods . . . they could do whatever they wanted, whenever they wanted. If Hapi didn't want hundreds of people to see that he had a baboon head, they wouldn't. I'd gotten too used to Horus, who wandered around the townhouse hanging out on his scratching post and playing with catnip toys. Not that I thought Horus was weak. Horus was one of the most powerful gods in existence. He just rarely let his powers show.

Henry and I, with our shovels—well, they just weren't going to work. After two blocks we had to take them from the handlebars and hold them straight up and down. It probably looked pretty weird, riding our bikes while carrying shovels, like we were some kind of cycling Grim Reapers, but I knew I couldn't count on the memory spells I'd relied on for so long. With my powers from Osiris acting so wonky, I couldn't count on anything. How had Gil kept people from knowing who he was? It would have been really great to know. But no. Instead he had to leave and then go get himself kidnapped. It was so not helpful.

We pedaled through Old Town, dodging cars and horse-drawn buggies and buses; Hapi even made us ride down a cobblestone road. Henry kept covering his head with one hand. He looked like he was going to have a fit every time a car went by. Maybe on the way back, I could find a makeshift helmet for him to wear.

"It's just on the other side of Old Town," Hapi said, not

bothering to turn and see if we were still following him. He kept looking up at the moon instead. It may have been my imagination, but I swear it looked dimmer than normal.

We pedaled ten more blocks out of Old Town, but even then, we didn't slow down. We biked past the marina and only stopped when we got to the marshy area beyond. Hapi hopped off his bike and leaned it against a huge tree that had fallen over, so I did the same.

"Why are we here?" Henry asked. He stayed back, near the path, even while Hapi waded into the tall cattails and swamp grass.

"Grave's up ahead," Hapi said.

"I've looked at lots of maps. There aren't any graves here," Henry said. "The nearest cemetery is half a mile back."

"I never said it was in an official cemetery," Hapi said, and a chill settled over the humid air around us. "And you aren't going to find this place on any map."

I trailed after Hapi, the shabtis on my shoulders, because if Hapi said there was a grave up ahead, then there was a grave up ahead. But with each step I took, the chill pressed harder in the air around us, and small whispers filled the empty spaces. Fog lifted off the ground, masking our feet and legs.

"Come on, Henry," I said.

He didn't budge.

"You shouldn't stay back there alone," I said. Thoth may be protecting Henry, but he wasn't around now. Henry was way better off being near Hapi, no matter where he was going.

Henry finally grumbled under his breath and then followed.

The deeper we trudged into the swamp, the louder the ghostly whispers around us became. Hapi waved his long arms around and mumbled words that sounded like spells.

"What are you doing?" I asked.

"I'm removing the protective spells," Hapi said. "This whole place is covered with them."

This whole place was covered with something. Things kept brushing against my legs as we walked through the fog and the marshy water. Bugs bit at my skin . . . bugs I normally should have been able to push away with a single thought. I couldn't remember ever having a mosquito bite, and now I probably had fifty.

Henry reached out and snapped off a cattail. Hapi spun around and bared his teeth right in Henry's face.

"The dead don't like being disturbed, Henry," he hissed, dragging out Henry's name. And if I were Henry I would have probably peed my pants because the entire world seemed to freeze around us in that moment.

Henry let the cattail fall from his fingers. "The dead?" he managed to say.

"They're everywhere," Hapi said.

Henry looked down into the dark swamp water we walked through. "They are?"

This thought didn't make me the least bit happy either, but I kept my mouth shut.

"This whole place," Hapi said, looking from side to side. "It's a huge graveyard."

Flashes of people fighting filled my mind. A war of godly proportion. And in the images, I saw Gil, standing at the front of the line, battling in a war of the gods. He was covered in blood and dirt, and his dark hair was matted against his head. Darkness filled the sky, pulsing with each moment of the battle. Gil swung two swords and evaded arrows and spears.

"Gil was here," I said, unable to believe my vision, but knowing it was true. "There was some kind of fight."

Hapi nodded his baboon head slowly. "Thousands of years ago, before you were ever born, Tut. The battle between the gods was fought all over the world, from one distant corner of the earth to the next. When they reached this place, the end was imminent. Gil fought bravely with us. He nearly died in this battle."

I gasped as the truth hit me. "It's when Gil got his scarab heart."

Hapi nodded. "Gilgamesh fought his way to the front lines, past others who had already fallen. Apep was ready to destroy everything. The world was being cast into darkness. It had nearly reached the point where we wouldn't be able to stop it. And Ra couldn't get near Apep. But Gil crept up behind Apep and distracted him, giving Ra the chance he needed to imprison Apep. But just before Apep was trapped by the sun disk, he struck out with a mortal blow, stabbing Gil directly in the chest. Gil—"

"It was the immortal-killing knife," I said.

Hapi nodded. "It's even more effective on a mortal. Apep had it. He used it in the battle."

"Gil was dead."

"Maybe," Hapi said. "He should have died then. Would have died. But Isis and Nergal worked together, casting the spell on him, healing him and making him the first immortal."

Gil was the first immortal? How had I never known that? I

always thought Gil got his scarab heart from Nergal and that was all there was to the story. I'd never really thought to question it. But here Hapi was telling me that Gil not only fought Apep before, but that Gil was responsible for Apep's imprisonment.

"It's why Gil was put in charge of protecting the knife," Hapi said. "He became the guardian from that point on."

"And Apep was defeated after that?" I said.

Hapi nodded, motioning all around with his hands. "All the bodies of the fallen lie in the swamps around us. The battle was fought. Ra imprisoned Apep. And then Ra went away."

"Apep has Gil now," I said. That must've been how Apep even knew about Gil in the first place. Apep would have remembered Gil. He'd have known Gil played a part in his imprisonment. And he would want revenge.

Apep hadn't been looking for just any immortal. He had been looking for Gil specifically, and the reasons were absolutely personal.

"He'll kill Gil this time," Hapi said, and the emotion again slipped from his face. But how could he be so emotionless about the whole thing?

"We have to save Gil," I said.

"No. We have to stop Apep," Hapi said. "Gil is irrelevant."

"He's not irrelevant." How could Hapi even say that? Even if he was a god, it made me want to punch him in the face.

"Apep is the concern, Tut," Hapi said. "Not Gil."

I didn't say a word. Hapi was wrong. That's all there was to it. Gil and Apep were both the concern. And I would take care of both of them.

"Um, not to interrupt, but where do we find the sun disk?" Henry said. He had to have felt the tension rippling in the air between Hapi and me.

I flashed him a quick smile in thanks. Henry would help me get Gil back, even if Hapi wouldn't.

Hapi kept his eyes fixed on me for one more minute. The shabtis bravely stood on my shoulders, facing him off. And then Hapi finally turned away and started walking again.

"It's just ahead," he said, smacking his lips together.

I nodded to Henry, and we silently followed, shovels in tow.

I'd never been in these swamps, and I wondered now if it was the spells around the place that had kept me away. It reached far out toward the Potomac, farther than should have been possible, and yet Hapi kept pushing through the tall grass. The swamp got thicker, and the bugs kept biting. And when I couldn't see anything, not even with the light coming from my scarab heart, the darkness broke, and a raised clearing appeared in front of us. It was an island of hard-packed dirt that rose a good five feet out of the swamp around it.

Hapi walked to the center of the small island and stomped his foot on the dirt.

"Here," he said. And then he stepped to the side.

Hapi's message was pretty clear. I moved to the spot on the ground and raised my shovel.

Colonel Cody launched himself at me and landed on my hands. He tried to pull them from the shovel. "Please, Great Master, this menial labor is totally unbefitting someone of royal lineage such as yourself. Perhaps Master's common friend could perform the service."

"There is no way I am digging alone," Henry said, scowling at Colonel Cody. "No way."

I couldn't help but laugh. "Don't worry. I'll help."

I lifted Colonel Cody from my wrist and placed him on the ground. He immediately started digging with his small hands.

"It's probably a good idea for you to protect the perimeter," I said. "You know, since Hapi took down the protective spells."

At this, Colonel Cody and the shabtis stopped digging. "Great Master is beyond wise." He snapped his fingers, and the three shabtis formed a protective triangle around the perimeter of the small island.

I dug my shovel into the dirt. It was packed hard, like it had been in place for hundreds of years—thousands of years—and Henry joined me. Given that I was an immortal, and Henry might be, it shouldn't take long.

"You never told us who's buried here," Henry said to Hapi.

"Not who," Hapi said. "What."

"Okay, what's buried here?" Henry asked.

Hapi picked something off his shoulder, like he was grooming himself, and placed it in his mouth. I tried not to act disgusted. He was part baboon after all.

"It's not your concern," Hapi said, and he continued watching us, as if that were the end of that. But Henry was not about to let it go.

"What do you mean, not our concern? We're digging up a

grave in the middle of an ancient Egyptian battlefield. We have the right to at least know who's—I mean what's—buried here."

"Did you dig the original grave?" Hapi asked.

"Um, no," Henry said.

"Were you in the battle?" With each question, Hapi took a step closer.

"No," Henry said.

"Did you fight against the most powerful evil ever to face this world?" Hapi said.

"You know I didn't," Henry said. "But that's not the point. We're digging up a grave. We should know what we're digging up."

Hapi leaned close, getting in Henry's face. "Let's just say this, friend of Tut. What is buried here isn't for mortals to know."

"But I'm not even sure I'm m . . ." Henry stammered, so I interceded.

"Okay, can you tell me?" I asked. "I'm immortal."

Hapi crossed his arms. "What's buried here is—"

But right then my shovel hit something hard. Hapi squatted down and began to brush the dirt from the top of whatever it was. And in less than a minute, we'd uncovered a dirty sphere. Of course we had to dig more until we could finally get it free. Hapi pulled it from the grave and rested it on the ground next to the hole we'd dug. And then he popped it open.

Mist escaped from it along with a hissing sound and fog like a vat of dry ice. This was it. This was the moment I would get Ra's sun disk. I loved when things worked out like they should.

Except the sphere was empty. There was no Sun Disk of Ra.

There was nothing that even slightly resembled the Sun Disk of Ra. Instead, the only thing in the sphere was a rolled-up piece of papyrus.

I grabbed the paper and unrolled it, smoothing it between my fingers. It hardly even crinkled, which meant that it couldn't be that old.

Handwritten on it was a message.

This artifact has been detected by the "Order of the gods." By the "Order of the gods," all artifacts must be cataloged and stored at the "Hall of Artifacts." Please refrain from stealing artifacts in the future. Doing so will result in being thrown in stasis for all eternity!

I only had to skim it to know who it was from. Imsety and Qeb, two of Horus's other sons. They were in charge of watching over and protecting the Hall of Artifacts.

Hapi read the note and flared his nostrils. I half expected smoke to start coming out of his ears.

"'Order of the gods,'" he said. "When my father hears about this . . ."

If Imsety or Qeb had been in the swamp with us right then, the battle between the gods would have been reenacted.

"They have no right to dig here," Hapi said. "No right to disturb this place."

It was not the time to disagree or makes jokes about Hapi's irresponsible brothers. So I kept my mouth shut and prayed that Henry did, too.

Thankfully for Henry, my prayers worked.

"The mere fact that they came in here, without consulting Granny, is a huge violation," Hapi went on.

I folded the piece of papyrus and stuck it in my pocket. And then I motioned at Henry with my head that it was time to go. But Henry shook his head.

Was he crazy? We had to get out of here. Being around an angry baboon was bad enough. Being around an angry baboon who was also an Egyptian god . . . well, let's just say it wasn't how I wanted the evening to end. Hapi could go back and report this to Auntie Isis or Nephthys or whoever he needed to report in to. In the meantime, I needed to visit the Hall of Artifacts.

"When Granny hears what those two have been up to, she's going to shrink them into shabtis. We'll see how they like that."

I cringed, hoping Colonel Cody didn't take offense at the shabti remark. My shabtis were awesome. I could imagine a whole heck of a lot worse things in life than being a shabti. At least none of them had baboon heads.

Hapi threw the sphere back into the ground, and without even touching it, the dirt piled back on top, packing down until it looked completely undisturbed. If he had powers like that, then why did we have to spend the last hour digging with shovels?

"I'm telling Auntie N," Hapi said, and he started back through the marsh. "She'll get the message to Granny."

He sounded like a great big baboon tattletale.

"We're coming with you," Henry said, hurrying after Hapi.

"What? No, we're not. We're done here." We were heading right to the Hall of Artifacts, that's what we were doing.

"I need to talk to Auntie N," Henry said.

"You can talk to her some other time," I said.

But Henry shook his head. "No, Tut. It's the perfect time."

"It's not the perfect time," I said.

But Henry pleaded with me with his eyes. I had no clue why he'd want to talk to Auntie N so badly. "Please, Tut?"

I tried to calm the anxiety running through me. I counted to ten before I spoke. Henry must have some reason he needed to visit Nephthys.

The seconds ticked by. I couldn't use the sun disk until tomorrow evening anyway. There was still plenty of time to get it. And we were sort of close to Dynasty Funeral Homes.

"Fine," I said. We'd talk to Nephthys and then visit the Hall of Artifacts. It was only a small detour.

15

WHERE I GET MY WORST FUTURE PREDICTED AT THE HOUSE OF THE DEAD

We waded through the fog and the swamps. It took even longer on the way back because Hapi had to keep stopping and putting the protective spells up around the place. When I saved Gil, I'd ask him all about this battle he'd somehow never told me about. I couldn't believe that this was where he'd gotten his scarab heart. His immortality. But the heart in my chest felt warmer than usual, almost like there was a link between it and this place.

Hapi didn't speak as he got on his bike and started pedaling. Anger seethed off him in waves. I understood sibling rivalry, sort of. My real older brother and I had fought, but I also kind of worshiped the ground he walked on, and not just because he would have been pharaoh before me. He seemed to do everything right, so unlike me back in the days of ancient Egypt. Me? I was more the kid who goofed around when I should have been studying.

We made it to Dynasty Funeral Homes in record time. Hapi wheeled his bike around back and parked it in the bike rack, securing it with a U-lock before walking to the side door.

Did people steal bikes from the gods? I guess other gods did. They stole things like scepters and sun disks, so why not bikes? There were two more locks on the rack, so Henry and I locked our bikes up, too. And that's when I finally let my mind wander from Gil to think about Tia. She could be inside also. I didn't know where else she'd be at midnight.

Hapi pulled the key ring from the chain that was looped to his black pants and unlocked the side door of Dynasty Funeral Homes. I heard the silly jingle playing over the speakers the second we walked through the door. And I smelled the cookies. They even distracted Henry, who obviously had something on his mind. He sniffed and walked immediately into the kitchen.

"I am so hungry," Henry said, grabbing an entire plate of chocolate chip cookies. "I'm starving. All the time. I never used to be this hungry, Tut."

"It's puberty," I said.

He threw a cookie at me in reply, which I, of course, caught with my lightning-fast reflexes.

"It's not puberty," Henry said. "It's all that energy from your scarab heart. Ever since . . . you know . . . I've been hungry all the time."

I had noticed how Henry was always wanting to go out to eat. And he'd eaten more scones at my townhouse than I had.

Hapi was already out of sight. He'd probably gone downstairs to the basement to tattle to Auntie N. I didn't want to go anywhere near the basement—that's where they kept the mummified bodies—so I grabbed a couple peanut butter cookies, and Henry and I walked into the salon. And Great Osiris, there Tia was, setting down a plate of cookies. She didn't have an apron on like I'd imagined. But she still looked really cute with her cargo pants and combat boots and jewelry-store-worthy collection of bracelets and necklaces.

"I had no idea you were such a Betty Crocker," I said, biting into a cookie. It was every bit as good as Hapi had said.

"Don't you say another word." Tia challenged me with her eyes, daring me to open my mouth.

I took another bite. "This cookie is amazing."

"They aren't for you." Tia walked over and grabbed the unbitten cookie from my hand. Her fingers just barely brushed against mine, and it sent all sorts of stupid shivers through me. This being fourteen stuff was getting really old.

"What are you two doing here?" Tia said. She tried to grab the plate of chocolate chip cookies from Henry, but he was too fast. He stepped back and shoved an entire cookie into his mouth. And then he tried to say something but it was impossible to tell what because his mouth was full.

"Nothing," I said. "We were hanging out with Hapi." I tried to sound all cool when I said it, like hanging out with the gods was something I did on a daily basis. Well, it was, but I didn't really count Horus.

Tia lowered her voice. "Why's he so mad?"

I still didn't want to tell Tia about the sun disk, so I came up with something on the spot.

"We went out to eat," I said. "But they messed up his order."

"Don't lie to me, Tut," Tia said.

"I'm not—" I started, but Henry cut me off.

"Do you think I can go downstairs and talk to them?" Henry said.

"In the basement?" I said. Henry had been here with me before. He knew what was down there. It was a giant crazy mummification experiment gone wrong. No one in their right mind would go down to the basement by choice.

"Auntie Isis isn't here," Tia said. "She went away."

"I know," Henry said. "But I want to talk to her sister."

"Where'd she go?" I asked, hoping to catch Tia off guard.

"I can't tell you that," Tia said, and I couldn't believe that she would know something like that when I didn't.

"So I can go downstairs?" Henry said. "I wanted to ask Auntie N something."

"Sure," Tia said, rearranging the cookies on the plates.

Hope filled Henry's face. "Great. Come on, Tut."

Was he serious? I couldn't think of a single reason why I would voluntarily go into a mummification parlor when I could stay here talking to Tia instead.

"I'm fine. You can go alone."

"You said you'd come with me," Henry said.

"I said I'd come with you here, to the funeral home," I clarified. "And here we are."

But Henry was having none of it. "Come on, Tut. I need you with me. Seriously."

And even though no part of me wanted to go with him, he was my friend. So I gave a quick smile to Tia, then followed Henry down the steps.

The heavy scent of natron hit my nose by the second step. I resisted the urge to plug my nostrils. What did Henry need to talk to Auntie N about, anyway?

Hapi stood near the center of the room, in between a couple open caskets. Next to the caskets sat the tables with the five canopic jars. I still didn't know what they were putting in that fifth canopic jar, and I didn't want to find out.

In front of Hapi, with her back to us, stood someone who could only be Nephthys. She was patting Hapi's head, like she was calming him down, but no sooner had our feet hit the last step than she whirled around to face us.

"Nephthys?" I said, wondering if I should go right for the casual "Auntie N" salutation. I hadn't seen her in a while, yet I would have recognized her in a second. Nephthys looked like some kind of Bohemian gypsy. Her hair was long and dark brown with a scarf tied around the top, leaving the rest to hang straight down, covering her shoulders. She wore patchwork pants that fit snugly around her wide hips and a long necklace of Buddhist prayer beads. This all seemed kind of normal, but Nephthys was far from normal. In the middle of her forehead was a third eyeball.

She pressed a palm to the extra eyeball. "Tutankhamun!"

she hollered across the room, like it was some sort of surprise party. At least she recognized me. It was a good start.

"Yeah, it's me." I avoided looking around the basement as I answered, because I knew it was filled with natron and hooks and knives and all the other creepy things needed for mummification.

I hated mummification. Whatever happened to me after I died, I was not going to have my brains pulled out of my nose.

"I saw you coming!" she yelled. She hurried across the room, bumping into caskets with her large hips. They wobbled but didn't fall over. Hapi cringed and hurried after her to steady them.

I thought she was going to hug me, but instead she grabbed both my shoulders and pulled me close. And then she fixed that third eyeball right on me and stared. I got the very weird, distinct feeling that she was looking directly into my soul. My scarab heart began to warm.

I heard Henry gasp behind me, but I didn't dare turn around. I couldn't pull away from Nephthys. Immortal energy flared in my fingertips, and all my old powers, which had felt like they'd been trapped for the last six months—my Osiris-given powers—broke free, like a dam had broken. I wanted to use them all, to do all the things I used to be able to do. The energy strengthened.

Then images of Gil began to fill my mind. Gil and I together, at our townhouse. Gil going away. Gil in the battle I'd just seen in the swamp. Gil being kidnapped. Held prisoner. And with each image, something pulled on my scarab heart, almost like it was being yanked from my chest. And yet it stayed warm and strong. And the energy continued to run through me.

Finally Nephthys pulled away, releasing my shoulders. Her third eye closed, though the other two remained open.

"I see how things are, Tutankhamun," she said. "I see exactly how things are. You want to be strong. You want to do this. But you can't. No matter how much you want to, you can't do it alone. And you are in danger. Severe danger."

I wasn't sure what she was talking about. I was immortal. I was more than capable of defeating Apep.

"If this is about Apep, then I am totally up for it," I said.

She slowly shook her head. "No, Tutankhamun. You are not. You will fail if you do this."

I hated her words. I hated even considering that I wouldn't get Gil back.

"Don't worry," Hapi said, stepping up next to her. "Tut isn't going to deal with Apep anymore. I'm going to retrieve the sun disk, and I'm going to imprison Apep myself."

"I have to do it," I said.

"Because of Gilgamesh," Nephthys said. "I see that's where your thoughts are. You are connected."

"Exactly. I am going to free Gil and then imprison Apep."

But Nephthys shook her head. "Not you, Tutankhamun. You don't have the power to do this. And don't forget the danger. It is coming for you. Because of the connection. It will take you. And then you will be lost to us also."

She was wrong. That's all there was to it. Danger or not, I was totally going to succeed. And I was going to do it before Hapi did, because Hapi had already as good as assumed that Gil was dead. If he imprisoned Apep, Gil would die, for real this time. But I kept my mouth shut.

"Enough about this," Nephthys said, pressing her palm to her third eye again. "How is that nephew of mine doing? I've seen dreadful things."

She had to be talking about Horus, since he was her sister's son.

"He's not doing so good," I said. "This whole thing with Apep . . . it's really got him . . . well, it's got him confused."

Her third eye closed. "So it's worse than I've imagined. Tell me everything, Tutankhamun."

So I told her about how strange Horus had been acting. I kind of minimized the parts about him nearly clawing my eyes out; I didn't want to worry her. I did mention how mangy he looked. Auntie N kept squeezing her third eye shut, like somehow she could actually see what I was saying and confirm it by my words.

"It's the impending darkness. The shifting of the world. Apep's chaos beginning to take hold," she said, when I'd finished. "Oh, his mother is not going to be happy at all. Not at all. But enough about that cat." She spotted Henry, and her third eye flew open wide. "What do we have here?" She pressed a finger to her thick lips.

"This is my friend, Henry." I didn't add that he was the whole reason we were here at all. If Auntie N found out I hadn't wanted to come, that was the kind of thing that could offend a goddess for hundreds of years.

But she spun on me. "I can hear your thoughts, Tutankhamun."

I took a step back, as she almost seemed to grow taller. And wider. "Yeah, about that—"

But thank the gods, Auntie N turned back to Henry. "We'll deal with you later. For now, Henry. Henry. Henry. I do see the problem."

"Problem?" I said. "What kind of problem?"

But Nephthys wasn't interested in answering my question. I figured Henry was in for the whole third-eye thing, too. But instead she grabbed him by the wrist and dragged him forward. Henry went with her completely willingly, even though I wanted to grab him back. I didn't want Henry to get mummified. I liked hanging out with him. But Henry must not have been worried, because he followed her to the far side of the room and lay down on a granite slab that was covered with all sorts of disgusting stains.

Did I mention that funeral homes were not a fun place to hang out? Why had I not found a way to talk Henry out of coming here?

I hurried over. "What's going on, Henry?" Maybe he was sick, and I just hadn't noticed. Except I would have noticed. I spent a lot of time with Henry.

"Shhh . . ." Auntie N said, placing her finger to her wide lips. Unlike Auntie Isis, Nephthys didn't wear any makeup or nail polish or anything like that. They didn't even look like sisters. Or act like sisters. Auntie Isis would have covered Henry in mummy wrappings by now. Auntie N, though she was probably an expert in the whole mummification thing, didn't seem to want to pull Henry's brains out through his nose. She grabbed a scarab-beetle amulet that was as big as my fist and placed it on Henry's chest. I guess his nervousness had finally set in, because he was breathing really fast, and his muscles were all clenched up. And then she grabbed a deck of oversize tarot cards.

"Try to relax, Henry," Auntie N said. "If you don't relax, we'll be here all day."

Seeing as how it was midnight—the start of a fresh new day—being here for the next twenty-four hours was not what I had in mind.

Auntie N flipped the tarot cards over, one by one, laying them on Henry's stomach. With her other hand, she pressed her palm onto the scarab-beetle amulet, and it began to glow a bright green. Underneath it, Henry started to glow also, not just from a scarab heart, like I do, but all over his body, like he had with the scorpion bouncers. Then Auntie N started reciting a bunch of Egyptian words. It only took a few of them for me to recognize them as a spell from the *Book of the Dead*.

There were lots of spells in the *Book of the Dead*. Hundreds. There were even some that had never made it to modern-day translation. But I still knew them. And I recognized this one after the first four words. It was a spell to Thoth, for not dying again. Seeing as how Henry had already kind of died once, and that Thoth was now protecting Henry, it made sense for Auntie N to pick this spell. But the longer she chanted it, the more Henry glowed. The entire room lit up around us as the green light shone from the scarab amulet and from Henry. Hapi hurried around Auntie N, handing her various incense burners and feathers that she waved over Henry. And Henry, for as nervous as he'd been only minutes ago, looked really relaxed.

I didn't dare speak. I didn't want to interrupt the work of the gods. I prayed to Osiris as Auntie N chanted, willing him to not let Henry get hurt. I still didn't know why Henry wanted to come here, but Nephthys obviously did. The light was almost blinding. Energy brimmed at the edges of my skin, like it had when she was looking into my soul. I opened myself to that energy, and my scarab heart began to charge. To fill with the immortal energy that kept me strong. I normally charged it at obelisks, but that's only because they collected this power from the gods. Auntie N was here now, generating the power.

I lost track of how long I recharged. I wasn't aware of anything going on around me. And when the green glow finally faded, I was sure I could do anything. I could jump to the top of mountains. I could swim under the sea. And above all, I knew I could defeat Apep, no matter what Auntie N said.

Auntie N pulled the scarab amulet from Henry's chest and handed it to Hapi. Henry sat up. He didn't look any different than before.

"So, what'd you find out?" Henry asked. He swung his feet off the side of the granite table like he was at the doctor's office.

Auntie N came around to face him. She grabbed him by the shoulders, and I knew she was giving him the third-eye stare.

"You, Henry, are a complete mystery, that's what you are."

This was not the answer Henry was expecting. "What do you mean, a complete mystery?"

She shook her head. "I mean that I just don't know. But don't you worry. I'll talk with my sister. We'll devote our time to researching the issue."

"What issue?" I finally said. I was sick of not knowing what was going on. This was my best friend we were talking about.

Auntie N tilted her head in my direction. "You don't know?"

I shook my head. What hadn't Henry told me?

"It's about my . . . immortality," Henry said.

"So are you immortal?" I said.

He threw his hands up in the air. "I don't know. That's why I came here. I wanted to ask the gods."

"And I should have been able to tell you," Auntie N said. "I was sure that the spell would tell us. But I've never seen anything like it. It seems that you are neither mortal nor immortal."

"But he has to be one or the other," I said.

Auntie N narrowed her third eye at me. "Why?"

"Well, it just makes logical sense. Either you're mortal or you're immortal."

"Well, when you make the rules, that's what you can decide," Auntie N said. "For now, it remains a mystery."

16

WHERE I ALMOST GO FOR A SWIM

It was two o'clock Sunday afternoon when we finally walked out of Dynasty Funeral Homes. Somehow, that whole tarot card reading/scarab beetle amulet spell that Auntie N had done had taken over twelve hours. Now it was way too late in the day to find the disk and trap Apep. It would be sunset in a couple hours. But I could at least get the sun disk. Then tomorrow there would be no stopping me.

"We're going to the Library of Congress," I said. There was no way I could let Hapi get to it before me. He wouldn't save Gil. He'd just imprison Apep and not worry about who died. At the thought of Hapi, a couple thorny vines sprouted from the ground and twisted around my feet, reaching toward Henry.

My Osiris-given powers! They were returning!

Whatever Auntie N had done, they were coming back. I tried to make a couple more vines grow, but it was like the more I thought about it, the harder it got. Still, it gave me hope that with time, all my Osiris-given powers would return. I'd be better than I'd ever been, what with the powers of both Osiris and Nergal at the tips of my fingers.

"Watch where you grow that stuff," Henry said, stepping to the side so the vines wouldn't twist around his ankles. "And I can't go with you."

"What do you mean you—oh, this is about your parents, isn't it?" I said, plucking one of the vines and running it between my fingers. It was the most beautiful thing I'd ever seen in my life.

Henry nodded. "They like you. A lot. I swear it's not you."

Of course it wasn't me. People loved me. It was part of the magnetism that came along with being pharaoh. It wasn't some weird mistake that the royal families always came to power. There was something special about the pharaoh lineage. We were descended from Osiris himself, if Horus could be believed.

"You can't get out of it?" I wanted Henry along, but I didn't want to wait. Hapi had stayed at Dynasty Funeral Homes as long as we had. He'd helped Auntie N. But now there was nothing to keep him from getting the sun disk himself. He could be getting closer with each second.

Henry shook his head. "I'm supposed to go to some musical."

"Like a real musical?" I said. Musicals were worse than cleaning cat litter. There was all that singing and dancing. Not that I cleaned cat litter. The shabtis did that for me. But I'd watched them clean it plenty of times. I'd smelled it.

"They got tickets six months ago," Henry said. "My mom bought me a new shirt and a tie and everything. I can't get out of it. Plus they promised to take me out to eat."

With the way Henry had been eating these days, I hoped his parents were going to bring some extra cash. I didn't say anything, but I would have suffered through a musical if it meant I had parents to take me.

We parted ways, Henry off to listen to singing for the rest of the night, and me alone to the Library of Congress. There must be some way I could get in to the Hall of Artifacts in the middle of the day without a whole bunch of people noticing. But around about the time I got to the Lincoln Memorial, my head started to swim. I blinked a couple times to clear it, but the world only got murkier. If it was another vision of Gil, I didn't want to miss a second of it. It might tell me where he was.

Chills ran through me. My scarab heart thrummed. Reality started slipping away, and little flashes filled the edges of my vision. Something black blurred around me, moving so fast I could barely see it. And then a voice sounded in my head.

"Are you there?" the voice said. It sounded a lot like Gil except kind of muffled.

Gil! This was great! He was trying to get in touch with me. He could have found a way to communicate through whatever link we had. Maybe it had something to do with my scarab heart being charged.

"I can't see you," his voice said, and this time, even though it was still muffled, it sounded even more like him.

"I'm here," I said, aloud. I wasn't sure if anyone around me could hear. The entire world had slipped away. I couldn't see anyone. Couldn't see anything but the Lincoln Memorial and the steps and the Reflecting Pool.

"Great Master, who are you talking to?" Colonel Cody asked.

I looked down for him, but I couldn't see him or Majors Rex and Mack either.

"It's Gil," I said to the shabtis. I didn't want them to worry.

The shabtis didn't answer.

"Let me see you," Gil's voice said.

I didn't know why Gil would want to see me. Maybe he wanted to make sure it was really me. But if he couldn't see me through the link, I wasn't sure what his plan was.

"I'm right here," I said. "I'm looking for you. Where are you? Are you okay?"

"Walk to the water," Gil said. "I can see your reflection there."

It seemed a little strange, but if he was suspicious, then I wanted to show him it was really me. I walked toward the water, but each step I took, the dizziness in my head became stronger.

From far away, only the monuments and stuff could be seen in the Reflecting Pool, but as I got closer, other images began to take shape. Trees and benches lining the pool. Clouds overhead in the gray sky. They crystalized in the still water, perfectly reflected, like a mirror.

Just like a mirror.

Like the mirrors in the funhouse.

I halted my steps.

"Why do you want to see me?" I asked, and skepticism filled my voice.

"Go to the water," Gil's voice said, except it had gone back to being muffled. Or maybe it wasn't muffled. Maybe it wasn't Gil's voice after all.

"Why?" I said.

"I need to see what you look like."

"No." I planted my feet on the ground and looked once more for my shabtis, but I still couldn't see them in the vision.

"Yes," the voice said. "You can't defy me, scarab heart."

Before I realized what was happening, my feet started moving again . . . without me controlling them. My scarab heart yanked me forward, step after unwilling step.

I pulled back, but I couldn't stop moving. And I knew, more than anything, that I couldn't let myself get to the water. This was Apep, communicating with me through the link. Trying to see me. I fought as hard as I could, but my feet kept moving.

I pulled for the powers in my scarab heart, but they didn't come. But even were I to manage to use my powers, I wasn't sure what I would do. This was a vision. I couldn't fight it with fire.

"Almost there," the voice said. It sounded nothing like Gil. It hissed like a snake and made me shudder. "Almost where I can see you."

Nephthys's words kept slipping into my mind. *You are in great danger.* This had to be exactly what she'd meant. I hated that she was right. But it made no sense. Why would Apep want to see me? Why would he want *anything* with me? He had Gil, immortal or not, and Gil was the one Apep had the vendetta against.

I tried to stay confident, but with each step, despair crept in. I kept walking. I kept fighting. The complete lack of control was infuriating. And then someone stepped in front of me, and sounds erupted in my ears.

It was like I'd been dropped in the front row of a rock concert, like there were huge oversize speakers that were blasting at top volume. They played some weird trance electronic music with all sorts of digital beats that sounded like a hacked-up version of rap music. Instantly my feet stopped moving. Relief filled me. I was still far enough away from the Reflecting Pool that my image wasn't visible.

I tried to raise my hands to my ears, to block out the noise, but I couldn't do it. All I could do was stand there and listen to the music. My ears would be ringing for days. But as the seconds ticked by, the world around me began to return. To fill in with tourists and joggers and everything else that belonged in Washington, D.C., in the middle of a Sunday afternoon. Finally, I was able to raise my hands. When they touched my ears, I discovered that I was actually wearing a pair of huge headphones.

I blinked my eyes and looked forward. There stood Igigi, with Humbaba next to him, body lowered, tail straight in the air in attack posture. Igigi motioned at me to keep the headphones on. So I did.

He roved his eyes around—all eight of them—watching the people pass us by. The Mall was packed, what with everyone getting ready for the Fourth of July. And they'd wheeled in giant towers of lights to help brighten up the place, since it was getting so dark so early.

My head cleared with each beat of the music, and my body relaxed. Igigi kept two of those eyes fixed on me, watching every twitch of my muscles. And after a solid five minutes had passed, he tapped his own ears and gave me a huge thumbs-up. I pulled off the earphones and let them hang around my neck.

"Got yourself in a bind, didn't you, King Tut?" Igigi said.

Humbaba finally relaxed. He sat back on his haunches and his snake tail wagged back and forth.

"How did you know?" I asked. I'd only met Igigi a few days ago. It's not like we'd exchanged cell phone numbers so he could track me via GPS. Maybe Igigi was more than a DJ working at The Babylon Club. Maybe Igigi was secretly working with Apep. He could even know where Gil was. Except for the fact that Igigi helped me break whatever spell had been placed over me.

Why had I been so eager to answer the voice in the vision, anyway? It was times like this that I was actually glad Gil wasn't around. He claimed I was always getting myself into trouble, and this kind of thing . . . well, it didn't do much to clear my name.

Igigi patted Humbaba's head with a giant hand. "Your monster-dog came and warned me. He said he saw you. Said you were acting funny. He roared at you a few times, and when you didn't respond, he came to the club and got me."

"It's true," Colonel Cody said. "It is exactly as the eight-eyed minor heathen god says. The monster nearly stepped on us in his efforts to get you to play. And then, when you wouldn't, he ran off."

I thought back to when the world had first slipped away. Humbaba could have been the blurriness at the edges of my vision.

"How did he know you were at the club?" I asked Igigi. "How does he even know you?"

Igigi shrugged. "Me and Humbaba . . . we go way back. He's been hanging out at the club recently. Pretty sure he missed me in these last few thousand years. Also, I think he likes the music."

It was either the truth or a really good cover story. I opted to consider it the truth, because my head might explode if I thought it out anymore.

"Good Baba," I said, which Humbaba must've taken as encouragement because he pounced forward and landed on me, knocking me to the ground. Drool dripped onto my face as he licked me. I wished I had a cookie from the funeral home to give him as a treat.

"It was Apep," I said, once I'd managed to roll out from under the Sumerian monster. "He was trying to see what I looked like." I kept my voice low, though I'm not sure why I bothered. If people around us hadn't noticed Igigi with his eight eyes along with a lion-headed monster, talk of an Egyptian god surely wasn't going to get us noticed.

"Did you let him?" Igigi asked. He started walking toward the Capitol, like he knew where I was going. I followed along next to him, happy to get as far away from the Reflecting Pool as I could.

"No. But almost. He was controlling me. I couldn't stop walking." The idea of the Egyptian god controlling my mind made me want to incinerate him on the spot. How dare he do that to me?

Humbaba must've sensed my unease, because he nudged his head so it was conveniently right under my hand. I scratched him between the ears.

Igigi tapped my chest with one of his big hands. "Through your scarab heart?"

"Yeah. I think so," I said. Which was just wonderful. There wasn't much I could do about that.

We walked in silence until we got to the Capitol. "Well, this is where we part ways, King Tut." He nodded to the north. "I'm headed that way. I got things to do."

I couldn't imagine what Igigi did in his spare time. I'd have asked him except I had other things on my mind. I had to get the sun disk.

"Thanks again," I said.

"I'm not looking for thanks," Igigi said. He shuffled his feet and waited, like he was expecting me to hand him twenty dollars or something.

"Oh," I said. "Your name." I'd almost forgotten, but now that he reminded me of it, I felt completely in his debt. He'd just saved me from some unknown fate over which I had no control.

"Yep, my name," Igigi said. "Did you find it? 'Cause if you didn't . . ."

I scrambled to think of something, because I didn't want to tell him that I'd come up with nothing. I also didn't want to go to the underworld without my hands and eyes. So I said the first thing that came to mind.

"Bob."

A few horrifying seconds went by when I was sure Igigi would start screaming and drag me off to the underworld. I tried to keep my face steady. But Bob? What was I thinking? I was a complete idiot.

But then Igigi's eyes lit up—all eight of them. He snapped his fingers.

"Yes! Bob! That's it! That's exactly it!"

"It is?" I said.

"Yes! It's a palindrome, just like Igigi, except it's my name. How did you know? Where did you find it?"

I couldn't believe I'd really gotten Igigi's name right. I pored over my memories, trying to figure out why I'd said Bob, and then it came to me. It was the word that Thoth had given me. Once again, he'd known exactly what I needed.

"It was a gift from the gods," I said.

Igigi—well, Bob, if we wanted to be technical—nodded his head. "I am forever in your debt, King Tut." And then he grabbed me in a bear hug that made me feel like my insides were getting pulverized with a meat hammer. I waited it out, because I couldn't move.

"Keep the dog with you," Igigi/Bob said. And then he snapped the headphones over his ears, did a couple little dance moves—including a pretty sweet moon walk—and walked away.

17

WHERE MY DOG GETS A BATH

Nobody else in D.C. knew it, but under the Library of Congress was one of the largest warehouses in the world: the Hall of Artifacts. Horus had told me about it six months ago. I'd gone to retrieve a scroll. And the way to get in was under a giant statue out front of the Library. Tia and I had found it. Well, I'd found it, and Tia had followed along. It's when she found out—or at least when she told me that she knew—who I was.

Humbaba, the three shabtis, and I headed around to the front of the Library, but the second we got there, my heart sank into my stomach. There used to be a fountain with a few statues, including a giant statue of Poseidon, Greek god of the sea. That statue led to the secret entrance to the Hall of Artifacts. But the statue was gone. The fountain was drained. And there was nothing but smooth cement underneath. Yellow tape surrounded the entire area, and signs were spray-painted with the words RENOVATION IN PROGRESS. BUILDING A BRIGHTER FUTURE. The estimated completion date was three years from now.

Three years! How could remodeling a fountain take three years? Apep would have destroyed the earth five times over by then. There was nothing bright about that future. I couldn't wait three years. But I also wasn't going to be able to get to the Hall of Artifacts the same way I had before. I needed a new plan. I needed Horus's help. But Horus was back at my townhouse. At least I hoped he was.

Humbaba trotted along next to me the entire way home, peeing on fire hydrants, sniffing the butts of dogs, all of which he towered over. I played around with my memory spells, making people think they were seeing a dog instead of a Sumerian monster. I just hoped Humbaba didn't eat any of the other dogs. That would be hard to make anyone forget. My powers got stronger each time I used them. I even tried using more of Gil's power, letting heat cascade off me. It worked brilliantly. I didn't summon any fireballs because I didn't want Humbaba to run away. After the whole Reflecting Pool incident, having him around might not be such a bad idea. Plus, it was kind of nice having a dog. Even if he wasn't really a dog.

When we walked into the townhouse, Horus was nowhere to be found. Aside from the fact that I needed to talk to him, this was actually a good thing because of Horus's whole "no dogs" rule. But Lieutenant Roy ran up to me and bowed low to the ground. "Great Master, it seems you've brought the monster back with you."

I scratched Humbaba's head, causing his tongue to slip out the side of his mouth. Drool dripped onto the wooden floor.

"Yeah, he's fine," I said. "He won't hurt anything."

Lieutenant Roy snapped his fingers and four shabtis ran over with a towel and started mopping up the drool.

"As you say, Great Master," Lieutenant Roy said. "Perhaps the monster would care for a bath?"

There was a rank monster aroma in the air, but I highly doubted the shabtis would be able to get Humbaba into the tub. I was wrong. At the word "bath," Humbaba started jumping up and down, hitting the ceiling as he did so, and letting out little growling yips, like a Yorkshire terrier.

Lieutenant Roy beamed. "Wonderful. If the monster would follow me this way." He headed for the upstairs bathroom, trailed by at least fifty shabtis. Humbaba bounded after them and vanished into the bathroom. The door closed behind them.

"Is Horus here?" I asked Lieutenant Virgil as I walked to the futon. He and Lieutenant Leon hurried over with a soda and a plate of scones.

"Yes, there is a problem with that," Lieutenant Virgil said, and his eyes drifted downward.

That's when I heard the low hissing coming from underneath the futon. I looked down, through my legs, so I could see what was beneath me. One glowing yellow eye stared back at me from the darkness.

"Horus?" I whispered.

The hissing continued.

"As I was saying, Great Master," Lieutenant Virgil said. "The cat seems to be under the weather. He's been like that for hours."

"Horus?" I said again. "You need to come out here."

Nothing.

"It's about the Hall of Artifacts. I need to know how to get in. The main entrance is gone."

The hissing only got louder.

"Come on, Horus," I said, and even though he was a god, I couldn't help the anger that crept into my voice. Gil's life was on the line here. Horus needed to snap out of whatever weird trance he'd entered.

"We've tried milk," Lieutenant Virgil said.

"And catnip," Lieutenant Leon added.

"Nothing has worked," Lieutenant Virgil said.

"Perhaps he needs time." Colonel Cody joined the other two on the coffee table. He must've finished briefing the other shabtis on everything that had gone on in the last twenty-four hours. Majors Mack and Rex had a bunch of their battle shabtis lined up and were already running drills.

"We don't have time," I said, sinking back onto the futon. This was a stupid mess. Hapi was a god. He would find some other way to get into the Hall of Artifacts. And it's not like I could ask Nephthys. She was on Hapi's side. She didn't think I was capable of going after Apep myself.

Just then the bathroom door flew open. I braced myself, ready for a dripping, furious Sumerian monster to come rushing out the door with shabtis clinging onto him for dear life. But instead, out pranced Humbaba like some sort of Pomeranian show dog. His curly black hair glistened. His face had been trimmed, making his eyes look super-big and innocent. And he had a bright red bow on top of his head, holding back his lion's mane.

Lieutenant Roy beamed next to him.

"Great Osiris, that can't be Humbaba," I said.

Humbaba thrashed his snake tail from side to side with happiness.

"May I present Great Master's pedigree show monster," Lieutenant Roy said.

"You did an amazing job! Was it hard?"

"On the contrary," Lieutenant Roy said. "The monster was most willing. Our estimates of the dirt under his nails suggests that he hadn't been bathed in four thousand years."

Four thousand years. Even Horus would want a bath after that long. The pipes were surely going to clog from all the dirt.

Humbaba jumped onto Gil's chair and immediately started digging a hole in the stuffing.

"No! Over here, Baba!" I said, and patted my side.

His monster ears perked up and he bounded over, knocking stuff from Gil's piles of junk on the way. I glanced under the futon again. Horus was still there, hissing. Humbaba got really interested in what I was doing and pressed his nose down onto the floor so he could see under the futon. And then he started doing the roar-bark thing again, trying to get Horus to come out. It didn't work.

So instead, Humbaba sank to the floor right there and rested his head in my lap, almost like, now that he had been properly bathed, he was going to protect both Horus and me. I wasn't sure which of us needed protection more.

I flipped through my notebook, hoping some sort of revelation would come to me, but it didn't. And as the seconds ticked by, haziness took over me, and I fell asleep. Or at least I thought it was sleep until I opened my eyes and realized that I wasn't in my townhouse anymore. I was back in the darkness. And I wasn't me. I was Gil, crawling along the floor. In the background, the two guards I'd heard before were still arguing, this time about sunspots.

"They're getting bigger," the one guard said.

"Not bigger," the other said. "That's the boss. He's pulling the light from it."

His words got harder to hear because I think Gil was getting farther away. And then he pressed his hands against the wall, but there was a handle, so he reached out to turn it.

"Have you seen the immortal?" the one guard said.

And then they started running across the floor, their footsteps getting closer. Gil knew he had to do something. He pulled on his powers, but they didn't come, because I had Gil's powers. And I willed them to move through whatever link we had, to give them back to him so he could defend himself and get out of there. I pushed heat out into the air around me. I summoned the fire. But it didn't work. The powers stayed with me, not with Gil.

The two guards grabbed Gil.

"You think we should tie him up or something?" the second guard said.

"We already did that," the first said. "He tried to choke us with the rope."

I grinned at that. Gil might be a captive, but he was still fighting.

"We need to give him that venom again," the second guard said.

"Boss won't like that," the first said. "He says it breaks some kind of link."

Link. They were talking about me.

I snapped out of the dream.

One glance at the clock told me it was already the next morning. I'd slept the entire night. I was still on my futon, but I was covered in sweat. My fingers brimmed with heat from the vision. Apep one hundred percent knew about the link between Gil and me. That was how he'd controlled me at the Reflecting Pool.

Colonel Cody stood vigil over me, standing on my chest. Humbaba still had his head on my lap, though his eyes were wide open. The doorbell rang, and immediately my sensors went on red alert. Apep was definitely after me. Me, specifically. He knew I had Gil's heart. I hated to admit that Nephthys was right, that I was in danger, but the signs definitely seemed to be pointing that way.

"Shall I answer it, Great Master?" Colonel Cody said.

I had a Sumerian monster at my side, over three hundred shabtis, and a really angry, crazy Egyptian cat god in my townhouse. I should be okay.

"Who is it?" I asked.

"Great Master, it is the beautiful mortal girl," Colonel Cody said, throwing the door open wide. The shabtis loved Tia, ever since the first time she'd met them and she'd called them cute.

I ran a quick hand through my hair and tried to make it look like I hadn't just woken up. But it would have been nice to at least have had time to brush my teeth.

"What are you doing here?" I glanced around instinctively. A bunch of Gil's stuff sat in piles around the townhouse and the shabtis were still mopping up the monster drool.

Behind her, a gloomy morning streamed through the open door. A gloomy morning with not much sun. And I thought of what the guards had been saying in the dream. *He's pulling the light from it.* If Apep wasn't stopped, gloomy skies would be only the beginning.

"Are you seriously sitting here on your butt?" Tia said. "Do you have any idea what's happening?"

That got my attention. I shot up from the futon so fast I accidentally knocked over the two shabtis who were guarding me. Humbaba jumped to his feet, ran over to Tia, and started sniffing her.

She glanced at him, but if she was surprised by the fact that he was a monster and not a dog, she didn't let on.

"What's happening?" I asked. I still wore the same clothes I had on the last time I saw Tia, over a day ago. She, on the other hand, had dyed the streak in her hair purple and wore a tank top to match.

She stormed into the townhouse, combat boots smashing

scarab beetles with every step. "Do you have any idea what that monkey is going to do?"

There was only one monkey Tia could be talking about.

"Hapi?" I said.

She nodded.

"Don't call him a monkey to his face," I said.

"Do you not think I know that, Tut? I've been living at the funeral home for six months." Tia flopped down in Gil's chair, causing a cloud of dust from deep in the cushions to erupt around the room. Lieutenant Roy, who was standing nearby on a shelf, gasped and jumped from the shelf. He flipped through the air, ninja-style, and landed on the floor, then trailed a tiny finger through the dust that was settling. With the claw marks and the burns and the stuffing coming out, they'd want to get rid of the chair for sure now.

"I know what he's going to do," I said. "He's going to the Hall of Artifacts. But he can't get in. I went by yesterday. The entrance is under construction."

Tia looked at me like I'd lost half my brain matter. "And you think that will stop a god? Of course there are other ways in."

My hopes, which had been so low they may as well have been the scarab beetles under Tia's boots, perked up. "Do you know them?"

"Maybe," Tia said. She tapped the toe of her combat boot and smiled.

Great Osiris, this girl drove me crazy.

"You do! You have to show me." I grabbed my gym shoes from under the coffee table and shoved them on. This couldn't wait any longer. I had to get there before Hapi. I knew I could talk his brothers into giving me the sun disk. Or at least I hoped so. There was this whole rule about no artifacts being removed from the place. But the fate of the world was hanging in the balance. They'd understand.

"Has he already gotten there?" I asked. If Hapi did know how to get in, he could already have the sun disk in his grubby little hands.

Tia picked at a loose thread on Gil's chair, and a huge chunk of it started to unravel. She twirled it around her finger and pulled at it some more. "Not yet. Auntie N kept going on and on about how he had to wait for the fullness of the noonday sun so Apep would be at his weakest. I've had about as many of her crackpot prophecies as I can take."

So Tia didn't put much merit in them either. That made me feel better, because I knew I was powerful enough to imprison Apep. I didn't care what Auntie N said.

"Forget the noonday sun. I'm going right now," I said. Hapi had as good as counted Gil dead. But I hadn't. I was not going to give up on Gil. If Gil died, I would never forgive myself.

Humbaba loped up to my side. He was prepared to save the world with me. He stuck his snake tail out straight behind him and dug his lion claws into the wood of my floor. But his red bow still looked really pretty.

"I'm coming with you," Tia said, standing up, avoiding the shabtis who had started vacuuming the floor around her.

"No you're not," I said. I may have been in danger, but it was going to stop there. I was not going to endanger anyone else just because the crazy Lord of Chaos was after me.

She placed her hands on her hips. "And you're going to stop me, Boy King?"

Even though she sounded completely sarcastic when she said it, she also sounded cute. Really cute. Like, if one person in the world could call me Boy King and get away with it, it was Tia.

"You can just tell me where the entrance is," I said. I would not be swayed by her cute factor.

"Not going to happen."

I stammered, looking for the perfect reason why she shouldn't come along. "It could be dangerous."

She pursed her lips at me. "Yeah? Imsety and Qeb? Dangerous?"

She had a point. Imsety and Qeb, alleged guardians of the Hall of Artifacts, were so harmless even Henry wouldn't have been afraid of them. I mean Henry from before. Henry now seemed to be getting braver with each day that passed.

"You probably have something else you need to do," I said.

"Nope," Tia said. "You're all I have on my agenda."

"Why do you want to go, anyway?" I asked. Sure, part of me entertained the idea that Tia just wanted to spend time with me, but I knew this was a bunch of baloney. Tia definitely had some ulterior motive.

"I just want to," she said. And then she smiled. And my insides went all wobbly because she had about the best smile in the world.

"Fine," I said, even though I knew she was keeping something from me. "But let me do the talking."

"Whatever you say, Boy King," Tia said.

I thought everything was settled. Then the doorbell rang again. With Tia here, that seriously narrowed the possibilities of who might be visiting. Next to me, Humbaba tensed.

"Ready for camp?" Henry said, the second Colonel Cody opened the door.

Great Amun, camp?

I knew he wasn't kidding, because he wore a shirt that read, Um : THE ELEMENT OF CONFUSION. I couldn't believe it. Here Gil's life and the entire fate of the world was in my hands, Henry knew this, and he still planned to go to science camp?

"I'm not going today." I didn't even try to make it sound apologetic. There was no way in all the realm of Anubis that I was going to camp.

Henry's face fell. I would have felt bad if I didn't have such a good excuse.

"But you promised, Tut." He eyed Humbaba warily, but the monster-dog didn't act like he was going to eat Henry.

Tia crossed her arms and waited to see what I was going to say. Perfect. Now I was going to sound like a complete jerk who was bailing on my friend.

"I promised last week. I went three times. That completely fulfills the promise. It more than fulfills the promise."

Henry looked to Colonel Cody for support, but the shabtis of course stood by me. Even if I had given Henry his immortal energy, they would always side with me.

"The promise was for two weeks," Henry said. "And if you do anything less, then . . ."

"Then what?" I said, waiting to see what kind of threat Henry could possibly pull out.

I guess he realized it was futile, too, so he tried for pure logic. "But it's at the Botanical Gardens today, Tut. You love plants."

I used to love plants, back when they did what I wanted them to. Now, I'd say my relationship with plants was somewhere in the range of lukewarm, but getting better with each hour that passed.

"You're kidding, right?" Tia said. "The Botanical Gardens?"

Henry nodded, inspired by her interest. "Yep. We get the behind-the-scenes tour. You know, they don't give that tour to just anyone. You have to get a special pass nearly six months in advance."

Tia grabbed my arm and pulled. It actually kind of hurt. "We're going to camp, Boy King," she said.

She may as well have just told me that we were going to cross-stitch for the rest of the day. I figured Tia would have been about as interested in science camp as she would be in macramé. But that said, she did like baking.

"We are?" I said, because maybe camp wouldn't be so bad if Tia was there. No, what was I thinking? I had to get on with things. I shook my head. "No, we're not. You promised you'd show me how to get into the Hall of Artifacts."

"Wait, you guys were making plans without me?" Henry said.

Now I had to worry about hurting Henry's feelings? To make matters worse, Horus's hissing from under the futon got loud enough for the neighbors to hear. It was only eight in the morning, and it was already a horrible day.

"She just got here," I said. "And she said she knew how to get in. I would have texted you." I figured this wasn't a lie. It might not have been the first thing on my list, but I would have let Henry know.

"So we can go after camp," Henry said.

Tia looked at both of us like we'd grown antennae. "Don't either of you get it?"

I hated to admit that I didn't get something, especially when she might as well have said, "Any idiot who does not understand what I'm talking about, please raise your hand." But the problem was that I really didn't get it. I had no idea what she was talking about.

"Okay, fine," I said. "I don't get it."

Henry shook his head, too. At least I had an ally in my ignorance.

"The entrance that I'm talking about," Tia said. "It's in the Botanical Gardens."

"Sweet!" Henry said, doing some awkward victory fist pump.

"No, it's not," I said. "You're just trying to stall."

Tia crossed her arms and shook her head slowly, as if she were talking to a small child. "Tut, tell me, what buildings make up the Capitol complex?"

"Duh. The Library of Congress."

"And?"

Well, there were a bunch, most of them small. But then there was also . . .

"The Botanical Gardens," I said. Since it seemed like more of a museum, that's what I mostly considered it. But it was actually part of the Capitol, not the Smithsonian.

"I knew you'd get it," she said, patting my cheek.

"Um, not to be a pain here, but can we hurry?" Henry said. "I don't want to be late to camp."

18

WHERE I VISIT THE MOTHER OF ALL PLANTS

Maybe Henry was right to be concerned. We were the last kids to get there. And no pets were allowed in, so I told Humbaba to wait outside. But he kept following me. He wouldn't let me out of his sight. So I did the only thing I could think of. I summoned a fireball and threw it with all my immortal strength.

Humbaba let out a bark-roar and then tore after the fireball, disappearing within seconds.

"Stop showing off," Tia said, and pushed her way past me. The closer we'd gotten to the Botanical Gardens, the more on edge she'd seemed. Or maybe it was my imagination.

When we walked in, Camp Counselor Crystal scowled at Tia, who crossed her arms and scowled right back at her, but she didn't say anything since she was about to start lecturing. I guess there were pretty big goings-on at the Botanical Gardens. One of the corpse plants was about to bloom. Thankfully it hadn't bloomed yet or we'd have all been plugging our noses.

"You know why they call it a corpse plant?" Blair said, rushing over to join us at the first possible second.

"'Cause it's dead?" Tia said, turning her scowl to Blair.

They were like complete opposites of each other. Blair had a curly blond mess of hair and was bouncy enough to be captain of the cheerleading squad. Tia, on the other hand—well, I was willing to bet cheerleading was pretty far down on her list of hobbies, just below macramé.

But Blair wasn't swayed in the least by Tia's sour attitude.

"No, silly," Blair said. "It's not dead."

"Blair's right," Henry said, totally backing her up. "Technically, for it to be blooming, it needs to be alive. Otherwise, it would be more of a mutation. Like a wart or something. Warts don't bloom. And you know that whole myth about hair and nails growing after death? It's totally not true. Nothing grows after death."

I shot him a look, hoping he'd get the idea that Tia didn't care. I cared, but that's because I really did like plants. I'd seen corpse plants here at the Botanical Gardens bloom lots of times before. I'd caused some of them to bloom. After all, I'd had power over plants for three thousand years. Just to see how my powers were doing, I reached out, barely touching a nearby vine, willing it to grow.

It worked. The vine started crawling up the side of the blue-tiled wall, snaking around the other vines already in place. It felt amazing, better than slaying a charging rhinoceros. And I was overcome with the urge to cause an explosion of blossoms in this entire place. To really make the Botanical Gardens come alive.

Tia smacked me on the arm, bringing me back to my senses. "Enough already."

Of course she was right. No need to call attention to myself. But it had worked. I'd focused on it, and the plant had grown. I loved that I had my powers back. Osiris was with me. It was such a positive omen that I almost didn't notice Blair staring at the vine. But I did, and she was. And then I pretended that I didn't see her, because I didn't want her to think that I thought she thought anything weird was going on.

"That stunk that you guys couldn't come over on Saturday," Brandon said, walking up with Joe.

Saturday night I'd been digging up a grave with Henry. I'd had the blisters to prove it, but then I'd healed myself. Henry still had them.

"Yeah, sorry. Something came up," I said.

"We got pizza," Joe said. "It was so good. And we drank, like, ten sodas apiece. But then Brandon's little sister overflowed the toilet, so we had to go to the bathroom outside for the rest of the night."

"Pizza sounds great," Henry said, totally ignoring the toilet part. If I ever did go hang out with Brandon and Joe, maybe I'd bring a few shabtis along in case there was another toilet disaster.

"Hey, we should come over to your house sometime, Tut," Brandon said.

"Henry's house is a lot more fun than mine," I said quickly.

I might at some point hang out with Joe and Brandon, but it would be a cold day in the underworld before I had kids from school over to my place for pizza. The last time I'd done that, the Cult of Set had delivered snakes to my house instead.

"Give me a word," Henry said to the two of them.

I looked at him like he'd lost his mind. I was about to tell him that he'd lost his mind. But before I got the chance, Joe answered.

"Pizza," Joe said.

"Farts," Brandon said.

I mentally groaned. Now Henry was running around acting like he was the Lord of Divine Words or something. I never should have let him and Thoth play Senet for that long.

"Good words," Henry said, but he didn't offer any back in reply.

Camp Counselor Crystal led us into the big main room, which was filled with trees that reached four stories high. Two upper levels of walkways ran around the outside glass, and water droplets fell from above. I'd spent lots of time here in the past, especially when I'd felt lonely. But now, even with Gil gone, I realized that it had been months since I'd had that sinking, lonely feeling I used to get so often. It was good to have friends . . . even if my best friend did currently have googly eyes for some girl.

Speaking of which, Blair grabbed Henry and dragged him to the front of the group. Well, I say "dragged." It wasn't like Henry needed that much persuasion. Tia and I fell to the back.

"So where is it?" I asked.

She leaned close. Really close. So close I felt her breath on my neck and the sweet smell of her lotus blossom perfume filled my nose. I focused my thoughts. Now was not the time to be thinking about how pretty Tia was.

"It's near the carnivorous plants," Tia whispered.

I thought about her words, not the perfect sound of her voice. She was helping me. We were in this together.

"Where near there?" I whispered back.

"There's a path," Tia said. "And a hidden door at the end of the path."

I nodded and then pretended to listen to Camp Counselor Crystal because she had stopped talking and was looking directly at me and Tia.

"Are we disturbing you?" Camp Counselor Crystal asked.

The truth was that yes, camp was disturbing me. It was getting in the way of me saving the world. But Camp Counselor Crystal didn't need to know that. Hopefully I'd make everything better and all the clueless mortals in the world wouldn't be any wiser. It wasn't the hero's reward that I might have dreamed of, but it would save Gil and the rest of humanity.

"Sorry," I called, waving my apology. After everyone turned away, I tried to motion to Henry, but Blair had clenched hold of his arm and was not letting go. So I texted him and told him to come back with us.

I know he saw the text. I saw him reach into his pocket and check his phone. He looked back. Nodded. And then continued to listen to the camp lady. We moved from the big room to the southern room, where all the American desert plants were kept. And I knew we were in the right place when Camp Counselor

Crystal started talking about Venus flytraps. I'd enlisted the help of many a carnivorous plant in my time. They were tricky and temperamental, but they did work exactly as promised, swallowing up anything that landed on them. I'd even threatened Horus with them on occasion.

I texted Henry again. This time, he whispered something to Blair, who finally let go of his arm. She didn't look happy at all about letting him out of her grasp.

"What'd you tell her?" I asked, once Henry finally joined me and Tia.

"That I had to go to the bathroom," Henry said.

The camp group moved forward, past the carnivorous plants. We fell behind a little more. Now was the perfect time. Except just then, someone strolled through the door we'd come through. Someone with the head of a baboon.

"Turn around," I hissed. Henry, Tia, and I turned back to Camp Counselor Crystal and took a few steps forward, pretending we were listening. Well, Henry probably was listening. Out of my peripheral vision I barely saw Hapi. He glanced around, and since he thought no one was watching, he stepped off the main walkway, onto a side path next to the carnivorous plants. And then he disappeared behind the greenery.

"It must be close to noon," Tia said. "We have to follow him." It was like she wanted to find this disk as much as I did. I loved that.

"Come on," I said, and I headed for the same path Hapi had taken. Tia was by my side. Henry cast one last glance at our science camp group, and then followed.

19

WHERE I LEARN MORE THAN I EVER WANTED TO ABOUT WHITE HOUSE CHINA

When we reached the end of the path, there was a hidden door, just like Tia had said there would be. It was already closed, meaning Hapi was well ahead of us.

"He can't get there before us," Tia said, pulling the door open. The hinges made a gods-awful screeching that they probably heard over in the White House. Stupid Hapi. He'd probably cast some spell so no one heard the door when he opened it. I looked back, but our group had already moved on to the next room.

"Why do you care so much?" I asked. I mean, sure, I was happy that Tia was willing to help me, but she had to have some ulterior motive here.

Tia pretended to look shocked. "Because I'm just a caring kind of gal."

Whatever. She could keep her secret. I'd find it out eventually.

After the three of us were through, we closed the door behind us. If anything, it was even louder than when we opened it. My muscles tensed with each second that went by. Hapi was probably listening to us breathe.

Ahead of us was a hallway lit by a flickering fluorescent bulb that looked like it hadn't been changed since the 1970s. It gave me a headache just looking at it.

"I don't hear him," Henry said.

I didn't either. That wasn't a good sign. Hapi was a god. He could probably move at superspeed. I tiptoed down the hallway, but I swear Tia's boots were clomping loud enough to wake the dead.

"Can you try to be quieter?" I asked.

"Can you try to hurry up?" she said.

So I walked a little faster and she walked a little quieter, and the three of us came to the top of a set of concrete steps. Tia immediately started down, like she'd been here a million times before. For all I knew, she'd been sneaking down, playing Mario Kart and enjoying hot chocolate with Imsety and Qeb. They were probably all BFFs by now. Maybe we could use that to our advantage.

There were a million steps ahead of us, illuminated by the fluorescent bulbs. It would have been better to have no light at all. We were all lit up in a ghastly zombie glow, and it gave me a headache. It felt like an eternity, but we finally reached the bottom. Far ahead, I heard something that sounded a lot like a door closing. Or maybe it was coming from above and just echoing down the stairway. It was hard to tell. Aside from turning back, there was only one way to go. And I was not going to turn back. I was still going to find a way to get the sun disk before Hapi. Or I'd steal it from him. We moved forward, and at the end of a hallway was a door.

There was no knob, so I pushed it open the tiniest amount. I had no idea what was on the other side. Hapi, waiting to tear our noses off? Imsety and Qeb, ready to put us in eternal stasis? When it was open a crack, I peeked inside and then stepped through, motioning for Tia and Henry to follow.

We were up on some kind of balcony that ran around the entire perimeter of the room below. I'd been in this exact room six months before, but I'd never noticed the balcony. Of course, I had been worried about getting my head shaved, so I had other things on my mind. I dropped low to the ground, so the railing would hide me, and I crept around until, through the slats, I had a good view of below. Tia and Henry were so quiet that I almost didn't know they'd joined me. Also, I was pretty focused because Hapi was definitely down there, and it looked like he was in some sort of deep discussion with Imsety and Qeb. Well, at least as deep of a discussion as Imsety and Qeb ever had, which may have been the source of the disagreement they seemed to be having.

Hapi kept putting his baboon head in his hand and shaking it back and forth.

"Why don't you understand?" I heard Hapi say.

"Calm down, bro," Qeb said. He was the one with the falcon head, which looked really funny with his jean shorts and Atari shirt. "We totally understand exactly what you're saying."

"Then you know I need it," Hapi said.

"Totally," Qeb said.

"Then why are you not placing it in my hands right at this very minute?" Hapi said.

I had to agree with his logic. If they had the sun disk and they understood, what was holding them back—not that I wanted Hapi to get the sun disk at all. Maybe they knew I needed it, and this was a ploy to keep it away from him and save it for me. Yeah, I knew this possibility was slim, but I couldn't help the small daydream. It would be so nice for something to really go my way, just once.

"That's just it," Imsety said, slapping Hapi on the back, like they were getting along like the best brothers in the world. Hapi was not the least bit amused. "We can't give it to you. We understand, but we just can't."

Hapi glanced at the sign on the wall, the one that threatened anyone who took an object from the Hall of Artifacts. "There is no such thing as eternal stasis," he said.

"Shhh," Imsety whispered. "Don't tell anyone."

Hapi threw up his hands. "Who would I tell?"

"That's why you were able to steal the scroll," I whispered to Tia.

She only smiled in reply.

Qeb narrowed his falcon eyes at Hapi. "I don't know. Who would you tell?"

It was ridiculous. I wished they would just get on with it.

Hapi must have had the same sentiment because he bared his teeth. "Give it to me now. You took it. It's mine. I buried it in the first place. I want it back."

"Yes, but all artifacts—" Imsety began.

"Now!" Hapi screamed. I'd never heard him scream in all my life. Never even thought it was possible. Him with his lack of emotions. But here, around his two extremely frustrating brothers . . . well, I guess it brought out the worst even in gods.

Imsety put his hands up. "Okay, here's the deal. And don't get mad when I tell you this."

Hapi took a step forward. We were beyond the point of mad.

"We don't have it," Qeb said quickly.

"What do you mean, you don't have it?" Hapi said.

"They don't have it?" Henry whispered.

"We don't have it, bro," Qeb said. "That's what we mean."

Hapi bared his teeth as if the entire conversation were worse than torture. "Then who does have it?"

Imsety made a calm-down motion with his hands. "Okay, that's the good news. What Qeb meant to say is that we don't have it . . . here."

Hapi looked from one to the next, as if he was trying to figure out which brother he could trust more. Or which he wanted to kill more.

"Then where do you have it?" he asked as calmly as possible for an angry baboon.

"Off-site storage," Qeb said. "That's where it went when we uncovered it."

Hapi looked like he was going to start pulling Qeb's feathers out of his head. "Why did you dig it up in the first place? It was fine where it was. Totally safe."

Imsety laughed in that cocky way that always grated on my nerves. "Safe? In that swamp?"

"That swamp is a sacred battleground," Hapi said. "You shouldn't be disturbing anything in there, let alone the very item that defeated Apep to begin with."

"Sacred battleground," Imsety said. "Did you think to even place one protective ward on it? Even one?"

"There were plenty of protective wards," Hapi said. "You shouldn't have been able to get past them. No one should have. No one even knew what was there."

Imsety chuckled. "Well, I guess that's where your logic is flawed, little brother. Because somebody did know it was there. They came here and told us about it. Asked us to . . . relocate it."

"Who?" Hapi said, keeping a completely deadpan face.

Imsety turned to Qeb and flicked his hands dismissively, like the answer was irrelevant. "I don't know. Some lady. Do you remember who?"

"Of course I remember," Qeb said. "She wasn't just some lady. She was the First Lady, married to the president."

"Which president?" Hapi asked.

"You want me to remember her name?" Qeb said. "Sorry, that's a little too much record-keeping, if you ask me."

Great Amun, it was a miracle Imsety and Qeb kept anything safe in this place.

"Okay, fine," Hapi said. "Do you at least remember when it was?"

I guess he couldn't let it go that someone had discovered his secret hiding place.

"Oh, yeah, sure," Imsety said. "That's easy. You remember when they opened Tut's tomb?"

I held my breath. Suddenly this conversation had turned to me. I knew very well when my tomb had been opened. Nineteen twenty-two. The headlines had reached America in days, but I had felt it, deep in my soul, as if some part of me had remained in that tomb for thousands of years and had finally seen the light of day. It's the day my uncle Horemheb had been released. The day my worldly possessions had started being photographed. And cataloged. The day my peaceful immortal life had changed forever.

"Of course I remember," Hapi said.

"Who was the president then?" Qeb said. "Harking? Harwell?"

"Harding," Henry whispered next to me, unable to keep his mouth shut. When it came to trivia, Henry would win any contest Imsety or Qeb put before him.

"Harding," Hapi said, almost like he'd heard Henry. I hoped he hadn't heard Henry. We did not need an angry baboon after us. Not today.

"Right. Harding," Imsety said. "So his wife comes here. She's the First Lady, you know. That means she's married to the president."

Hapi made a motion with his hand for Imsety to hurry up.

"So anyway, she stops in to visit, coming through the side entrance like she's been here a million times. And she tells us about this object. How it's buried in some swamp over across the river."

"That's impossible," Hapi said. He scratched behind his ears as if this whole conversation blew his mind.

"Not impossible," Imsety said. "And she says that we have to get it for her."

"So you got it," Hapi said. "Where is it?"

Qeb scratched his feather head. "That's the weird part. She told us that we couldn't keep it here, 'by order of Ra.'" He said it all funny and spooky and used finger quotes as if to mock Ra. "Like anyone's seen or heard from Ra."

"That dude's totally never coming back," Imsety said.

"Never coming back," Qeb echoed. "But hey, we're not stupid. What if it is Ra? It's not like we want to get on the bad side of that guy. So we give it to the lady—"

"She was really cute," Imsety said. "You remember how cute she was?"

"She was married," Qeb said, silencing his brother. "Anyway, we give it to her, and you will not believe what she does with it."

"What?" Hapi said. He was trying really hard to keep his temper; I'd seen him enough that I could tell. "What did she do with it?"

Imsety laughed. "She used it as her 'First Lady China.' You know how all those presidents' wives have their special dishes they eat their doughnuts off of each morning for breakfast? She turns Ra's sun disk, possibly the most powerful Egyptian artifact in the world, into a plate."

Hapi didn't say a word. I wasn't sure what he would say, anyway. A plate? The sun disk was a plate?

"So let me be really clear here and ask a simple, straightforward question," Hapi finally said. "And I want you to do your very best to answer it. Just answer it."

Imsety and Qeb nodded. "Sure, bro," Qeb said.

"Good," Hapi said. "Where exactly is the sun disk right now?"

It was the question that should have been asked ten minutes ago. Finally we were going to get an answer.

"Oh, that's what you want to know," Imsety said. "That's easy."

Hapi waited. Henry, Tia, and I watched silently from the balcony above.

"It's in the First Lady Plate Collection," Qeb said. "Like we said, off-site storage."

"That's in the National Museum of American History," Henry said, and he looked like he wanted to jump up right then and run over to the museum and grab it.

"Thanks for your help," Hapi said, and he turned to walk away.

"Oh, but the same rules apply, bro," Qeb called after him. "You can't take anything from the Hall of Artifacts. Not even from off-site storage. Doing so will result in stasis for all of eternity."

Hapi didn't bother responding. He had no intention of listening to that stupid threat, and neither did I. Now I just had to find a way to get to the sun disk before Hapi.

20

WHERE HENRY MAKES A TRIP TO THE HOSPITAL

We held our breath, waiting until Hapi tore up the stairs, but the second he was out of sight, I dashed after him. I had to get the sun disk before he did. Otherwise, Gil would be as good as dead. I ran up the steps, taking them three at a time. Henry and Tia both kept up, even given my immortality. When we got to the top of the stairs, I shoved the maintenance door open, not caring if the entire world heard.

There was no sign of Hapi, curse that stupid baboon. But Blair was right there, as if she'd been waiting for us.

"There you guys are," she said. "Where have you been? You're missing the best part of this place."

I didn't care about science camp or whatever botanical revelation I wasn't hearing. All I cared about was getting Gil back.

But then it occurred to me how weird it was that Blair happened to be right here, waiting for us. We'd been gone for at least a half hour.

"We were looking for the bathroom," Tia said, stomping past Blair and back onto the main path. I followed her, but blood pumped through me so fast, I started to lose control of my powers. Powers I barely had regained control over. Vines on the ground sprouted new leaves. The points on nearby cacti doubled in size. And the carnivorous plants began to grow, which was not going to end well. They were already as big as my fist. Any bigger and people were going to start losing hands.

"Stop it, Tut!" Tia said.

I tried. I really did. But all I could think about was Gil and how I was going to lose my chance to save him. And if I didn't do something, I'd never get another chance. Mortal meant mortal. There was no coming back from the dead. It would be the end for Gil.

The carnivorous plants kept growing. The vines continued to twist.

"I can't," I said. Henry was still back near the door talking to Blair. They hadn't noticed anything weird was going on. But the more I tried to stop it, the less control I seemed to have. I tried to reach for a fireball, for Gil's powers, but they slipped out of my grasp.

"Tut!" Tia said. "What are you doing?"

"They won't stop," I said, trying to focus on something else. But it was useless. The Venus flytraps were now big enough to devour a rat. A large rat.

I squeezed my eyes shut, hoping that would help. And it did, because before I knew what was happening, Tia kissed me, an amazing, awesome, see-stars kind of kiss right on the lips, sending all sorts of crazy emotions through me. I couldn't think about anything else.

My heart pounded. My face got really hot. I wanted it to last forever.

But once again, I didn't get what I wanted. Tia pulled away and stepped back.

"Well, that worked," she said, nodding at the carnivorous plants, which had stopped growing.

Here my heart was pounding faster than a jackhammer, and Tia was acting like nothing had just happened. Or was her face just the tiniest bit red? Great Osiris, why did Tia have to be so perfect and so complicated all at the same time? It made everything so confusing.

"Um . . ." I said, because nothing else would come out of my mouth.

Thankfully I was saved from any further embarrassment because Henry and Blair had joined us. His Um shirt was never more appropriate. I should have been the one wearing it today.

"I had no idea there was something between the two of you," Blair said.

"That's because there isn't," Tia said. And that was the end of that. She continued down the path and back to our science camp group.

We'd missed nearly forty-five minutes. It was lunchtime, so everyone was sitting out front eating their brown-bag lunches.

Well, except for Joe and Brandon, who had Spider-Man and Bat-man lunch boxes, respectively. A huge black stretch limousine pulled up in front of the Botanical Gardens.

"Oh, there's my dad," Blair said, nearly jumping up and down. "He's bringing me lunch. I'll be right back, you guys." And she ran off, over to the limo.

"We need to leave," I said. "We need to get to the museum before Hapi."

Henry shook his head and mumbled something, but it was hard to hear because his mouth was stuffed full with half his sandwich.

"Can you please speak English?" Tia said.

I tried not to look at how pretty she was while she talked. I tried not to think about the kiss. The last thing I needed to do was sit around staring at her. I had to focus.

"We need a distraction," Henry said, swallowing his food so this time we could understand him.

"Who are we going to distract?" I couldn't really see Camp Counselor Crystal tearing off after us if we decided to skip out of camp. Sure, we might get blackballed from ever signing up again, but I was totally cool with that.

"Hapi," Henry said. "Who do you think?"

Huh. I hadn't even thought of that. Distracting Hapi would actually be a great idea.

"How?" I started thinking of ways to do this, but Henry was way ahead of me.

"Don't worry." Henry pulled out his phone. "I have this taken care of." He typed in a quick text and smiled.

Less than a minute later—seriously, no kidding: a minute—Thoth skated up and plunked down next to Henry like they were old pals or something. It was weird, my best friend just hanging out with the gods like that was a normal thing. But it was also kind of awesome.

"'Sup, Henry," Thoth said. He looked like he'd only been using red and black paints today. They covered his gray tank top.

"'Sup," Henry said.

Henry had gotten to this point with Thoth?

"I'm crushing you in Words with Friends," Thoth said.

"I'm gaining on you," Henry said.

"You guys are playing Words with Friends?"

Thoth studied his fingernails. "It passes the time."

"Passes the time," Henry scoffed. "Thoth challenged me. I couldn't back down."

I hoped Henry knew what he was getting into. Challenges with gods were always matters to be taken seriously.

"Give me a word, Boy King," Thoth said.

I was still reeling from Tia's kiss, so the first word that popped out was "soul mate." It was so lame and pathetic that I wanted to crawl under a nearby bench, but there was no taking it back once it was out of my mouth.

Thoth, to make it worse, chuckled. My face must've been redder than the paints on his shirt.

"You, Henry?" he said.

"Polyglot," Henry said.

A huge smile popped onto Thoth's face. "Now you're catching on."

233

The only thing I was catching on to was that Henry was becoming more of a word snob than Thoth.

"Polyglot?" I said.

"Soul mate?" he replied.

Okay, that was fair. I shut my mouth.

"And you, Tia," Thoth said, turning to Tia. I guess he knew who she was.

"Tut," she said.

I was completely floored. Here she acted so cool all the time, like she never thought about me or anything, and the first word out of her mouth was my name. I would have loved to have said something, but a really smart voice in my head told me to keep my mouth shut.

Henry raised an eyebrow at me and I gave him an almost imperceptible shake of my head.

"Good words," Thoth said. "And I got one for you guys. Zeiss."

"Zeiss? Like the microscopes?" I wasn't sure what that had to do with anything except that it was one more science thing. Probably another bonding thing between Henry and Thoth.

"You mentioned a game in your text," Thoth said, leaving his word just like the others he'd delivered: unexplained. "Are you challenging me again?"

"Not me," Henry said. "But we're hoping you'll challenge someone else."

"Why?" Thoth said.

"Because he was talking trash about you," I piped in, now that I'd figured out Henry's strategy.

"Who was?" Thoth asked.

"Hapi," I said, trying to keep my face from betraying me. But I really needed Thoth to do this.

"The monkey?" Thoth said. "That guy hates games."

"No," I said, because I wasn't sure Henry was up to lying to Thoth. With the protection thing and all, Thoth might know. "He loves them. In fact, we heard it on good account that he was boasting that he could beat you."

"He was not!" Thoth said.

"I was as shocked as you," I said. "But that's what the rumor is."

My ability to twist the truth would impress even Colonel Cody. Maybe Thoth believed me. Or maybe he read my mind but didn't care, given the possibility of a challenge.

Thoth stood back up. "Well, if that's how Hapi wants to play it, consider it game on. Catch you all later." And without another word, he skated away, as fast as immortally possible—which was really fast.

"Henry!" someone called.

I looked toward the voice, and there was Blair, still standing at the window of the limousine. She pointed at us, I guess for her dad, and waved. And it would have been completely rude, even for me, not to wave back, so I did, even though I couldn't see whoever was in the car. Maybe they waved. Maybe they didn't. It wasn't at the top of my concerns list.

"You know her dad's going to run for Senate," Henry said. His eyes were super-wide, as if somehow being a senator was cooler than being an immortal.

"I'm not going to vote for him," I said. It was a technicality that I'd never be old enough to vote. I grabbed half of Henry's sandwich, because he'd managed to buy us a little time, and food helped me think more clearly. If I'd known I'd be at camp all day, I would have had Lieutenant Virgil pack me some bacon scones or something.

Out of the corner of my eye, I finally saw the limousine drive away, and I knew Blair would be coming back. Henry would once again be captivated by her girlie charms, or something like that. But I'll be completely honest. My mind was fixed on Tia, who was completely avoiding looking at me. I still couldn't believe she'd said my name.

Someone screamed, an eardrum-piercing shrill sound that probably would ripple through the air for miles. When I turned to look, Blair was lying on the ground, near a short retaining wall.

Henry was up in a second and running over to her.

"Are you okay?" he asked.

But she obviously wasn't because she was clutching her ankle and crying and really making a show of it. It looked like she might have tripped on the retaining wall.

"I think it's broken!" she wailed.

Camp Counselor Crystal was there after Henry and called for an ambulance because Blair's dad's limousine was already gone. Henry never left Blair's side. And when the ambulance finally arrived, Blair begged and pleaded with Henry to ride along with her to the hospital.

"I have to go with her, Tut," he said, glancing at the medics who were lifting Blair onto a stretcher.

"What a drama queen," Tia said. "You'd think the world was ending. She probably just sprained it."

"She really hurt it," Henry said with such earnestness, I knew he believed it.

"It's fine," I said. "Tia and I will go to the museum. You can catch up with us later."

Henry nodded and ran off, back to Blair, who clutched his arm like it was her life raft.

Two people would be way easier than three, anyway. Plus, after the whole kiss thing, I didn't mind spending a little extra time alone with Tia.

21

WHERE I MAKE A SOLEMN VOW
IN EXCHANGE FOR COOKIES

With Henry gone, there was zero guilt making me stick around for the rest of camp. I ditched it the first time Camp Counselor Crystal looked the other way. Tia and I set out from the Botanical Gardens. I thought about texting Captain Otis and having him send a couple shabtis along, but with Hapi out of the picture, there shouldn't be any obstacles. I'd snuck into plenty of museums in my time. The Smithsonian Museum of American History was no different. Sure, they'd remodeled a few years back and upped the security, but I was an immortal. I wasn't worried.

But immortal or not, even though I'd been the pharaoh of Egypt, even though I'd lived for thousands of years, walking with Tia alone after the whole kiss and then the words thing . . .

it was completely awkward. I had no idea what to say. Tia had that effect on me.

"Your cookies were pretty good," I said. "Maybe you can make some and bring them by my townhouse sometime." Lieutenants Virgil and Leon shouldn't have a problem with that. They were always looking for great new recipes. They'd been fixated on the scones thing for a while now.

"Don't hold your breath, Boy King," Tia said.

"Oh, come on," I said. "Don't I at least deserve a plate of cookies?"

She stopped walking and turned to me. "For what?"

Was she kidding? "For stealing that stupid scepter for you."

"Hmmm . . ." Tia said, like she had to really consider it.

"You'd never have gotten it without me," I said. "It's my immortal skills."

"It's your immortal something," Tia said. "So this plate . . . you think they'll just hand it over to you?"

"Of course not," I said. "But I have a plan."

Tia's eyes grew wide in mock surprise. "Oh, please do tell, Great Pharaoh."

"Well," I said, trying to sound as confident as I could. Using my pharaoh voice around Tia was just awkward. "I'm going to find the nearest guard. And I'm going to ask him to unlock the case."

Tia laughed. "You're just going to ask him to unlock it? And you think he'll listen?"

"Of course he'll listen," I said. "You forget, I have spells."

"Right," Tia said. "Those spells you tried to cast on me? To make me forget who you were? Those worked pretty great."

"You already knew," I said, only losing a small bit of my confidence. "It's not like I can erase an entire memory. I work more on a short-term basis."

"Ah," Tia said. "So once the guard unlocks the case, then what? You ask him to give you the plate?"

"Sure," I said. "Just a short-term loan. I'll promise to give it back."

"No, you won't," Tia said.

"Of course I will." I had no need to keep the Sun Disk of Ra. Once I'd saved Gil and imprisoned Apep, I'd be happy to return it.

"Um, no, Tut," Tia said. "You're not putting it back."

"Wait, why do you care?" I said. And then a lightbulb went on in my brain. "Oh, I get it. You want the sun disk, too. For your little quest you're on. I'm right, aren't I?"

"It's not a little quest," Tia said. "It's really important. And yes, as a matter of fact, the Sun Disk of Ra is one of the objects I'm out to get."

"So you think I should just hand it over to you?"

She stopped walking again. We'd gotten to the bottom of the steps leading up to the museum. And her eyes got really wide. "Please, Tut?" she said.

I swear my insides went all gooey again. I'd have given Tia the throne of Egypt in that moment if there was still such a thing.

"Would you stop doing that?"

"Doing what?" she said, batting her eyelashes. And she smiled so sweetly that all I thought about was making her happy. It was like Tia had these mystical, magical powers that made me do anything she wanted. It was totally unfair.

"Trying to use your female charms to get what you want." I forced myself to look away from her and started up the steps. I was not going to fall into her trap so easily.

"I'm not using any female charms," Tia said, hurrying to catch up to me. "But do we have a deal?"

"A deal?" I said. "I don't remember you offering up anything in return, and the last time I checked, that's how deals normally work."

"Fine," Tia said. "What do you want?"

I didn't even hesitate. It's not like I wouldn't give the sun disk to Tia once I was done with it. With Apep imprisoned, there would be no immediate need for it, and hey, if I could help the greater good and bring the gods together, then why shouldn't I? I was all about helping others.

"Cookies. Fresh-baked by you, delivered to my townhouse," I said.

Tia rolled her eyes, but I could see how she was trying to hide her smile. "Fine. Cookies."

"Every day for a week," I finished.

"Oh, that is so not fair," Tia said.

"Take it or leave it," I said. I had no intention of backing down. I wanted cookies, but seeing Tia for a week seemed pretty cool, too.

And so we had a deal.

We headed into the museum and up to the third floor.

It was afternoon in the summer near the Fourth of July. The museum was packed. There was actually a line to get into the exhibit. I hated waiting in lines, so I figured it was the perfect opportunity to test out my newly regained spells. A guard stood at the entrance, letting a couple people in at a time. Tia and I walked up. I was sure I could get him to let us in.

"No line-cutting," he said, not even looking at me.

"It's okay for us to cut the line," I said, and I summoned the spells that I used to know so well. Certain scents, working together, had amazing powers over the brain.

Or at least they should have.

"It's not okay for you to cut the line," the guard said.

So I tried again. "It's fine. We don't want to wait in the line."

"Nope," the guard said, and he finally looked me in the eye.

"Imsety?" I said. "What are you doing here?" Not an hour ago I'd seen him in the Hall of Artifacts.

"Duh," Imsety said. "Protecting national treasures. What do you think?"

"But . . . but you were just . . ." I pointed back in the direction of the Library of Congress.

"Yeah," Imsety said. "And I know you were eavesdropping. You and your little girlfriend."

"Not his girlfriend," Tia said, crossing her arms.

I forced myself not to respond to her comment. But I would be an awesome boyfriend. I was the pharaoh, after all. At one point, I'd been the most important person in the world. I was perfect boyfriend material.

"And we weren't eavesdropping," I said.

"Yeah," Imsety said. "Like we're going to believe that. What? You're just here by coincidence?"

"Well, of course not," I said. "But you know Hapi is going to come here."

"Exactly," Imsety said. "Which is why Qeb and I are guarding the place. Just because storage is off-site doesn't mean that we aren't responsible for the security of it."

I didn't think Imsety and Qeb were responsible for much. The fact that they were here, that they'd actually connected the dots and realized Hapi would come after the sun disk . . . well, it skewed my whole view of them.

"Just let us cut the line," I said. I went over in my mind all the possible ways I could convince them to let me have the sun disk.

"No way, Little Tut," Imsety said.

I cringed at the nickname. Tia elbowed me. I would've died of embarrassment on the spot if I wasn't immortal.

"Can we at least see it?" Tia said. "Please?" She clasped her hands together and batted her eyelashes in the exact same way she'd done only minutes earlier when she was trying to get me to give her the sun disk. But this time it was working completely to my advantage.

Imsety softened instantly. He glanced back over his shoulder. Through the room, I spotted Qeb with his falcon head standing near a glass display case.

"Well," Imsety said. "I guess it couldn't hurt to let you guys cut the line, just this once."

Was there anything Tia couldn't do?

"But Qeb's watching you," Imsety said. "So don't go touching anything."

"Of course not," Tia said with such earnestness in her voice, I almost believed her.

Imsety was a complete pushover. He stepped aside and let us pass. Only a few people grumbled behind us. The line was pretty long. They'd probably been waiting an hour. Which I still couldn't get over. Who would wait an hour to see a bunch of dresses and plates? I don't care who they'd belonged to.

Tia and I walked past the line, right over to where Qeb stood. No one noticed his falcon head. He stood in front of a glass case displaying tons of plates and cups and all sorts of china that would probably break if someone spooned their soup the wrong way. Sure, I had special dishes at home. Colonel Cody had insisted upon it, stating that only solid gold was befitting a king. I'd refused the gold, and we'd squabbled back and forth, finally settling on Fiestaware.

"Little Tut," Qeb said.

Tia snickered.

"And Little Tut's girlfriend," Qeb said.

This made her stop laughing. "Not his girlfriend." She pointed to herself. "Seriously. Not. His. Girlfriend."

"You don't have to be so emphatic," I said. I couldn't help myself.

"Obviously I do, Little Tut," she said.

That was when I knew I was way out of my league. I was up against a god and a girl. I had to drop it.

"So what are you guarding?" Tia said, looking around behind Qeb.

"Oh, you know, just some plates," Qeb said.

"You're sure doing a good job of guarding them," Tia said. "You know, you and Imsety are probably the best guards this place has ever seen."

"Can we please just cut to it?" I said. I did not have time to waste with ridiculous chitchat. "You know exactly why we're here."

"'Course I do," Qeb said. "It's why we're here."

I put my hands up in front of me. "Here's the thing. We really need the sun disk."

"I don't think that's such a good idea," Qeb said.

"No, you don't get it," I said. "We really, really need it. Like the world is going to end if we don't get it."

Qeb flicked his wrists at my petty words. "The world is always going to end. Every other day there's some crazy threat. This god or that god wanting to take over."

"There is?" I said. I had no clue what Qeb was talking about.

Imsety walked up to join us.

"Well, not quite," Qeb said. "But there could be. That's the point. And if we, as the guardians of the Hall of Artifacts, just let anyone come and take stuff, well, what kind of guardians would we even be?"

"The responsible kind?" I said. "The kind that doesn't want the world to end?"

Imsety shook his head. "The world is not going to end."

"You know," Tia said, "not to side with Tut here, but he's actually right. There are some pretty big issues right now."

"Yeah, like you guys' dad. When's the last time you saw him?" I asked.

Imsety looked to Qeb and they both shrugged. "No clue? A few months ago, maybe."

"Right," I said. "Well, the last time I saw him, he tried to kill me." I could still feel Horus's claws digging into my scalp.

Imsety's eyes grew wide. "Our dad did? You're sure?"

I nodded. "Of course I'm sure. This whole thing with Apep. It's driving him insane. He can't take the darkness. It's like his new-moon curse, but permanent."

"Oh, that's not good," Qeb said. "Dad is bananas during the new moon."

"But I can fix it," I said. "All I need is the sun disk. If you let me borrow it—I promise I'll bring it back—I can make everything better." I'd save Gil and save the world.

Qeb narrowed his falcon eyes at me. "If that's true, Little Tut, then why don't we just give it to Hapi? He is a god, after all."

It was a good question. And I wasn't sure my answer would convince Imsety and Qeb. They weren't the biggest fans of Gil.

"Here," I said. "Ask me some questions. We can do the whole trivia challenge thing again." Last time I needed something from them, I had to answer a bunch of ridiculous trivia questions with even more ridiculous answers.

"Play the same game twice?" Imsety said. "No way. You'd know all the answers."

I shook my head. "You can ask me different questions."

"Hmmm . . ." Qeb seemed to consider this.

"I don't think that's an option," Imsety said. "It's too easy."

There had been nothing easy about my last trivia match with Horus's sons. I'd nearly lost everything.

"We could make it harder," Qeb said.

Not a good idea. So I went for the truth. "It's because of Gil."

"Gil?" Imsety said. "That stick-in-the-mud you're always hanging out with?"

"Yes!" I said, though Gil wouldn't like me agreeing with that. "Apep has him as a prisoner. And he's going to kill Gil if I don't free him."

"Gil's kind of annoying," Qeb said.

"That doesn't mean he should die," I said. "And if your brother Hapi gets the disk and goes after Apep, he's not going to worry about Gil. Gil will die. It's why I have to do it. I'm the only one who can save him."

I erased Nephthys's words from my mind. That I would fail. That I wasn't strong enough. There was no place for those words here and now.

"You remember that time he tattled on me to Horus?" Qeb said.

"Which time?" Imsety said. "There were about fifty."

"Come on, guys. Gil can't die." And my voice kind of cracked, but I didn't care because I had to get the sun disk.

Something must have worked because Imsety's face softened. With Qeb and his falcon head it was hard to tell.

"You make a compelling argument, Little Tut," Imsety said, and I knew it was going to work. They'd give me the sun disk, and I'd get on with saving the world.

Except then every siren in the museum started blaring.

22

WHERE I PICK THE PERFECT DISH

Emergency lights flashed and everyone started screaming. Tia grabbed hold of my arm. I barely noticed. Something was way wrong.

"What's going on?" I asked Qeb and Imsety.

"No clue, Little Tut," Imsety said. They actually looked worried. Whatever was happening was not planned. And never before had they looked so serious. So godlike. It was easy to forget these two really were gods sometimes, because of how they acted, but now, they seemed to double in size and awesomeness.

Something huge pounded on the ground below us, shaking the entire floor. The plates, so well secured in their display cases, rattled and fell from the wall, crashing below. People all around us ran for the exit. The pounding from below came again, as if something huge was coming up the stairs, right for us.

"We need to get the sun disk and get out of here," I said. Whatever was happening, this was not Hapi coming for the sun disk. It had to be Apep. Somehow he'd found out about my plan.

Imsety looked to Qeb. "Based on the circumstances, Little Tut may be right."

"I am right," I said. "This is what I was talking about. You may not want me to have it, but if you don't give it to me, then Apep is going to get it. And it's not like he's going to imprison himself."

The display cases rattled again, and more plates fell. Around us, the mannequins wearing the fancy First Lady dresses fell over, toppling through the broken glass of the cases. People tripped on them and landed on the ground. And then, just when I thought things couldn't get any worse, all the lights went out.

"Chaos is coming!" a voice screamed in my head. But not just in my head, because when I let some light escape from my scarab heart, I could tell that Tia, Imsety, and Qeb had all heard it, too.

"You'll keep it safe?" Imsety said, fixing his eyes on me, daring me to say no.

"I promise," I said. "I'll make things right."

"You'll bring it back to us?" Imsety said.

I forced myself not to look at Tia. "Yes." I crossed my fingers behind my back.

Imsety looked to Qeb, who nodded. And then Qeb slammed his fist into the glass of the display that hadn't yet broken, shattering it everywhere. He grabbed the only plate still hanging on the wall. It was dull brown, with chips and cracks all around the sides. It couldn't be the Sun Disk of Ra. But he shoved it my way.

"Do what you need to do, Little Tut," Qeb said. "Just get out of here. Now." And then he and Imsety ran toward the entrance of the exhibit.

Something landed in front of them. It was the monster from the mirror trap at the funhouse. It had the body of a snake, the head of a bird, and tons of tentacles waving around in the air. It lashed out its tentacles and grabbed Imsety, wrapping him around the waist.

Qeb jumped for Imsety, but another tentacle latched onto him. They struggled against the monster as it flailed them around in the air. I started back for them, but Tia grabbed hold of my arm.

"We need to go, Tut," Tia said.

"We need to help them!" They could die. The monster in front of them was as tall as the ceiling.

"They'll get out of this," Tia said. "We need to get the sun disk out of here."

And even though I hated her words, I knew they were right. Imsety and Qeb were gods. They had their path in this, and I had mine.

I looked around the exhibit room for a way out that wasn't toward the monster, but the back entrance was blocked where part of the wall had collapsed. There was no getting out that way.

"Go, Little Tut!" Qeb screamed. He'd bitten off part of the

tentacle that had been holding him with his beak and freed himself, but this had made the monster really angry. It thrust its own beak head down at him and he dodged it.

I glanced upward, scoping out the ceiling. Fiber tiles fifteen feet up. No problem. Before she could argue, I grabbed Tia around the waist and jumped.

"Tut . . . !"

We busted through the fiber tiles, sending pieces everywhere. I set her down on one of the ceiling supports.

"Warn me next time," Tia said, stomping her foot on one of the tiles. This wasn't a good idea because her foot punched through, and she lost her balance and started falling.

I grabbed her arm and caught her. "Don't fall through," I said, and we took off, making sure only to run on the supports and not the tiles. One wrong step and the monster would find us. Also, Tia was mortal. She could die. I didn't want either of those things to happen.

It felt like forever that we ran, but I didn't stop until we were as far away from the monster as possible. At the far side of the museum, we reached a hatch. I grabbed hold of the cover and yanked it off. It punched through the ceiling tiles and clattered onto the floor below.

"Chaos is coming!" the voice screamed again in my head.

"Come on!" I pulled Tia through the hatch. I didn't need the extra threats of the world ending to hurry me, but they certainly did make the situation seem more immediate.

The sirens weren't as loud up here in the attic, and we twisted and turned our way through the shelves. Endless row after row of stuff. But we didn't slow down. What Tia and I needed to do was get out of this museum and back to my townhouse. Horus's wards would protect us there . . . I hoped.

We got to a back staircase and ran down without stopping. Once we hit ground level, we tore out the back door of the museum. Outside was chaos, just like the voice had said. But not just because all the museum alarms were still blaring. The museum wasn't even the half of it. The sun, which should have been bright and full like it had been only hours before, was about two-thirds of its normal size, and even though it wasn't possible, it seemed to shrink more with each second that went by.

I turned to Tia, about to tell her the importance of finding Apep, but whiteness flooded my mind, and I fell to the ground. Searing pain ripped through my thoughts, and I knew it was pain that Gil was feeling. We were sharing it, through the scarab heart in my chest. He'd thought that he was saving me by giving me his scarab heart. But what he'd really done was linked himself to me, forever. And with each wave of pain, I was sure that my immortality was not secure. If Gil died, I would die, too.

23

WHERE I MAKE A WAGER ABOUT THE FATE OF THE WORLD

W hat's wrong with you?" Tia said, yanking on my arm.
I sat on the ground, propped up against a building. Cars
drove by, horns blaring as they cut around each other.
My head pounded with the vision, still so fresh.

"Nothing," I said, letting her pull me to my feet. I had the
sun disk, so at least I had that going for me. I hurried over to the
nearest street vendor and bought a drawstring bag, which I then
shoved the sun disk into.

"Nothing? It didn't seem like nothing." She narrowed her blue
eyes at me and bit her lower lip, like she was actually concerned.

"I'm fine."

"Can you just stop lying?" Tia said. "I won't judge you. I
won't think you're weak. Just tell me what's going on."

It was like Tia could see into my soul. I hated being weak—hated that there was something I had no control over. But I also wanted to tell Tia. I wanted to share it with someone.

"It's just this weird thing with Gil. This connection I have."

"Connection, like you know where he is?" she asked. We hurried down the street, away from the museum and back toward my townhouse. Gil wasn't at the museum. Apep wasn't even there. The monster had been the same servant of Apep from the funhouse, this time out to stop me from getting the disk.

I shook my head. "Not quite. I can't see anything in the visions. But I can hear things. And smell things. And feel things." Gil was in pain. It made me feel so helpless. But I was not helpless. I was the great Tutankhamun. Pharaoh of Egypt. I would find Gil and make everything better.

"Have you asked Auntie N about it?" Tia asked.

"Auntie N," I said. "She told me I was going to fail. She doesn't want me doing any of this at all."

Tia shook her head. "Maybe she's wrong. We should go back and talk to her."

Of all the things I should do, going back to Nephthys was not one of them. She would take the sun disk away from me and give it to Hapi.

"There is no way I'm doing that," I said.

"But the sun . . ." Tia said.

"I see the sun. And I'm going to fix it. I'm going to re-imprison Apep. But first I have to find Gil. Because there is no way I am taking care of Apep before I'm sure Gil is safe."

"Just talk to her," Tia said, and her eyes pleaded with me,

almost like she really was concerned for me. And that's when I realized what was going on. She didn't think I was strong enough to do this either.

"You go talk to her," I said. "I'm going to find Gil." And before she could bat her eyelashes or tilt her head just the right way to make my thoughts go all wonky, I walked away. I had a plan, and so far it was going perfectly.

When I walked into the townhouse, there wasn't a shabti in sight. Not one. That had never happened before. From under the futon, I still heard Horus, but it sounded more like a hyperventilating, frantic purr. Maybe he'd scared the shabtis away.

"Colonel Cody?" I called.

Nothing.

"Major Mack?"

Not a sound.

"Lieutenant Roy?"

There was no reply, but Horus stopped making noise for a second, long enough for me to hear sounds coming from the hall closet. I shoved aside the camel seat that had been pulled up against it to barricade it, and I threw open the door. Hundreds of shabtis tumbled out; they'd been packed in there like cockroaches. Colonel Cody tumbled down the stack and stood at attention.

"Did you forget to invite me to a party?" I asked.

Colonel Cody looked back at the troops, and with practiced

precision, they broke up into their legions and stood ready for orders. "Great Pharaoh, we were having a meeting."

I raised an eyebrow. "What kind of meeting?" Seriously, what would the shabtis get together to talk about? New tactics for destroying scarab beetles?

Colonel Cody bowed low in front of me. "We are thinking about making an offering to a god."

"An offering?" I said. "To what god? Horus?" He'd started his purring back up at full force, making it hard to hear the shabtis.

Colonel Cody balled his fists in frustration. "Oh, Great Master, everything is dreadful. The cat won't stop making that horrifying noise. The heathen heart still beats in your chest. The sun is vanishing from the sky. What are we to do? Please impart your great wisdom on us."

I was glad Tia and Henry weren't around to hear that. And it probably didn't even register on Horus. But the thing was that aside from the heathen-heart thing, the shabtis were right. Things were looking pretty grim.

I pulled the sun disk from the drawstring bag and laid it on the ground in front of Colonel Cody. "I got it. And I'm going to use it to make everything better."

The shabtis' eyes got super-wide, like cartoon characters'. "The Sun Disk of Ra," Colonel Cody whispered, and every single shabti fell prostrate to the ground.

Horus stopped purring. The townhouse fell into silence. The very air around us seemed to freeze in place. And I knew that this was going to work. I could do this. What I needed was a solid plan of attack.

I picked the sun disk up and walked to the futon, tripping over a pile of Gil's stuff on the way. A couple stone tablets fell, but the shabtis hurried to set them back in place. Once Gil got home, all this stuff was going back into his room.

I set the sun disk on the coffee table.

"Horus, are you going to come out here and help me?" I called down under the futon.

He let out a low purr in reply, but he didn't answer and he didn't come out. And I knew I couldn't count on him. He had passed the point of no return. If I didn't stop Apep, then Horus would be lost forever.

"Will you bring me a map?" I asked Colonel Cody.

He snapped his fingers, and ten shabtis ran off. They returned less than a minute later with piles of maps. I should have been more precise. I sifted through them until I found the most recent one. Even at that, it was still five years old. Paper maps were going out of style faster than dial-up Internet. But paper helped my mind work better. It was easier to see the whole picture. I grabbed a pencil from Lieutenant Roy and got to work.

I was still awake the next morning when the doorbell rang. I'd pored over the maps all night, labeling every possible place Gil could be based, on the information from my visions. I would check them out, one by one, until I found him.

"I'm not going to camp!" I yelled through the door. I knew it was Henry.

I couldn't hear Henry's muffled reply.

"We should barricade the door," Colonel Cody suggested. "Then you won't find yourself with this dreadful science camp dilemma."

"That's a great idea," I said.

"At your command," Colonel Cody said.

But Henry was persistent. He kept ringing the doorbell until it was driving me crazier than Camp Counselor Crystal's droning voice.

"Fine. Let him in," I said to Colonel Cody. I dragged myself off the futon and went upstairs to the bathroom. But I couldn't understand why Henry was here so early. The sun wasn't even up.

"Tut, you're not going to believe it," Henry said, rushing up the stairs. Gil's door was still blue and gold, even though I'd asked the shabtis to repaint it. I'm sure it was on their to-do list, just not anywhere near the top. There would be plenty of time to deal with it later, once Gil was back.

"Try me," I said. At this point, I'd believe almost anything.

"Camp is canceled today," Henry said. It must've been a complete surprise for him, too, because he'd already gotten dressed for the occasion, a bright green shirt that read, Th In K .

Think. Think. Think. That's exactly what I had to do. I had to figure out where Gil was. There were so many possible places. I needed a way to narrow them down.

"Good," I said, and I grabbed my toothbrush. My teeth were super-healthy, part of my immortal perks, but bad breath was never in style.

"Good?" Henry said. "Don't you want to know why it's canceled?"

"Sure. Why's it canceled?" I kept brushing so it came out as a mumble, but Henry still understood.

"Have you even looked outside, Tut?"

I spit out the toothpaste. All I'd looked at for the last eight hours were maps.

"What's outside?"

Henry dragged me to a downstairs window that faced east. It was dark, like just before the sun rises or just after it sets, not quite pitch black. But the problem was, although the sun was still in the sky, it looked like someone had taken a giant straw and placed it near the sun and then started drinking, like every bit of sunlight was being sucked away. A huge funnel had formed between the sun and whatever was pulling at it.

"Why is it doing that, Tut?" Henry said. "This can't be Apep."

Prickles of energy ran through me. Not only could it be Apep, it had to be Apep. Yesterday had just been the beginning. Just a hint at what was to come. Today was the real thing. At the rate the sunlight was vanishing, within days there would be no more sun at all.

"I can't believe it's already gotten this bad," I said. "Great Amun, I have to stop this."

"It's not just camp," Henry said. "The entire government is talking about closing down. Fireworks are going to be canceled. I had to sneak out of the house today because my mom told me not to leave. Can you believe that? I snuck out."

It was a little surprising. Henry never bent the rules.

"Oh, and did you get my text?" Henry said. "About Blair?"

"What about Blair?" I hadn't checked my phone. I'd been too caught up looking at the maps.

"Her dad invited us over for dinner," Henry said. "Well, he invited me, because I helped Blair yesterday when she hurt herself. But Blair said that it was totally cool if you come along also. It was her idea, so you should definitely go."

"Dinner?" Food was so far down on my priority list right now. "I'm not going to dinner at Blair's house. I have bigger things to worry about. Like the sun? Apep?" I pointed out at the mess in the sky.

Henry shook his head. "No, that's the thing, Tut. Do you know what her dad does?"

"He's running for Senate," I said. "She told us, like, five million times. There's no way I could possibly not know."

"Yes, he's running for Senate," Henry said. "But he has a ton of side businesses. You know, like the carnival. Remember?"

There was no way I was forgetting the carnival. Stupid funhouse disaster.

"And one of his businesses is a research lab," Henry said. "They spend a ton of money doing solar research. Blair says that he knows what's wrong with the sun."

"It's Apep," I said. "I told you that."

But Henry was not convinced. "It's not Apep. And Blair says that her dad has a completely scientific explanation."

That, I wanted to hear. Maybe there was a scientific explanation. Maybe I was the one who was wrong. Maybe we could mix together a few elements from the periodic table and solve everything. And maybe pigs could fly.

"There's no scientific explanation, Henry."

"Tut, you are wrong," Henry said. "And I'll make you a bet. Go to dinner with me. If her dad's explanation has any merit, then I win."

"Win what?" I said.

"I get to borrow half your shabtis," Henry said.

At this, Colonel Cody clutched onto the leg of my jeans. "Please, Great Master, don't get rid of us. If we have done something to offend . . ."

"Shhh . . ." I said, silencing him. "And when we find out her dad is full of baloney? What do I get out of it?"

"If her dad is wrong, and it really is Apep, like you say, then I never again question your Egyptian gods," Henry said, making an X over his heart.

"They're your Egyptian gods now, too," I said. "Whether you want them to be or not."

"I'm still skeptical."

Henry was always skeptical. I didn't think, even when he found out that Apep was behind trying to destroy the world, that would change. But his whole wager, the way he put it out there . . . well, it was weird, but I felt compelled to agree. Like deep in my gut, I had to do it.

"Fine," I said. "It's a deal."

"Blair said she can have her dad send a limo for us." He looked like he was going to fall over with excitement.

"I'm not riding in her dad's limo," I said.

"But I've never ridden in a limo," Henry said. "And seriously, when will I ever get another chance?"

I didn't trust Blair enough that I wanted her to know where I lived. She was weird and too friendly and it was crazy that she'd been right outside the secret entrance to the Hall of Artifacts yesterday. And the more I thought about it, the more I was sure something was off with her.

Okay, that was ridiculous. I was probably subconsciously jealous of Henry because she was paying so much attention to him and not to me. Just because Henry was getting all the notice and I wasn't didn't mean that Blair was some agent of the enemy. But I still didn't want to ride in her dad's limo.

"No limo," I said.

"Fine," Henry said. "Can we at least take a bus? She lives across the river in Virginia."

We agreed on the bus. Henry checked in with Thoth to see how Hapi was doing, but his lack of a response made me think that, if they were playing a game, it was still going on. That was good. I didn't want Hapi anywhere near me or the sun disk.

I sat back down on the futon and pointed to the map.

"Oh, I have her address," Henry said.

"It's not about Blair," I said. "I'm working on new theories to figure out where Gil is, trying to use information from my visions."

"What do you know so far?" Henry asked, plunking down next to me. Horus let out a huge squawk from under the futon that sounded like someone had stepped on him. It was encouraging to have him act dramatic. "Oh, and do you think . . . ?" Henry looked to Lieutenants Leon and Virgil, who then looked to me.

"Make it two sodas," I said, and the two shabtis ran off, returning less than a minute later with two cans of soda, two cups of ice, and a plate of jalapeño scones.

"Well, it's round," I said, making a circle with my finger on the map in front of me. The problem was there were tons of circular things in D.C.

"Okay," Henry said. "What else?"

"It's really loud," I said. "Like I'm pretty sure there's construction or something nearby. And there are these guards that sit around bickering all the time. Oh, and there are lots of seats."

"Like a theater," Henry said. "I didn't see anything weird at the theater the other night."

"Yeah, like a theater, but it might be outside," I said. "The guards were arguing about the stars this one time." Their idiotic discussion about the names of the constellations drilled through my mind.

"Maybe an amphitheater," Henry said, grabbing a nearby Sharpie. He started making small circles on the map, adding to my already numerous possible locations. "There are a bunch of outdoor theaters nearby. Oh, or maybe it's a football stadium. Or baseball."

It was baseball season right now. I didn't think Apep was keeping Gil in Nationals Park. But Henry marked it on the map, anyway.

"We'll have to check them out, one by one," Henry said, tracing his finger on the map from one possible location to the next.

And so we finished our scones and sodas. I stuffed the map and the sun disk in the drawstring bag because no way was I leaving it here. I had no idea if any of Horus's protective spells were still in place. Time was running out. For Gil. For the world. I squatted down so I could look under the futon and tell Horus what our plan was, but he hissed at me and swiped out with his claws.

"I'll make everything better, Horus," I said. "I promise." An angry Horus was still Horus. It was better than him being gone.

We searched from one place to the next, and each minute that passed, standing in what should have been a bright afternoon in D.C., doubled the urgency. Apep was destroying the world. The sun was like a black-and-white pencil sketch of itself. The funnel had doubled in size. Or else the sun had shrunk even more. Neither was a good option. The sky, like the sun, was gray and dull like an old newspaper. And the wind howled through the streets, like the atmosphere was being stripped away, too. We hurried down the sidewalk, but we were alone. The only people out were dashing around in cars, preparing for the apocalypse.

Six hours later and our search had come up blank. We'd checked every single outdoor-theater thing that even kind of might be where Gil was, but I hadn't felt the slightest hint in my scarab heart that he was near. And I knew I would.

"We should check near the Masonic temple," I said. It was next on our list.

"It's time for dinner," Henry said.

Dinner. That's right. Maybe something Blair's dad would

say about this whole scientific explanation thing might actually give me a clue as to where Gil or Apep was. Except that would be another day gone. Another chance lost to defeat Apep.

Henry hurried to the bus stop, but after twenty minutes of standing there, it was pretty obvious that the bus wasn't coming. Maybe public transportation had been shut down. Come to think of it, I hadn't heard a single plane fly over the entire day, and being this near to the airport, that was definitely not normal. The birds still flocked and circled, like black clouds filling the empty spaces of the sky.

"We need to walk," I said. Which wasn't a bad plan. There were a couple places on our list that we'd go right past.

"We should have started walking a half hour ago," Henry said. "Do you have any idea how late we're going to be? We should have just taken the limo."

"Well, too late for that," I said, hoping Henry wouldn't whip out his cell phone and remedy the situation. He and Blair had to have exchanged numbers. Or maybe she didn't have a cell phone. I'd never seen her use one. Which was really odd. Everyone had a cell phone, even the third-grade little know-it-all girl who lived two townhouses over. But thankfully Henry didn't call Blair, and even with our two stops and the increasing wind, it only took us about a half hour to get there.

24

WHERE MY DOG FINISHES UP MY DINNER

Blair's house was across the river, in a super-old part of Virginia with all sorts of estate houses. There were tons of huge trees, pressing in from above, all around the fence, which was twenty feet tall and made of iron like it belonged at a prison. Security must be a pretty big deal if you're running for Senate.

Henry and I walked up to the gate. Two guards sat in a little building nearby. They glanced over and shook their heads as if we were just one more annoyance to have to deal with on an already bothersome day.

"What do you two want?" one of the guards said. He was tall, skinny, and bald, like he'd been stretched out on a board and plucked. And his voice had this thin, high edge to it, almost like his vocal cords had been stretched, too.

"We got invited for dinner," Henry said.

That was weird. They should have known about us coming. Guards were supposed to be informed of stuff like that. The crazy weather must have had them flustered.

"You hear about dinner guests?" the tall guard said to the other guard.

"Lemme check," the other guard said, and he picked up an old-school phone receiver. A minute later he gave a huge thumbs-up. "They're good to go!" His voice was deep and gruff, like he was angry all the time.

Our tall guard gave us the same thumbs-up. "You kids are good to go!" he said, like we'd won some kind of lottery.

The other guard stood up, or at least I think he did. He was shorter than a ten-year-old and at least three times as wide. He yanked on a lever and the gates swung open.

I looked back after we'd walked through. The two guards, short and tall, stood watching us. My scarab heart hummed with caution. Something was off with those two. Something was also kind of familiar with them. But I couldn't put my finger on it.

The driveway was paved with antique bricks. And even though there were trees around the entire fence, at least as far as I could see, there were none inside the fence, which made for a perfect view of the house.

Given the neighborhood and the iron fence and all that, I would've expected some historic mansion perched in the middle of the yard. But instead, there was a super-modern-looking house made almost completely of glass. It was three stories high, with the stairs completely visible through the many windows, and in the center of the house, it reached two stories higher, like there was some kind of penthouse balcony up there or something.

"I didn't know carnivals made so much money," Henry said.

Wherever Blair's dad got his money, it wasn't just from the carnival, especially since that was for charity. Maybe the lab research did a better business. Out front, in a circular driveway, sat the black limousine we'd seen yesterday at camp.

No sooner had the house come into view than the front door flew open. Blair stood there waving like a crazy person with a huge cheerleader smile plastered on her face.

"Does that girl ever not smile?" I said.

"Never," Henry said, somehow missing the sarcasm in my voice. "At the hospital, when they were twisting her ankle around to see if she'd hurt it, she smiled and talked the whole time, telling them all about her dad's charity work. The doctors couldn't believe she was really in pain. She's like a superhero or something."

"Or something," I said.

Henry smacked me in the stomach.

Blair's ankle must've felt a whole lot better because she bounced down the steps from the front door to the driveway to meet us.

"You guys are late! I was so worried. I thought maybe you got lost." Her eyes were wide with concern. Also, she didn't blink.

Henry turned two shades redder. "We got a late start." Thankfully he didn't mention anything about our searching D.C. all day.

"I am so glad you could still make it," Blair said. "And don't worry about a thing. All the food is still okay."

The food was the least of my worries. Gil and the disappearing sun were way more of a concern. The first thing I was going to do was ask her dad about the sun.

"I can't wait for you guys to meet my dad," Blair said, and she bounded back up the steps and inside. Henry was right at her heels, but I dragged behind.

I walked slowly through the entryway. On every interior wall, which weren't that many since there were so many windows, there was at least one mirror. They were all different sizes and shapes. Some looked like antiques. Some looked like pictures. They covered the place. And the uneasy feeling in my stomach grew.

Blair and Henry were already out the back door, so I hurried after them. In front of us was a huge patio surrounded by bushes and shrubs that looked like they'd died. They were brittle, skeletal remains with bark chipping off them. Blair's dad definitely needed to call the gardener. With my returned powers, I could have brought them back to life, but if Blair's family didn't want to take care of their topiary, I wasn't going to jump in and save it.

In the middle of the patio was an outdoor table set for dinner with silverware and water goblets. Unlit candles sat in the center of the table, and at the head of the table stood a man who had to be Blair's dad.

He wore jeans and a T-shirt and didn't look like any senator I'd ever seen. His hair, which was as blond as Blair's, was cut into a perfectly groomed mullet, like he had it trimmed every day. I'd worn a mullet only once, for a couple years back in the eighties. I made Captain Otis destroy all evidence of it by throwing any pictures down the incinerator chute. Her dad's black T-shirt had the logo for AC/DC with a huge lightning bolt running through it, and his skin was pale, like an albino's. When Blair ran up and gave him a hug, it made her skin look even paler, too.

"Guys, this is my dad, Mr. Drake," she said. "Daddy, these are my friends."

"Then they're my friends, too," her dad said, and he motioned for us to sit down. He pressed a button and heavy metal music started to play over some speakers that must've been hidden in the dead bushes because I didn't see them anywhere.

The skinny bald guard showed up, but instead of a guard uniform, he now wore black pants and a white shirt like a waiter at a restaurant. He carried a tray that looked like it would knock him over with its high center of gravity if the wind blew too hard. Which, come to think of it, wasn't blowing at all here inside the fence. Or maybe it had died down everywhere. But when I looked to the tall trees beyond the fence, the branches still swayed and their leaves flew off by the hundreds.

"I got the first course here," he said, and he started putting plates in front of us.

I had no intention of eating. The only reason I was here was because of what Henry had said.

"So, Mr. Drake, I hear you have a solar research lab," I said.

Blair's dad fixed his eyes on me. And like Blair, he didn't seem to really blink. Maybe it was a genetic non-blinking thing they had going on. Henry was bound to have some explanation.

"Totally, I have a solar research lab," Mr. Drake said. "And I have a carnival. And a museum. And, oh, have you heard about that new restaurant that just opened?"

I didn't care about his restaurant. Mr. Drake was getting creepier by the second. But Henry, with his never-ending appetite, said, "Which one?"

"Some Like it Raw," Mr. Drake said. "We serve everything raw. Raw meat. Raw vegetables. It's going to be the new rage."

That I wasn't so sure of, but I also didn't think it would matter what the rage was if the world ended.

"Sounds . . . interesting," Henry said. It was the first time in six months that he hadn't drooled at the mention of food.

"Blair says you know what's going on with the sun," I said.

"I know exactly what's going on," Mr. Drake said. "It's all we've been researching. We have top-of-the-line solar telescopes. German ones. They're the absolute best." He still hadn't blinked. I forced myself to break eye contact because it creeped me out.

"It's a solar flare issue, I bet," Henry said. "That's what I've been trying to tell Tut. Solar flares occur all the time. Some get really big."

Solar flares did not suck the sun from the sky.

Overhead, the birds flocked around in circles. Also there were bats. I would have recognized their horrible screeching anywhere.

"You are smart, Henry, just like Blair said," Mr. Drake answered. "It is a solar flare."

Henry turned to me. "I told you, Tut." He lifted the lid off his plate and kind of frowned at whatever was inside. "Is this raw?"

"Totally raw," Mr. Drake said. "A specialty from our restaurant. It's Blair's favorite. She requested it just for you."

Henry poked at whatever it was with his fork. I could almost see the battle in his mind. It would be crazy-rude to not eat it now, after that, especially if he wanted to make a good impression on Blair. But instead of taking a bite, he set his fork down and took a huge sip of water.

"What's causing the solar flare?" I asked.

"Solar flares are caused by all sorts—" Henry started, like he was dying to give me the answer.

I shook my head. "I know what causes normal solar flares. But this one is different."

"Yes," Mr. Drake said, and his unblinking eyes widened. "It is different. That's what makes it so special." At his words, the music, which was already pretty loud, increased in volume. Gil loved heavy metal music. Me? I wasn't such a fan. Sure, I'd gone to concerts with Gil and things like that, but that's because I wanted to spend time with him. To do what he wanted to do.

"Why is it different?" I asked, finally pulling the cover from my plate. In front of me was some kind of appetizer that was pink and slimy and looked like pieces of chopped-up baby squirrels. I'd eaten my share of exotic foods in my immortal life, but I was willing to bet that if this was the kind of food Blair's dad was serving at their restaurant, it wasn't going to stay open very long.

"Well, that's easy," Mr. Drake said. "The solar flare is happening because of a magnetic pull on the sun, coming from somewhere else."

Henry snapped his fingers. "That's why it looks like a funnel, right?"

"Exactly," Mr. Drake said.

It was all a bunch of hogwash. Weird things were going on, and I was not going to write them off scientifically. The gods were one hundred percent at work here. I'd had about as much of this dinner as I wanted to waste time on.

I stood up and scooted my chair out. "I need to use the bathroom," I yelled over the music.

"Oh. Blair will show you where it is," Mr. Drake said, pressing his lips together into a thin line. He stuck his tongue out the smallest amount, like there was a tiny crumb he wanted to get.

I shook my head. "No, that's okay. Just tell me where it is." I didn't plan to stick around here any longer. I needed to find Gil.

"Sure," Blair said, smiling as if she was thrilled no matter what. "It's just back inside, down the hall on the left."

"Thanks." I headed back into the house. I'd cut out of here and text Henry later. He could finish the disgusting raw-food dinner and meet me later. I was about to head for the front door, but the two guards stood there, the skinny one back in his guard uniform. He couldn't have changed that fast. It was like he was a clone. Still, whether they were guards or waiters, I didn't want to have to make excuses. So I took the hall to the left, toward the bathroom. I'd find a side door out of this place.

I pretended to go into the bathroom, just in case the guards were watching, but at the last minute, I crouched low and moved down the hallway, opening doors as I came to them. There was one room that looked like a weird style salon, with four different mannequins dressed in outfits I was sure I'd seen Blair wear to camp, including the O Mg shirt she and Henry had both had on. Mirrors lined the walls, reflecting the headless figures everywhere. The heads, not attached to the bodies, sat on a shelf with blond wigs on them. Two of the wigs looked just like Blair's curly blond hair, and two of them were mullets, exactly like Mr. Drake's heavy-metal-rocker style. It was hard to imagine that Blair and her dad were both bald. Maybe they shaved their heads, like in a religious ritual or something like that.

I closed the door, leaving the creepy mannequins behind. One glance back told me that no one was following me, but I hadn't been gone very long. I could definitely still be in the bathroom. I checked the next door and then the next. A couple of the rooms were empty. One was an indoor swimming pool. I also found the kitchen, which looked like some kind of stainless-steel butcher shop with knives and raw meat everywhere. My stomach turned. Finally I reached the door at the end of the hallway. The last door. It had to be the way out. I tried to turn the knob, but it was locked. Even better. A little extra immortal strength, and the knob turned easily. But I must have miscalculated. The knob came off in my hand.

"That's okay," I said to myself, and I set it down on the ground next to the wall. Then I pulled the door open and stepped inside. Immediately my foot went down a step. I grabbed hold of the door, causing it to hit against the wall, making a huge sound.

But it didn't matter. It's not like I was a thief trying to steal something. I was just trying to get out of here. If this was a basement there could be a door leading to the outside. I went down, holding onto the walls on either side. It was dim but not pitch dark, so I didn't need to add any extra light.

I counted twenty steps before I got to the bottom, and the light got brighter with each step. Once I was at the bottom, I saw why. In the center of the room was some sort of telescope-looking thing, like those telescopes you see out in the middle of the desert in Arizona. It had a giant receptor that looked like an upside-down umbrella with a bunch of antennas in the middle. It fed into some sort of tank that then led to a giant pipe that went directly into the ground.

It made sense that Mr. Drake would have something like this, given that he owned a solar research laboratory. Maybe he did know what he was talking about. Except the weird thing—the really weird thing—was that coming into the antenna array on the top of the receptor was a steady stream of light. It funneled in from the skylight way up high in the ceiling, maybe a hundred feet above. This must've been the really tall part of the house I'd seen from the outside. But when the light came in through the receptor, I could see it pouring into the glass storage tank, bubbling around like some sort of super-hot liquid metal. I dared to reach a hand out and touch the tank, expecting it to burn, but it was completely cool to the touch. And then, from the storage tank, the metallic liquid was being sucked out through the pipe in the ground.

Little pieces began to come together in my mind. This satellite was collecting something that was coming in through the sky. Through a skylight. And the stuff . . . it was bright yellow. Yellow like the sun.

Clarity hit me like a herd of elephants. This wasn't just any research satellite. This thing before me, satellite or telescope or whatever it was, it was a collector. And what it was collecting was exactly what was disappearing from the world. It was collecting light from the sun.

My heart pounded in my chest. I knew now it hadn't been just jealousy on my part. Blair totally was an agent of the enemy. I wasn't in any normal house. I was in the home of Apep, the crazy god bent on casting the world into eternal darkness. Mr. Drake was Apep, the Lord of Chaos.

I pulled out my phone. I had to text Henry. To tell him to get out of there. He was not safe. No one was safe. Not Henry. Not Tia. Not Horus. Not Gil. Not the entire world. This was my chance. I had to get back outside and stop Apep. Here I'd been so worried about finding Gil that I had failed to see the enemy when he was right in front of my face. And if Apep could fool me, the world had no chance.

"What do you think of it?" a voice said.

I whipped around and came face-to-face with Blair. She beamed at me. I stepped back, around the weird sun-collecting machine so I wouldn't trip on it. On the back was printed the brand of the telescope: Zeiss.

Zeiss, like Thoth had told us.

"Um, I got lost, I think," I said. Did she know that I knew? I couldn't tell by looking at her. Her face was filled with its normal bubbly happiness, but like always, she wasn't blinking. And she kept sticking her tongue out of her mouth.

No wonder she didn't blink. If she was related to Apep, she was part snake! Not human at all. That explained everything. The weird room with all the wigs and clothes. She had to dress up as a teenager every day.

"It's really cool, right?" Blair said. "My dad's been working on it for months."

"That's great," I said, and I took a few more steps back, searching for a door. Osiris was with me, because on this far side of the basement was another set of stairs. "I'm just going to step outside for a little bit," I said, and I ran up the steps, hoping she didn't have some kind of laser eyes that could incinerate me from behind.

"Wait, Tut!" Blair called after me.

But there was no way I was waiting. I ran to the top of the steps and busted through the door. The dull dredges of whatever day was left hit me. The sun was low in the sky, getting near sunset. What worried me was that if it did set, would it ever rise again? Based on the machine I'd just seen, I'd bet all the gold in Egypt against it.

I had to do something. I had to get rid of Apep now. But my mind kept playing tricks on me. Without Apep, I might never find Gil. Gil would die, wherever he was, and no one would ever know.

Far off to the left was the table where we'd just been having dinner. Henry and Mr. Drake were nowhere to be found. I whipped around, facing Blair, who was just now bouncing up the steps behind me.

"Why are you running, Tut?" she said. "We wanted to talk to you."

"Where's Gil?" I said. She had to know.

"That's what I wanted to talk to you about," Blair said.

"Okay, then talk." I had no time to waste. The sun was getting lower with each second that passed.

Even out here, against the walls of the house, were more mirrors. They were everywhere else also, decorating the dead shrubbery like garden gnomes.

"I know exactly where Gil is," Blair said. "We thought he was immortal. There is no other way he could have survived that battle so long ago. He told us he was immortal. But he lied to us. Can you believe that? He lied to my dad. Nobody lies to my dad. Nobody."

"Just tell me where he is," I said. "We can talk about his lying after that."

Blair shook her head, making her curls bounce around like miniature Slinkys. "I can't, Tut. Did I mention how upset my dad was?"

I nodded, even while I kept looking for Henry and Apep.

"But the good news is that my dad is willing to put the lie behind us. He's going to forgive Gil."

"That's great," I said. "Then just let him go."

"Oh, no," Blair said, stopping any hope I'd felt at her words. "We can't let Gil go."

"Why not?" I asked, not sure I wanted to hear the answer.

"Here's the thing," Blair said. "My dad got out of that

horrible, awful prison he was in, and he started out wanting re-venge on Gil. Gil was a huge part of why my dad got imprisoned in the first place. That's why he took Gil. But then he found out that Gil wasn't even whole. That part of Gil was missing. Gil doesn't have his scarab heart. And my dad wants that scarab heart. It's the only thing that will make Gil complete."

And once Gil was complete, Apep could kill him. Com-pletely. That was so not going to happen.

If Blair noticed my horror, she didn't react. Instead, she went on. "At first I thought Henry had it. The immortal energy was rippling off him in waves. And then I thought you had it. And then I thought Henry had it again. And then I wasn't sure. I got really confused, and you guys were always together. I could never get you apart. But yesterday, at the hospital, I finally got Henry alone, and I realized that Henry didn't have it. He didn't smell quite right." She licked her lips.

Oh. This was not good and it was getting worse by the second.

"Do you have any idea where I can find Gil's scarab heart?" Blair asked, clasping her hands in front of her like she was pleading, which she definitely wasn't. She completely had the upper hand here. She knew where Gil was. And she knew I had the heart. At least Henry wasn't in immediate danger.

"Maybe if you take me to Gil it will help me remember where the scarab heart is," I said.

This was a brilliant plan, if I did say so myself. I could play along. And once I knew where Gil was . . . boom! I'd grab Gil, imprison Apep, and be done with this whole mess in time for dessert.

"Hmmm . . ." Blair said. "That could work."

The plan was going to be perfect. Finally. Except then something bounded out of the trees and over the fence and landed on the ground in front of Blair. Humbaba growled at her and lowered himself to his front paws. Drool slipped from the sides of his mouth.

"Back, Baba," I said, but I don't think he was much in the mood for listening, because his tail was straight up in the air and his claws dug into the ground and he let out a roar that shook every bone in my body. Humbaba thought I was in danger, and he was not going to stand for it.

I was so close to finding Gil. I had to stop him. "Baba, no!" I said more forcefully, and I summoned a fireball, sure that would distract him. I did not need him doing this. Not now. I pulled my arm back and threw the fireball, far into the gray sky. It flew off like a shooting star.

Humbaba didn't even look at it. Instead he let out a roar that shook the ground around me. He roared again, louder this time. Blair screamed and covered her ears, like the sound was deathly painful to her. And then Humbaba pounced on Blair, a direct hit to her chest.

They flew through the air, then both slammed into the mirror behind her.

There was a giant explosion of light as Blair and Humbaba hit the glass. I covered my eyes because it was like looking into pure sunlight. And when I opened my eyes, even though the mirror was perfectly intact, Blair was gone. Wiped from existence.

But so was Humbaba.

25

WHERE I FAIL IN THE MOST EPIC WAY POSSIBLE

No, Baba! Come back!" I screamed at the mirror, but it didn't help. Humbaba and Blair were gone. I'd been so close. But now my hopes of finding Gil slipped away.

The sky began to blacken. The funnel doubled in size. And a horrible hiss filled the air around me.

"Tut!"

I heard Henry's scream from the left, and I took off. I couldn't do anything for Humbaba now. He'd given his life defending me. He'd taken down Blair, daughter of Apep, a monster of epic proportions. It would be the stuff of legends. I would never forget it.

"I'm coming!" I yelled, running past the table where we'd been sitting only minutes before. Around the corner I found

Henry, facing off against Mr. Drake. Except Mr. Drake was definitely not himself. His face had flattened into the jaw of a snake. His neck had widened, his whole body thickened. And then his arms began to shrink. There was no doubt that the creature in front of me was Apep, Lord of Chaos.

"You still think there's a scientific explanation for all this?" I asked Henry.

"What did you do to my daughter?" Apep hissed, elongating with each second that went by. His legs melded together and stretched across the ground, ending in a point that flickered around like a tail.

"Where's Gil?" I screamed back at him.

"Gilgamesh," Apep hissed. "He's already dead. And when I kill you, it will end his immortality forever. Then I will have my revenge."

Already dead? It couldn't be true. I would have felt it. I would have known. But Apep's words taunted me. If Gil was dead, then that would be it. I would have failed.

"He's not dead!" I screamed. I had to hear the words. I had to know if Apep was lying.

"You die next, Tutankhamun." The snake slithered and hissed and moved around on the ground, circling us with his long body. "And then the world will be cast into eternal darkness. It is going to be an era that will never be forgotten. I'll rule the world like I should have so many thousands of years ago, before Gilgamesh got in my way."

"You have to stop him," Henry said to me. His entire body glowed with immortal energy. It poured off him. And I knew that once Apep killed me, he'd come after Henry. And then Tia. Everyone would die.

No matter how much I wanted to find Gil, to make sure he was still alive, saving the world was more important. Stopping Apep. Even if it meant never seeing Gil again. Even if it meant dying myself.

"This stops here. Now!" I screamed. I fumbled with the drawstring on my bag, trying to get it undone, but it was knotted, so I yanked it apart. And then I pulled the sun disk from inside. This had to work. The world didn't have much longer.

I held the disk up, catching the last of the sunlight, reflecting it off the dull metal, directing it right at Apep.

It was perfect aim, right to his chest. Apep hissed so loudly and deeply that it felt like worms were digging into my skin. Henry and I covered our ears. This was going to work. But instead of the disk trapping him, as we watched, Apep sprung from the ground, straight into the air, and vanished from sight.

"Great Osiris!" I grabbed the torn bag from the ground and shoved the sun disk back inside. "We have to go after him."

"Why didn't it work?" Henry asked.

I glared at the sun, pouring all my fury out through my eyes. "Because there's not enough light to catch his reflection. We'll have to find another way."

"What other way, Tut?" Henry said.

"We need sunlight." I grabbed Henry's arm. "Come on. I need your help."

Henry and I flew down the steps to the basement. At the

bottom, the satellite device still collected sunlight, though it was starting to make a sucking sound like a straw at the bottom of a glass. There was almost nothing left for it to collect.

I didn't have to explain anything to Henry. He took one look at the machine and immediately understood what was going on.

"It's collecting the sunlight," Henry said. "I knew there was a scientific explanation."

"This is not science," I said.

"It's pure science," Henry said. "It's a magnetic receptor that's pulling on the elements."

"We need to figure out where it's going."

Henry dropped to the ground and started looking at the connection between the storage tank and the pipe that was taking the sunlight away. I scanned the room, searching for some sort of clue, but there was nothing.

"Zeiss," Henry said.

"It's the telescope brand," I said. "Thoth told us that."

But Henry shook his head. "It's not enough. The word is still burrowing into my brain. It still means something."

Zeiss. He was right. The word was still there, nudging at my skull. With the other words, no sooner had I used them than they'd gone away.

"What else does Zeiss make?" I said. I knew they were a German company that had been around for ages.

Henry started ticking things off on his fingers. "Microscopes. Telescopes. Camera lenses. Planetarium projectors. Medical la—"

I put my hand up. "Wait. Planetarium projectors?"

The second the words were out of my mouth, we both knew. Everything fit together. The circular seats. The stars in the sky. The construction sounds.

We ran as fast as we could because there was no other way to get there. The Air and Space Museum was closed, like everything else in D.C., but I yanked on the door, and Henry and I ran inside, up the escalator, and to the doors of the planetarium.

My scarab heart clenched up, almost like it was being pulled from the other side. The sign still hung on the door: RENOVATION IN PROGRESS. BUILDING A BRIGHTER FUTURE. I'd been here only a week before, in this exact spot. I'd been so close. That's why I'd felt weird back then. I'd thought I was nervous, but it was totally because Gil had been so close.

I yanked the chains from the door, and Henry and I went inside. The door slammed closed behind us.

It was crazy-dark inside except for the smallest bit of light escaping from a covered tank in the center of the room. It had to be filled with the stolen sunlight. Rows of chairs circled around the covered tank, and mirrors were plastered on every wall, but they didn't seem to show any reflection at all. Only blackness.

"Gil!" I screamed. He had to be in here. This was exactly what I'd felt in the visions. I'd been here, as him. I felt him close. My heart pumped in my chest.

"Tut!" Gil yelled back, from behind me.

He wasn't dead! I'd gotten here in time. Except when I spun around to see him, something moved in the darkness, slithering between the chairs. I couldn't let Apep get to Gil before I did. Everything had come down to this moment.

I ran to the center of the room and yanked the cover from the collection tank. Brilliant light exploded around the room, bouncing off every wall and mirror and surface in there. I kicked out with all my immortal strength, aiming my foot right for the glass storage tank. My aim was solid. The tank cracked from the force, and sunbeams blasted from the small fissures in the glass.

"Get the roof, Henry," I yelled, and then I jumped over the chairs to where Gil stood. Apep was almost there. I yanked the sun disk from the bag and held it in front of me. In front of Gil, protecting him for once. Sunlight from the tank hit the disk, and I aimed the reflection directly at the giant snake-god.

It was a solid hit. It should have worked. But nothing happened except my scarab heart started pounding and bouncing around in my chest like it was going crazy. Sweat trickled down my forehead. This had to work. This was my only chance. Except it wasn't working.

Nephthys's words filled my head: *You want to do this. But you can't. You don't have the power to do this.*

She'd been right. Doubt clouded my mind.

I tried again. I focused all my immortal energy, but nothing felt different. Nothing changed. Apep flicked his horrible tongue forward, brushing it against my arm. I refocused the beam of light. It still didn't work.

But then Henry yelled a single word across the room: "Synergy! That's the word Thoth gave me, Tut! It's 'synergy'!"

Synergy? Synergy . . . Wait, that was it! Synergy was teamwork. The doubt cleared. Nephthys was right. I wasn't strong enough to do this—at least not alone. As long as I kept trying by myself, I would fail. But I didn't have to do it alone.

"Grab hold, Gil!" I yelled over the hissing sunlight.

Gil reached forward and touched the sun disk also. The second his hand connected, energy flashed through me. Apep screamed in pain. The beam of light flared and flickered like it was made of flames. Apep started smoking and shriveling. His screams filled the planetarium around us. I wanted to cover my ears, but I also knew that I couldn't take my hands off the sun disk until this was done. The burning continued. Apep fought. And when he could fight no longer, the sun disk sucked him in like a straw sucking in a piece of fruit at the bottom of a smoothie.

Henry was still fumbling with the roof controls, but he finally got them to work. The roof began to peel back and open, exposing the blackened sky above. And then Henry gave the glass storage tank a kick of his own, and the already weakened tank shattered.

Sunlight blasted through the open ceiling of the planetarium, back into the world, and as we watched, it filled the sky and daylight returned.

I let the sun disk fall from my hands as I grabbed Gil in a hug so fierce, I almost cut off his circulation.

"I am so mad at you," I said.

He mussed my hair in reply, and started to make some perfect witty Gil comeback, but in that moment something burst from one of the mirrors on the wall.

It was Blair.

26

WHERE SNACK TIME SAVES
THE WORLD

Blair's blond wig was gone, exposing a bald head, and her face, like Apep's, had flattened to look like a snake. Makeup streaked down her pale skin.

"I'm going to get him back!" she screamed, and she dove for the sun disk, reaching it way before I even had a chance to react.

"Put it down, Blair," Henry called. He looked torn, like he was half ready to run over to her and half horrified by her appearance.

"No!" she screamed. Tears streamed down her face. "That was my father. My daddy. Do you have any idea how important he is? Any idea? He was going to run for Senate." Gone were any signs of her cheerleader bubbliness. Gone was all talk of her dad's charity and the good it would do. Blair was nothing but a crying, heartbroken snake-monster.

I almost felt bad for her, except for the fact that her dad was trying to destroy the world.

I inched toward her.

"Keep him away from me, Henry!" Blair cried. "Help me get my dad back!"

Henry looked from Blair to me and then back to her again, and for a split second, I worried that he might side with her. That he liked her that much. But my worries quickly vanished. Henry shook his head. "Blair, your dad was sucking the sun from the sky. That's not a good thing."

"It's a great thing," she said. "He would have re-formed the world. Made it better."

"Just give me the sun disk," I said, and I jumped out and tried to grab it from her. But she ran around the perimeter of the room, and with all the mirrors, I couldn't tell where she was. It was like the funhouse except this time, the consequences were going to be apocalyptic. If she managed to free Apep, the world wouldn't have a second chance.

Gil, Henry, and I tore after her, but everywhere I thought she was, it was just a reflection. And in those reflections I saw Blair lift the sun disk and catch the sunlight on it, bouncing it around the room. I didn't know if she could really free Apep this way, but I also didn't want to find out.

I dove for her, but before I could reach her, Humbaba leapt from the same mirror Blair had come through only moments before. He bounded across the chairs of the planetarium, jumping and gliding like it was some sort of parkour course. And then he stopped dead and roared so loudly that all the mirrors fell from the walls of the planetarium. They shattered when they hit the ground. Then Humbaba leapt forward, opened his huge mouth, and swallowed Blair whole.

"Good boy!" I said, and I ran over to him and started scratching his head.

Humbaba's tail wagged and his tongue hung from the side of his mouth.

"You tamed Humbaba?" Gil said. "Guardian of the Cedar Forest? Devourer of both the living and the dead? I imprisoned him. He's dangerous. You can't tame him."

"Sure, I can." I scratched the monster under the chin. "I'm King Tut. I can make fireballs now, too." I'd been waiting to tell Gil that for over a week.

"I can't believe he ate Blair," Henry said. "She was so nice."

I'd never seen Henry look so sad. It was like a kid who'd just dropped his ice cream cone on the ground.

"Blair was the daughter of the Lord of Chaos," I said. "She was trying to destroy the world."

"I know. But I really liked her." He looked wistfully at Humbaba. "Why did she have to be evil, anyway? It totally stinks. I was going to ask her to a school dance this fall."

"You can do way better," I said. "Trust me."

"You really think so?" Henry said.

"I'd bet the throne of Egypt on it."

Anything would be better than Blair. But I still felt kind of sorry for Henry. He had seemed to get along with her pretty well.

A rumbling noise started coming from Humbaba, deep in his giant stomach. It crept up his body, through his throat, and then Humbaba let out the hugest burp I'd ever heard in my immortal lifetime. The sun disk flew from his mouth, having been devoured with Blair, and landed on the ground, rolling to a stop in front of me.

I reached down and picked it up. I'd promised it to Tia, and it was a promise that I intended to keep.

27

WHERE THE FATE OF THE WORLD COMES IN THE FORM OF A WORD

The sky was filled with sunlight. Apep and Blair were conquered. But the planetarium was a disaster. I didn't want to stick around and have to explain anything to the authorities. So Henry, Gil, and I hightailed it out of there and headed back for the townhouse as fast as we could. Humbaba trotted along beside me, growling at anything that moved the wrong way.

"I should have known you'd have a perfect plan all worked out," Gil said.

I hadn't realized how much I'd missed his sarcasm.

"You know, if you hadn't left, none of this would have ever happened," I said. "I still can't believe you did that. Without even asking." My voice cracked, just the smallest bit.

"I'm sorry, Tut," Gil said. "It was a mistake. I thought if I left you alone, that if you didn't have me watching over your every move, it would help you grow. That you would be better off without me, especially now that I'm no longer immortal."

"Better off without you? Why would you even think that?" I said.

Gil ran a hand through his dark hair. "I don't know. I figured you could live your life, be independent, and do whatever you wanted to do and not have to worry about what I thought or worry about me growing old and dying. I was trying to make things better, but all I did was make things worse. And . . ."

I waited.

"And I'm sorry I hurt you," he said. "I'm really sorry."

I tried to think of some witty comeback, but the lump in my throat was too big. So instead I crossed my arms and smiled. There was a lot more to be said. The conversation was far from over. But I was too happy to see Gil again to press it anymore right now. As far as I was concerned, we had an eternity ahead of us to argue about it. An eternity because I totally intended to find a way to make Gil immortal again, whether he wanted to be or not.

Gil and I opened the door to the townhouse and Horus jumped onto the cat platform by the door. I walked in first. Henry was still dragging his feet, out on the sidewalk. I guess he was bummed about Blair.

"How you feeling, Horus?" I asked.

Horus stretched out super-long, like he'd just woken up from a nap befitting Sleeping Beauty. "Amazing, all things considered."

His fur was washed and brushed. His claws were trimmed. His good eye shone bright.

"What do you mean, all things considered?" I asked. "I saved the world. I restored the sunlight. Apep has officially been re-imprisoned." When I listed it out like that, it sounded pretty impressive.

"Yeah, don't get ahead of yourself, Tut," Horus said. "Oh, and the no-dogs rule still applies."

"He's not a dog," I said as Humbaba rushed past me into the townhouse, knocking a couple feather fans from the wall as his snake tail wagged. "So the rule is irrelevant."

"First time he tries to chase me around the townhouse, he's outta here," Horus said. "And if he pees on my scratching post, trying to mark his territory or anything like that, I'll stick him back into the Epic of Gilgamesh forever."

It was nice to see that Horus was back to his normal grumpy self.

"Speaking of the Epic of Gilgamesh . . ." I said.

Gil peeked his head in the door and grinned. "Okay, I admit it. It's nice to be home."

"The heathen lord returns," Colonel Cody said, and jumped in front of me. It must've been a precautionary measure, just in case Gil decided to attack me or something.

"It's about time," Horus said. "You surprised me this time, Gil. I expect Tut to get himself into huge messes. You?"

"Hey!" I said. "I do not get into huge messes." Messes just seemed to have a way of finding me.

"What in the name of Nergal happened to my door?" Gil

said. He stared up the steps at the blue door with the gold stripes and star. His hands balled into fists.

Colonel Cody looked to me, wondering if he should answer.

"The shabtis wanted to redecorate," I said, so Colonel Cody wouldn't have to. "They were turning your room into a media room."

Gil did not look amused. "No media room. I want my door painted exactly the way it was. And why is my stuff piled all over the family room?"

"They were going to burn it," I said. "You should thank me. I saved it from sure incineration."

Gil fixed his eyes on Colonel Cody. "All of it: back in my room. Now."

Colonel Cody again looked to me. "Should we do as the heathen lord commands?"

I loved that things were back to how they should be.

"Yep, do what he wants," I said. "Unless Gil plans on leaving again anytime soon." I fixed my gaze on Gil, challenging him with my eyes. "Do you?"

He shook his head and smiled. "I wouldn't dare. I made that mistake once, which is already too many times. Anyway, someone has to keep an eye on you."

"You're the one who got kidnapped," I said. "I saved your butt."

He mussed my hair. "And for that I'll be eternally grateful."

Colonel Cody summoned his shabtis and they got to work, carting everything back up the steps to Gil's room. Gil's eyes drifted next to his chair. I cringed. But Gil smiled.

I dared to glance over. The chair looked perfect. Between Humbaba drooling and shedding all over it, the shabtis setting it on fire, Tia pulling it apart, and Horus digging his claws into it and hacking up a hairball on it, I thought it was beyond repair. But the shabtis had made it look brand-new.

Gil flopped down in his chair and let out a huge sigh of contentment. Or at least half a sigh, because then he frowned.

"My chair feels different," he said.

"Just be happy it's still here," I said. "And don't ask any questions."

Gil raised an eyebrow but kept his mouth shut.

Henry finally walked in the front door. "We have a problem." He held up his cell phone, like he was going to show us a picture. But instead it was a screen shot of Words with Friends, the game he'd been playing with Thoth.

"Don't we always have a problem?" I asked.

"Not like this one," Thoth said, walking in behind Henry. I guessed the game with Hapi was finally over. It was like a regular party in my townhouse: two Egyptian gods, a Sumerian monster, and three somewhat-immortals. All we needed now were balloons and streamers.

"Are you sure?" Horus said from his perch. He sat up and flicked his tail back and forth.

"We'll see. I need some paper," Thoth said to the nearest shabtis.

Thoth's uncanny power over them prevailed again. They ran off, returning with one of my unused spiral notebooks from school. Thoth ripped a few pages out and handed us each a piece.

"Write down a word," he said. "But don't tell each other what your word is."

One of my shabtis handed me a pencil, and I scribbled down the first thing that came to my mind. Henry, Gil, and even Thoth himself did the same thing.

"Now show us your word," Thoth said once we were all done.

We flipped our papers around. I couldn't believe what I was seeing. We'd all written the same word.

"Ra."

"So it's true," Horus said. His tail stopped moving. It wasn't a good sign.

Thoth nodded. "It's true."

"What's true?" I held up the sun disk. "We used it to capture Apep. Everything is better."

"Maybe for now," Thoth said. "But things have gone too far."

"Things like what?" Gil said. At least I wasn't the only one who didn't realize what was going on.

Thoth lifted his hand and started counting off on his fingers. "Things like Horemheb and the Cult of Set nearly taking over the world. Things like the immortal-killing knife cutting the fabric of the universe. Things like Apep casting the world into eternal darkness."

"Yeah, but we've taken care of all those things," I said.

"You've patched them," Thoth said. "Sure. Just like the shabtis patched Gil's chair."

Gil frowned and looked down at his chair.

"But why are they happening in the first place?" Thoth said.

"Because . . . some of the gods are power-hungry?" I said.

"Because the gods are fighting," Thoth said. "And as long as the gods keep fighting, things will only get worse."

"This is about Tia's quest," I said.

All eyes turned to me.

"What exactly do you mean by that, Tut?" Horus asked.

"She has this quest," I said. "To reunite the gods." And I told them everything I knew. About the objects she'd been collecting. And her grand scheme to make sure everyone got along.

"And you think my mom is helping her with this," Horus said.

I shrugged. "It's all I can figure out."

Horus seemed to consider this. "That would tie in with why my mom went away."

"Where did she go?" Henry asked.

"She went searching for Ra."

Ra. The name we'd all written.

"She was convinced that by finding Ra, the battles between the gods would stop," Horus said.

"So did she find him?" I asked.

Horus shook his head. "That's the problem. I don't know. I can't get in touch with her. Nobody can."

"So we need to find Ra," I said.

"Seems that way," Gil said.

"Where is Ra?" Henry asked.

We all looked to Thoth. Of all the gods, Thoth would know.

Thoth put up his hands in defense. "I don't know where Ra is. Or where your mom is either, Horus."

"That's impossible," I said. "You said you knew where anyone was at any given time."

"I do," Thoth said. "Unless they're shielded from me. Which in this case they are. Wherever they are, they don't want to be found."

"Or somebody doesn't want us to find them," I said. "But we will. We'll find Ra, and we'll set everything right."

It seemed like a pretty big job, but after what I'd been through, I knew I could do it. Well, as long as I had a little help, which, looking around the room, I knew I did.

28

WHERE WE WATCH THE MOST
EPIC FIREWORKS IN HISTORY

Tia brought cookies over the next day. I gave her Ra's sun disk in return. Lieutenant Virgil insisted on trying a cookie first. He said he was worried about me getting poisoned, but I think he just wanted to sample the recipe. After finishing the entire cookie, he declared the batch safe and ran off to record notes. I figured he was going to try to duplicate Tia's secret formula.

Gil sat in his chair and listened to my entirely awkward conversation with Tia. She annoyingly left me speechless. But finally Henry showed up and saved me from myself.

"I brought you a T-shirt, Tut," Henry said, throwing a red bundle across the room to me.

I caught it and unrolled it. It read, HENRY IS A GeNiUS.

"No way am I wearing this," I said, throwing it back at him. Henry caught it effortlessly. "It's that or lending me half your shabtis. I won the bet."

My mouth dropped open. "What are you talking about? I won the bet. Apep was totally behind everything."

But Henry shook his head. "The Zeiss satellite was collecting the sun, using magnetic force. That is a scientific explanation if I've ever heard one." He threw the shirt back to me. "Now put it on."

Colonel Cody jumped onto the coffee table. "Great Master, might I recommend you wear the shirt? The shabtis and I were discussing this matter, and it would make us most unhappy to be placed on loan to master's questionably immortal best friend."

I looked at the shirt and then at Colonel Cody's earnest little face. He pleaded with me with his eyes. But still? *Henry is a genius.* Ugh.

"Please, Great Pharaoh," Colonel Cody said.

He'd always been there for me. And Henry did make a compelling argument, though I had no intention of telling him this.

"Fine," I said, letting out an exasperated sigh. "But only for one day."

"Every day for a week," Henry said.

"No. Possible. Way." I pulled the shirt over my head. I had to admit that it was a pretty nice fit.

"Red is definitely your color," Tia said.

"Oh, and don't forget that the next camp session starts up again on Monday," Henry said.

"No more camp," I said. "It was horrible."

"Camp was fun," Tia said. "Maybe I'll go instead."

"Oh," I said. That certainly changed matters. "By 'horrible,' what I meant was that—"

"Shut up while you're ahead, Tut," Gil said. "And just say that you'll go to camp."

"Fine. I'll go to camp," I said. Tia better have been serious. Otherwise I'd just signed myself up for two more weeks of extracurricular tedium.

"Look what Thoth gave me." Henry dropped a book onto the coffee table. A color-blind person would have recognized the bright yellow cover.

"*Senet for Dummies,*" I said. "I think Thoth is trying to send you a message."

"Of course I'm trying to send him a message," Thoth said, walking in next.

"What message?" I said.

Thoth grabbed a cookie off the platter. I resisted the urge to tell him to put it back.

"Henry will figure it out," Thoth said. He looked around. "Horus isn't back yet?"

"He went to check on those loser sons of his," Gil said. "I still can't believe Hapi was going to leave me for dead. I am going to find a way to get back at that monkey."

"No, you're not," Horus said, sauntering in the window from the fire escape. "You're going to be nice and civil."

"Nice and civil," Gil said. "Maybe after I pull his baboon teeth out."

I didn't say anything, but Gil had every right to be upset. Hapi wasn't top on my list of favorite gods right now either.

Horus hissed. "You have no idea what I had to go through to get him to calm down."

Nor did I want to.

"What about Imsety and Qeb?" I asked Horus. "They're okay?" Last I had seen them, they were fighting the monster in the museum.

Horus licked at a paw and then jumped up onto the top of his scratching post so he could look down at all of us. "They're fine. They fought the Crick. Crazy monster. I can't imagine where Apep dug that thing up from."

"I'm glad they're okay," I said.

"Well, they are mad at you, Tutankhamun," Horus said.

"Me?" I'd saved the world. How could anyone be mad at me?

"You said you'd give the sun disk back," Horus said.

"He's not giving it back," Tia piped up from the futon.

"I didn't say he should," Horus said. "I only said they were expecting Tut to. Keep that in mind next time you ask them for a favor. Oh, and they mentioned something about shaving your head in retribution."

I smoothed my hair and hoped I wouldn't have to ask them for any favors in the future, but with the search for Ra ahead, I had no idea what to expect.

We all went to watch the fireworks: Henry, my possibly immortal best friend; Gil, the best big brother in the entire universe; Horus, my grumpy cat god; Thoth, a god who seemed to have his sights set on Henry; Humbaba, my Sumerian monster-dog; Colonel Cody and twenty other of my valiant shabtis; and Tia. I still wasn't sure what she really was. I'd thought she was just the unfortunate sister of the Cult of Set, but every time I talked to her, I was sure she was something more. I'd figure out what eventually.

We sat on the steps of the Lincoln Memorial. Lieutenant Virgil had packed us a picnic basket full of scones. And even with everything that had gone on in the last couple weeks, the fireworks went off without a hitch. Things could go right every once in a while. Tia even reached over once the fireworks started and grabbed my hand, lacing her fingers through mine. It was without a doubt the best night of my life.

And as for finding Ra, I was formulating a plan. It was going to be brilliant. It was going to be perfect. I'd defeated Set and Apep both. Finding the hiding place of the most important Egyptian god in existence should be no problem.

ACKNOWLEDGMENTS

To Susan Chang, Kathleen Doherty, and the entire amazing team at Tor, for giving the Boy King a chance . . .

To Tricia Lawrence, for believing in me and my potential . . .

To all the wonderful Texas librarians, for loving King Tut stuck in middle school as much as I do . . .

To my amazing writing friends, especially Jessica Lee Anderson, Christine Marciniak, fellow retreaters at the Lodge of Death, the Texas Sweethearts & Scoundrels, and Austin SCBWI, for your enthusiasm . . .

To my wonderful family, especially Riley, Zachary, Lola, Dad, and Mom, for your undying support and inspiration . . .

Thank you!

GLOSSARY

Ammut—crocodile goddess who devours unworthy hearts at the entrance to the Egyptian underworld

Amun/Amun Ra—king of the gods

Anubis—jackal-headed god of the underworld

Apep/Apophis—snake god who embodies chaos; Lord of Chaos; devours the sun each evening

Bast—cat goddess

Bes—god of luck

Duamutef (Dua)—jackal-headed god; one of four sons of Horus; in mummification, protected the stomach

Hapi—baboon-headed god; one of four sons of Horus; in mummification, protected the lungs

Hathor—goddess of love

Horus—son of Osiris and Isis; most often seen with a falcon head (but takes form of a cat in *Tut: The Story of My Immortal Life* and *Tut: My Epic Battle to Save the World*); lost one eye in fight with his uncle Set

Imsety—god (with a normal head); one of four sons of Horus; in mummification, protected the liver

Isis—mother goddess; mother of Horus; wife of Osiris

Khepri—dung beetle god who pushes the sun across the sky each day

Maat—goddess of justice and truth; judges the dead at entrance to Egyptian underworld

Nephthys—protective goddess of the dead; sister of Isis and Osiris; wife of Set; mother of Anubis

Osiris—god of fertility, death, and the afterlife; carries a crook and flail; most often depicted green and partially mummified

Qebehsenuef (Qeb)—falcon-headed god; one of four sons of Horus; in mummification, protected the intestines

Ra—god of the sun

Sekhmet—lion-headed goddess

Set—god of chaos, disorder, storms, and infertility; brother and slayer of Osiris

Thoth—god of writing, knowledge, and science; often has the head of an ibis

SUMERIAN GODS/MONSTERS

Anu—king of the gods

Enlil—god of storms and wind

Humbaba—monster from the Epic of Gilgamesh; Guardian of the Cedar Forest

Igigi—lesser/younger gods of Mesopotamia

Nergal—god of war and the sun

PEOPLE

Akhenaton—father of Tutankhamun; used to be known as Amenhotep IV; introduced monotheistic religion to Egypt, which made him really unpopular

Ay—advisor to Tutankhamun while he ruled Egypt; it is thought that Ay ruled Egypt after King Tut

Enkidu—best friend of Gilgamesh back in ancient Sumer

Gilgamesh (Gil)—former Sumerian king

Horemheb—commander in chief of the Egyptian army during Tutankhamun's reign; advisor to Tutankhamun

Howard Carter—English archaeologist who discovered King Tut's tomb in 1922

Smenkhkare (Smenk)—older brother of Tutankhamun

Tutankhamun (King Tut)—Egyptian pharaoh; often called the Boy King since he took the throne when he was only nine

PLACES

Fields of the Blessed—equivalent of heaven in the Egyptian afterlife

Valley of the Kings—valley in Egypt where over sixty tombs have been discovered, many of these for pharaohs of the Egyptian New Kingdom

THINGS

Ankh—ancient Egyptian symbol which represents eternal life

Book of the Dead—ancient Egyptian funerary text containing spells to assist a dead person on their journey through the underworld and into the afterlife

Canopic jars—jars used during mummification to hold the liver, lungs, stomach, and intestines

Eye of Horus—ancient Egyptian symbol of protection, good health, and power

Sarcophagus—a funeral box, often carved of stone, which formed the outer layer of protection for a mummy

Shabti—small figures which were placed in tombs to act as servants for the dead person in the afterlife

Sun Disk of Ra—headdress worn by the god Ra

Tiet—ancient Egyptian symbol; often called "Knot of Isis"

KING TUT'S MOST EXCELLENT GUIDE
TO ALL THINGS SHABTI

Three-hundred and sixty-five shabtis. It's a lot to keep track of! I'm not kidding when I tell you that it took me years to keep them all straight. But I've gotten pretty good at telling them apart. My secret? It all comes down to finding one special thing beyond their painted exterior. One unique quality that sets them apart.

In the event you want to know more about the shabtis, I offer up this simple guide.

COLONEL CODY

I know, I know. A parent shouldn't have a favorite kid. But it's just that Colonel Cody has been with me through everything. When I almost lost him in the underworld . . . well, let's just say that was a pretty low point in my immortal life. I don't know what I would have done without him. Sure, he offers to end his existence if I imply in even the slightest way that something's not quite perfect, but I find that kind of endearing.

- **Appearance:** Gold clothing and gold face
- **Role:** Leader of the shabtis
- **Special info:** Sometimes I'm sure Colonel Cody has telepathic abilities. He seriously knows what

I'm thinking before I even do. But it's not just me. He's the same way with Gil, Henry, and even Horus. Also, Colonel Cody is part of a shabti poker group that meets in my hall closet on Wednesdays at midnight. He always wins. Always.

MAJOR REX

At times it feels like I can't leave the townhouse without at least three shabtis in tow. Along with Colonel Cody, Majors Mack and Rex are almost never left behind.

- **Appearance:** Green clothing, golden arms, small sword and bow/arrows
- **Role:** Weapons specialist; first line of defense for the pharaoh; often placed in charge when Colonel Cody is gone
- **Special info:** Uses every opportunity to drill his troops on fighting techniques and battle maneuvers. Has ninja stealth skills. Practices kung fu. Can construct an arrow out of a toothpick in five seconds flat. Is often found reading *The Art of War*.

MAJOR MACK

Sure, Majors Rex and Mack are a ton alike, but if you spend more than five minutes with these guys, you'll never confuse them again.

- **Appearance:** Green clothing, golden arms, small sword and bow/arrows
- **Role:** Member of the pharaoh's special fighting unit
- **Special info:** Though skilled with both the sword and the bow, Major Mack definitely prefers the sword. His sword is pure black and named OBSIDIAN ANNIHILATION (he picked the name). When he thinks I'm not watching, he throws peanuts in the air and slices them in half.

LIEUTENANT ROY

My townhouse has got to be the cleanest place in all of the United States. Maybe even the world. But if you think there's a cleaner place, please don't tell Lieutenant Roy. He's already way too concerned about every loose hair or speck of dust. Still, it's nice to never worry about mildew in the bathroom.

- **Appearance:** Purple
- **Role:** Number one in charge of cleanup efforts around the townhouse
- **Special info:** Lieutenant Roy can smell dust. I'm not kidding. I see him sniff the air at least once every five minutes. Sometimes I even hear him when I'm sleeping. It kind of freaks me out. Please don't tell him about that either.

LIEUTENANT VIRGIL

I will never starve to death—at least not so long as Lieutenant Virgil is around. And this scone thing he's got going on . . . yum! In addition to scones, Lieutenant Virgil is all about snacks and appetizers. Some nights, for dinner, I have mini-quiches and cheese sticks. He also makes sure I never run out of ranch dressing.

- **Appearance:** Solid blue; often wears an apron and a chef hat
- **Role:** Drinks and snacks for the pharaoh
- **Special info:** His favorite day of the year is March 14, also known as Pi Day. This past March 14, he baked thirty-one pies, one for every day of the month. Henry and I tasted as many as we could, and then we finally convinced him to let us take some to the food bank. Lieutenant Virgil never realized what a great feeling it is to help those less fortunate. Now he makes ten pies a week that we deliver to the local soup kitchen.

LIEUTENANT LEON

If Lieutenant Virgil is more the snacks guy, then Lieutenant Leon is the shabti who makes sure I am properly nourished. I could eat nothing but scones and bacon all day long and be happy. I suggested this to Lieutenant Leon once. Big mistake. He got Captains Otis and Otto to print out a bunch of information on proper diet, and then he did a crash course in nutrition.

Now he's constantly rambling on about healthy living tips. He even keeps track of how many glasses of water I drink each day. I feel like a camel. Sometimes, when he's not watching, I dump the water into the plants. Thankfully, just like me, he loves bacon.

- **Appearance:** Solid blue
- **Role:** Drinks and snacks for the pharaoh
- **Special info:** Plans to write a diet book, but claims he has writer's block. His current working title is *Build a Better Body with Bacon*. I think it has huge potential.

CAPTAIN OTIS

The hardest thing about being immortal? Making sure one of my neighbors doesn't walk up with a school yearbook from thirty years ago and point to my picture. Thankfully, I have Captain Otis. He's managed to destroy all evidence of my past, including horrible yearbook pictures. He also took care of that awful mullet thing I had going on back in the eighties.

- **Appearance:** Silver clothing, silver skin
- **Role:** Lead hacker, computer expert
- **Special info:** Besides hacking, the thing Captain Otis loves the most is video games. He plays them constantly. His current favorite is *Minecraft*. He even created a server to go along with my stories. And he wrote a video game called *Escape from King*

Tut's Tomb. It's really hard to get through all ten levels. You can find both on this really cool website he created, www.pjhoover.com.

CAPTAIN OTTO

Another hard thing about living an immortal life? I always need new documents to prove my existence. The world demands them. So every few years, Captain Otto makes me a new birth certificate. That and a social security card. I can't get into school without either of them. Hmmm . . . maybe that's not such a bad thing.

- **Appearance:** silver clothing, silver skin
- **Role:** Lead hacker, computer expert
- **Special info:** He spends hours watching movies and episodes of TV shows online. His favorite movies are those awful early horror movies, especially the mummy ones. Maybe it reminds him of all those years he was locked in my tomb.

NAME A SHABTI

Obviously, that's not all of my shabtis. And as much fun as I've had naming them, I'm sort of running out of ideas. I could definitely use some name suggestions. So if you've got a great name for a shabti, connect with me through www.pjhoover.com and let me know what it is!

SENET FOR DUMMIES

Everyone loves board games, but people get sick of playing Monopoly and Scrabble. Why not introduce a new game to the mix (or in this case, an old game)? Senet! What? You don't know how to play? Trust me, it's easy. You'll have no problem mastering it, and then you'll be able to ~~beat~~ teach your friends. Think how impressed they'll be. Just a note that there are lots of different ways to play Senet. I'm showing my favorite below.

Fun Fact: Did you know another name for Senet is The Game of Passing Through the Netherworld?

THE GAME BOARD & PIECES

Your board should look something like this. Sketch it. Paint it. Draw it with Sharpie marker on your kitchen table. (Okay, don't really do that last one.)

For the game pieces, coins work great. Go dig through your sofa cushions and find five pennies and five dimes. The dimes are the white pieces. The pennies are the black pieces. Arrange them with white and black alternating along the top of the game board (so space one gets a white piece, space two gets a black piece, and so on).

You're supposed to have two-sided sticks, but in case you don't, coins again work great. Find four coins that you can mark on. Take that same black Sharpie and color one side of each of the coins dark.

BASIC PLAY

Your goal is to get all your pieces off the game board first. White goes first. Toss the four sticks (or coins) and see how they land.

- 1 light side up—Move one piece 1 space and get an extra turn
- 2 light sides up—Move one piece 2 spaces
- 3 light sides up—Move one piece 3 spaces
- 4 light sides up—Move one piece 4 spaces and get an extra turn
- 0 light sides up—Move one piece 5 spaces and get an extra turn

RULES

- There can only be one piece per space.
- If you land on your opponent's piece, that is an attack, and your pieces swap places unless your opponent's piece is "protected" or unless it is in spaces 27–30.

- If a piece is attacked when it is in spaces 28–30 (by a piece in space 26), it is moved to Space 27 unless a piece is already in Space 27. Then the pieces swap as normal.
- You can't land on a space with your own piece on it.
- You have to try to move forward first. If you can't move forward, then you have to try to move backward, and you lose your extra turn (if you had one). If you can't move backward either, then your turn is over, and you lose any extra turn you may have had.

PROTECTION

- For your piece to be protected, it must be adjacent (numerically) to another of your own pieces. This works side by side horizontally and around corners if the corners are adjacent (for example, spaces 10 and 11 are adjacent, but spaces 9 and 12 are not. Also spaces 1 and 20 are not adjacent.).
- Pieces that are in the last four spaces (spaces 27–30) are no longer protected and can't protect other pieces either.

SPECIAL SPACES

There are some special spaces with equally special rules.

- **Space 15: The House of Second Life**
- **Space 26: The House of Beauty**

All pieces must stop here on an EXACT throw of the sticks. This spot may never be skipped by any piece.

• Space 27: The House of Waters

If you land on this space, you lose any extra turn you may have had. Sorry!

If you're starting your turn on this space, you don't have to throw the sticks. You can move your piece to Space 15 if you want. If there is another piece already on Space 15, it gets moved BACK (numerically) to the first open space on the board.

If you want to try your luck and throw the sticks, you must throw a four (all light sides up). If you do throw the four (and trust me, the odds are against you), then your piece is off the board and you get your extra turn.

• Space 28: The House of Three Judges

A piece on this space can't be moved forward or backward. Its only option is if you make an exact throw of three. Then it escapes the game board.

• Space 29: The House of Two Judges

A piece on this space can't be moved forward or backward. Its only option is if you make an exact throw of two. Then it escapes the game board.

• Space 30: The House of Horus

Great luck! ANY throw gets a piece on this space off the game board.

See, I told you it was easy. Now go share the love of Senet with the world!

Visit www.pjhoover.com for a downloadable Senet board and printable instructions.

CARING FOR YOUR SUMERIAN MONSTER

You've read about all the fun I've had with Humbaba. Now you want a Sumerian monster of your own. I'll tell it to you straight. Taking care of a Sumerian monster is no small task. But that doesn't mean you should give up on your dreams. In fact, in order to help, I've come up with some of my best tips for caring for your Sumerian monster.

Potty training—Let's start with the big one. Consider the mess that puppies can make. Now multiply that times one hundred. A Sumerian monster will need to be taught proper potty training. A big part of this is having a designated spot for your Sumerian monster to use the potty. I suggest the front yard of those neighbors who've been complaining about you walking across their grass or throwing the ball in their yard. That would be the perfect spot to train your Sumerian monster to use the potty. One look through the window at your Sumerian monster, and I'm pretty sure your neighbors will stay inside. Also, they should thank you. Monster dung makes great fertilizer.

Proper diet—Sure, every Sumerian monster loves doughnuts and cookies, but a diet of baked sweets won't help him (or her) grow into the strong, healthy monster you want him to be. What every Sumerian monster needs is a proper diet. Start with the basics. Humbaba loves bacon, and I'm sure your Sumerian monster will, too. Protein is the most important part of any monster's diet. But take care to make sure your Sumerian monster does not eat your neighbors. That may make them unhappy. I suggest an alternate protein source. Make friends with your local butcher. Find out what animals in your area are pesky and out of control (feral hogs? Coyotes?). Your Sumerian monster can become a problem solver and find dinner all at the same time!

Playtime—As far as high-energy pets go, a Sumerian monster tops the list. If your Sumerian monster isn't eating or sleeping, then he will want to play! Be prepared for this playtime. Save up your energy. Make sure there is a park nearby with lots of space for running. And make sure you have running shoes. Also you'll need toys. Normal puppy toys will not do. Your Sumerian monster will only eat these. When you are thinking toys, think big and tough. Fetching a stick? You'll need a tree branch. Frisbee? A metal trash can lid will do. Squeaky toy? Keep your neighbors away from your Sumerian monster and use a giant clown doll instead. Making sure your monster has proper play toys will keep him from chasing cars instead.

Discipline—Don't bother.

Sleeping—After a busy day playing, your Sumerian monster is going to want to sleep. Unless you want him crushing you in your bed, he'll need a bed of his own. Doggie crates aren't made in sizes that will fit your Sumerian monster. I wouldn't suggest crating your monster anyway. This won't make him happy and he may pee on you for revenge. Instead, a second mattress, on the floor near your bed, works best. I suggest a mattress protector since your Sumerian monster will drool a ton in his sleep.

Grooming—Your Sumerian monster loves to look his best, almost as much as he loves to roll in the mud. This is a problem because all that dirt could clog your pipes, which won't make your parents happy at all. The best way to bathe your monster is with the garden hose. Or in your neighbor's swimming pool (late at night is best, once your neighbor is asleep). Use plenty of soap, but watch for chemicals. They will only dry out your monster's skin. Also, here's a great tip for making your monster's hair look its shiniest: coconut oil. It works like magic.

Treats—My only advice? Never run out of them.

Good luck with your Sumerian monster! I hope you'll be the best of friends.

HENRY'S PHRONTISTERY

Hey, Tut fans! Henry Snider here. I asked Tut for ten pages at the end of the book where I could share all sorts of interesting information. He agreed to one. I'll take it. It's not every day I get to spread my knowledge across the world.

I offer up to you words that may come in useful when hanging out with an immortal teenage prior pharaoh.

apricate—to bask in the sun; if Apep has his way, we'll never get to do this again!

dysania—when you have a hard time waking up in the morning; some mornings, especially on weekends during daylight savings time, this is totally me.

jettatura—the evil eye; Horus gives me this all the time.

octonocular—having eight eyes . . . like Igigi!

ophiomormous—snakelike.

phrontistery—a place for thinking or studying (kind of like school!)

podobromhydrosis—stinky feet.

serpivolant—flying serpent; yes, just like Apep.

That's all we have time for! But I'd love to hear some of your favorite words. Connect with me through www.pjhoover.com.

TUT: PICK YOUR OWN QUEST GAME

You are about to embark on a great adventure as King Tut, Pharaoh of Egypt. Whatever you do, don't turn back. Once you make a choice, it cannot be changed! One path may lead to you saving the world. Another may lead to your doom.

CHOOSE WISELY :)

It's a big job being pharaoh, but somebody has to do it. And let's face it, life as pharaoh is awesome. People treat you like a rock star! Still, forget taking nice, leisurely walks along the Nile River. Everyone bows to you and wants you to bless their children. But it's good to be famous. You don't mind the attention.

Yet deep in Egypt there is a conspiracy, and you are the only one who can get to the bottom of it. Your people are counting on you. Egypt is counting on you. And the gods are counting on you! Visit www.pjhoover.com/tut_games.php to see if you have what it takes to save Egypt!

ABOUT THE AUTHOR

P. J. Hoover wanted to be a Jedi, but when that didn't work out, she became an electrical engineer instead. After a fifteen-year bout designing computer chips for a living, P. J. decided to start creating worlds of her own in books such as *Solstice and Tut: The Story of My Immortal Life*. When not writing, she spends time with her husband and two kids, and enjoys practicing kung fu, solving Rubik's Cubes, watching *Star Trek,* and playing too many video games. P. J is also a member of the Texas Sweethearts & Scoundrels. She lives in Austin, Texas.

For more information about P. J. (Tricia) Hoover, please visit her website: www.pjhoover.com.